SPECIAL MESSAGE TO READERS

This book is published under the auspices of

THE ULVERSCROFT FOUNDATION

(registered charity No. 264873 UK)

Established in 1972 to provide funds for research, diagnosis and treatment of eye diseases. Examples of contributions made are: —

A Children's Assessment Unit at Moorfield's Hospital, London.

•

Twin operating theatres at the Western Ophthalmic Hospital, London.

•

A Chair of Ophthalmology at the Royal Australian College of Ophthalmologists.

•

The Ulverscroft Children's Eye Unit at the Great Ormond Street Hospital For Sick Children, London.

You can help further the work of the Foundation by making a donation or leaving a legacy. Every contribution, no matter how small, is received with gratitude. Please write for details to:

THE ULVERSCROFT FOUNDATION,
The Green, Bradgate Road, Anstey,
Leicester LE7 7FU, England.
Telephone: (0116) 236 4325
In Australia write to:
THE ULVERSCROFT FOUNDATION,
c/o The Royal Australian and New Zealand
College of Ophthalmologists,
94-98 Chalmers Street, Surry Hills,
N.S.W. 2010, Australia

SAVING WILLOWBROOK

When Ella discovers that her husband Miles plans to sell their farm without her agreement, it's the final straw: her marriage, already on the rocks, is over. Determined to save Willowbrook, and to protect her daughter Amy from a father who doesn't love her, Ella embarks on a mission to build the farm into a successful bed-and-breakfast business. But Miles, an ambitious and ruthless man, has other plans for the property development, which has been in Ella's family for centuries. And when Cameron O'Neal, a rival property consultant, arrives in the Wiltshire village and offers to help Ella, she finds herself torn between a fear of getting hurt again and a powerful attraction to a man whom both she and Amy instinctively like . . .

Books by Anna Jacobs
Published by The House of Ulverscroft:

OUR LIZZIE
OUR POLLY
OUR EVA
CALICO ROAD
PRIDE OF LANCASHIRE
STAR OF THE NORTH
BRIGHT DAY DAWNING
HEART OF THE TOWN
FAMILY CONNECTIONS
TOMORROW'S PROMISES
KIRSTY'S VINEYARD
YESTERDAY'S GIRL
CHESTNUT LANE

ANNA JACOBS

SAVING WILLOWBROOK

Complete and Unabridged

CHARNWOOD
Leicester

First published in Great Britain in 2009 by
Severn House Publishers Ltd.
Surrey

First Charnwood Edition
published 2009
by arrangement with
Severn House Publishers Ltd.
Surrey

The moral right of the author has been asserted

Copyright © 2009 by Anna Jacobs
All rights reserved

British Library CIP Data

Jacobs, Anna.
    Saving Willowbrook.
    1. Family farms- -England- -Wiltshire- -Fiction.
    2. Bed and breakfast accommodations- -England
    - -Wiltshire- -Fiction. 3. Love stories.
    4. Large type books.
    I. Title
    823.9′14–dc22

    ISBN 978–1–84782–876–7

Published by
F. A. Thorpe (Publishing)
Anstey, Leicestershire

Set by Words & Graphics Ltd.
Anstey, Leicestershire
Printed and bound in Great Britain by
T. J. International Ltd., Padstow, Cornwall

This book is printed on acid-free paper

With love and gratitude to my niece Louise and her family, husband Kevin, children Archie and Scarlett, who have helped me with the research for Spinal Muscular Atrophy and given me an understanding of how it affects people.

And with warmest wishes to all families whose children have been affected by SMA.

1

Ella picked up the mail from the post office box, muttering in annoyance when she saw how battered and torn the largest envelope was. Whoever had sent it should have used more secure packaging.

It was addressed to her husband and Miles really hated anyone to open his mail, even circulars. She'd found that out the hard way early in their marriage when she accidentally opened one of his letters. It had been their first quarrel — but not their last.

As she walked out of the post office, a youth running past bumped into her and knocked the letters flying. Before she could pick them up a policewoman chasing the lad trampled on them. Ella was pleased to see a passer-by trip up the fugitive and end the chase.

The torn envelope had burst open and its contents were jumbled up with the other mail, some pages marked by a dirty footprint. As she sat in the car, smoothing out a crumpled letter, the words on it jumped out at her:

With regard to finalizing the sale of Willow-brook . . .

She couldn't move for a moment, so shocked was she, then she read the letter carefully, close to tears at what it revealed. Miles was trying to sell the home that had been in her family for centuries, and without telling her! When had he shown these people round? Oh, yes. Two months ago he'd insisted she and Amy spend a weekend at the seaside while he went away on a business trip. It could only have been then.

She'd been touched by his thoughtfulness, only he'd been lying to her, tricking her!

By the time she'd finished reading, blazing anger had taken over from the urge to weep. She'd learned to control her temper years ago, so she breathed deeply and did nothing till she was calm enough to think straight. That took a while.

She and Miles hadn't been getting on for some time, didn't even share a bedroom any more, but she'd hung on to the tatters of their marriage for their daughter Amy's sake — and with a vague hope that things might improve. And he could be charming when he wanted, even now. But Ella had never thought he'd try to cheat her. Had he forged her signature? What did 'finalizing the sale' mean? They couldn't do that without her, surely? Willowbrook was hers alone. She'd owned it before they married and made sure it would stay hers legally.

At first Miles had pretended to love the country lifestyle, but he'd gradually grown weary of commuting and had suggested she sell the farm and invest the money. She'd refused, of course she had, because the farm wasn't hers to sell. It had been in her family for several generations and she regarded it as a sacred trust. She was merely the person who looked after it in this generation of Turners, as her daughter Amy would in the next.

She shook her head in bafflement. *How could*

2

Miles expect to get away with this? Perhaps he thought she'd change her mind if he presented her with a good enough offer. He was always optimistic about his own powers of persuasion — and about the power of money. It was what made him a good salesman and ideas man — well, ideas that might make money, he wasn't interested in any other sort.

In the end there was only one thing to do. She went to see the lawyer who'd dealt with her family's business until — stupidly, in the first flush of love! — she'd let Miles persuade her to move her affairs into the hands of his London lawyer and leave things to him. At least she'd never signed anything without reading it, even if that had caused more quarrels. She wasn't that stupid. Not quite.

Grimly she started the car and drove to the other end of the village, parking outside the old-fashioned 'rooms' where the Hannows had done business for as many generations as the Turners had farmed at Willowbrook.

Arthur Hannow came out of his office, walking stiffly but still escorting a client to the door with his usual old-fashioned courtesy. Then he turned to her with a beaming smile. 'Ella, my dear girl, how delightful to see you again!'

She tried to smile back, couldn't, and saw his eyes narrow. He might look like everyone's favourite grandfather, but he was as shrewd as they came. She let him usher her into his cosy office overlooking the main street of the village and sighed as she sank down on the worn oxblood leather armchair.

'Something's clearly wrong, Ella. Can I help?'

'I hope so. Will you take me back as a client, me and not my husband?'

'Yes, of course.'

She explained to him what Miles was trying to do and, by the time she finished, she was in tears again. She couldn't take the end of her marriage lightly.

Mr Hannow pushed a box of tissues towards her and waited quietly until she'd stopped crying. 'I'll have to ask my nephew to handle this, if it's all right with you, my dear.' He gave her a wry smile. 'I'll be seventy-five next month and it's more than time I retired.'

'I'm sorry you're leaving. You'll be greatly missed. I didn't know you had a nephew working with you.'

'Ian's only been with us for a few months. He's young but he's smart. He's been in London for a few years gaining wider experience. You'll be safe in his hands.'

Ian Hannow joined them, a slimmer, younger version of his uncle, mousy hair already thinning, but with the same gentle smile. 'Young fellow' was a misnomer. He must have been at least forty, ten years older than her.

'I'm happy to help you, Mrs Parnell.'

'It's Ms Turner from now on. I'm resuming my maiden name.'

'What exactly do you want to do about this?'

She sighed. 'For Amy's sake I'd rather settle everything quietly. Miles is still her father, after all. I just want him to leave Willowbrook and not come back.'

4

'Do you hold the property as joint tenants?'

'No, it's mine alone. I inherited it from my father before I even met Miles.'

Old Mr Hannow leaned forward. 'We drew up a list of property and possessions before Ella married and he signed it.'

Ian nodded slowly and thoughtfully. 'Good. And you never authorized your husband to sell Willowbrook, or gave him the impression you might be interested in considering selling, Ms Turner?'

'Please call me Ella. And I definitely didn't authorize Miles to sell the property, though he's suggested it a few times. It was one of the things we quarrelled about. It might not be a legal trust but it's a sacred trust, which is why my father left Willowbrook to me, not my mother.' She frowned and added, 'Miles put money into the tourist chalets we've built at Willowbrook. I can't pay that back now, obviously, so we'll have to come to some arrangement about it.'

'Very well. We can't keep these papers, of course. You should send them back to your husband, including the torn envelope with the sticker 'damaged on receipt', explaining how they came to be opened.'

'I'll send them via his London lawyers.' And she'd make photocopies of the papers first. But she didn't say that.

Ian cleared his throat, looking suddenly very wooden-faced. 'You're not still — um, sharing a bed?'

'No, we haven't been for a while. Miles comes down every second or third weekend, but he has a service flat in London. He said he was sleeping badly, didn't want to disturb me. We both knew it was a lie, but there was Amy to think of. Now . . . Well, I'd like to get a divorce as soon as I can.'

'I see.'

She shrugged. The anger was subsiding, her main emotion sadness that it should come to this — and to her surprise, she felt deeply relieved to be done with the pretence. Miles's visits over the past few months had been full of arguments and bristling silences. Even four-year-old Amy had noticed that and no longer hurried to meet her father or show him things.

Ella would never forgive Miles for this. Never! He wasn't just trying to steal the inheritance from her, but from his own daughter. She was quite sure he'd have been getting a huge kickback from any sale of Willowbrook. He'd not have bothered to arrange it otherwise.

The thought of all the lies he'd told recently made her feel physically sick. She'd seen him use his charm on others, hadn't realized at first that he was using it on her too, that there was nothing behind his endearments.

She looked at her watch. 'It's time to pick Amy up from my cousin's. Is there anything else we need to do now?'

'We'll need to have an in-depth discussion about the details of the divorce — and the money your husband invested in Willowbrook. Perhaps you could make an appointment to do that?'

After she'd said goodbye to old Mr Hannow,

Ian escorted her to the door in the same way his uncle did. That was comforting. A small continuity in a changing world.

★　★　★

A couple of weeks later Ella heard a car drive up to the farm and come round towards the rear. Putting down the potato she was peeling, she went to peep out of the window at Amy, who was playing with the dog. When the car came into view, Ella exclaimed, 'Oh, no!' She wasn't ready for this confrontation.

Miles parked and walked towards the back door. He waved to the child, who had turned towards him, a hopeful smile on her face, but he didn't stop to speak. The dog had stiffened into an alert, watchful stance. Porgy had never accepted Miles, nor had her husband liked having a dog around.

It hurt Ella to see Amy's face crumple with disappointment as her father walked briskly past. What would it have cost him to stop and say a few words to his daughter?

He came into the huge kitchen without knocking, smiling as if nothing was wrong. 'Hi.'

She folded her arms and glared at him, waiting.

He cocked one eye at her questioningly. 'Surely we can talk about this in a calm, adult way?'

'I'm past the talking stage. Just take the rest of your things and get out! And don't ever come here again. I want a divorce.'

He studied her and sighed. 'Very well. But we should make this divorce amicable, for Amy's sake, don't you think? How about a coffee? It's a long drive from London.'

'I'd not give you a drink of water if you were dying of thirst.'

'Dear me. How melodramatic!' His smile didn't falter, but his eyes were cold and watchful. 'You always were rash, Ella. Typical redhead. That temper of yours will be your undoing one day.'

'How could you possibly think I'd sell Willowbrook?'

'I thought when you found out how much they were offering, you'd see reason. We could have made a fortune.' He looked out of the window towards the six holiday chalets they were building as the first stage of a venture into tourism. 'I started those chalets to tempt buyers to the farm and they've done that. If you read those papers you opened — '

'I did *not* open them!'

'However you came by the information, you'll know what a big fish we had on the hook, Skara Holdings was offering enough to set you and Amy up in comfort for the rest of your lives, even after I'd taken my spotter's share. Look at that!' He gestured to the view. 'A private lake, woods, land zoned for agriculture that can't be built on. It's perfect for a major tourist development.'

'We had trouble getting even limited development permission from the council.'

'But those chalets got our foot in the door, planning-wise. That's how it's done these days,

8

create a precedent. It wouldn't be hard to push the council for more if someone went about it the right way. As it is, you're going to be left in the mire, Ella, my pet. How are you going to finish the chalets without my money? I'm definitely not paying for something which won't benefit me.'

She'd been worrying about that. 'None of your business now. I'll manage.'

'You're being stupid as well as stubborn. What about Amy? She's only going to get worse. Wouldn't a disabled child be better facing life with money behind her? She may never be able to work and — '

'How many times do I have to tell you there's nothing wrong with Amy's brain? Her problem is physical and children like her are usually smarter than average, so she'll be able to do a desk job as well as anyone else, probably better than most. And if by the time she grows up, she's using a wheelchair to get around — which isn't always necessary for people with her problem, remember — well, the world is used to people with disabilities and technology is getting better at helping them all the time.'

She clamped her lips together. It was no use talking to him about their daughter. The minute they'd found out that Amy had spinal muscular atrophy, in her case the milder version known as SMA3, Miles had withdrawn mentally and physically, not only from their daughter but from Ella as well. And yet, the defect only showed up if both parents were carriers, so why he always blamed her for it, she didn't understand.

9

Actually, she did understand. She'd come to realize that he never admitted being in the wrong, always found someone else to blame. It was part of the way he dealt with every aspect of life.

'The child would get help more easily, if you had money,' he said slowly and with heavy scorn, as if speaking to someone stupid. 'You do realize my medical insurance will no longer cover you from now on?'

'You'll cut Amy off it too? I was hoping . . . ' Ella bit back further words, annoyed at having betrayed her feelings.

'Now that *you* have ruined this project, I'm damned if I'm helping you in any way. You've not only turned down a good offer — you always were stupid financially — you've lost me a top job with the same company. It'll be a while before certain people have confidence in me after this fiasco.'

'So why did you waste petrol money coming down here?'

'Haven't you been listening? *We need — to reach an agreement — about the chalets.* You and I, not some damned lawyers. *I* borrowed the money to build them, so I could still close you down and force a sale if I demanded repayment.'

'And if you did that, I'd tell Skara Holdings you were trying to sell my house without my permission, which would further damage your reputation in that wonderful business world you inhabit.'

The look he gave her was briefly vicious but was quickly replaced by a cool expression. 'You

10

won't do that, though. For our dear daughter's sake. Anyway, I'm not going to foreclose. I'll treat it as an investment and let the money you owe me stand for the moment, for Amy's sake — I do care for my child, whatever you believe. But you'll need to buy me out one day — and not in twenty years' time, either. Let's agree that you'll pay me back within five years — with annual interest at current mortgage rates? What could be fairer?' He looked at her questioningly.

'Ten years would be better.'

'I'm not a bloody philanthropist. And what's more, I'm not paying maintenance for Amy as well as losing the chance to use my own money. Is it a deal or not?'

'Probably.' She'd manage somehow, pay Miles back, do whatever it took. She didn't intend to be the Turner who lost Willowbrook, even though she was the first not to farm it. She'd no interest in raising beef cattle and had leased the fields out after her father died, keeping only the land around the lake. Her mother had moved back to Lancashire to be near her elderly parents and was now remarried, to a great guy.

Miles smirked at Ella and she pulled her attention back to the present.

'You'll have to get the chalets up and running without my help.' He reached into his inside pocket. 'I've drawn up an agreement. If you could just sign it and — '

'Send it to my lawyer.'

'I thought we were going to keep this between ourselves. It's all perfectly straightforward, just read it.'

'I'm signing nothing without Ian Hannow's say-so. I trust him; I don't trust you.' She gestured towards the door. 'If that's all, we'll say goodbye. Don't come back here again, Miles. You can make any further arrangements through my lawyer. If you want access to Amy, he'll arrange that too.'

He shoved his hands in his pockets. 'I might have known you'd go back to the Hannows. They're as stick-in-the-mud as you are. Right, then. I'll go up and pack my things, then I'm off.'

He was out of the kitchen and up the stairs before she could stop him.

She followed him up. 'Your clothes are no longer here; they're packed and waiting for you out in the barn.' She hadn't been able to face sharing a wardrobe for one hour longer with his precisely arranged row of designer jeans and trousers, expensive shirts and tops.

'You don't mind if I check that you've got everything?' He moved towards the wardrobe and stared inside, then opened the drawers that had been his one by one. 'You were very thorough, weren't you?'

'It was a labour of love.'

Before he went downstairs he flicked a scornful finger towards her jewellery box. 'You should put that away. It's stupid leaving it in full view. Any burglar would go straight to it. As I said, you have no financial sense.'

She shrugged and followed him downstairs.

He looked at Amy. 'I'm leaving now. Be a good girl.'

But he didn't touch the child or even wait for her answer, simply moved on across the yard to the structure they still called the barn, though it stood empty now, housing only her car and a few old farm tools. She gestured to the pile of rubbish bin bags to one side. 'There you are. Every single thing that belongs to you. I doubt anything's missing, but if it is, tell me and I'll send it on.'

'You realize I'll need to have them all ironed after they've been stuffed into those bags and dumped out here.'

She shrugged. Whether his suits and shirts would need ironing had been the last thing on her mind. He dressed well, she had to give him that. No woman took more care with her appearance than he did.

For a moment he continued to glare at her, then he picked up a couple of the bags and carried them out to his car.

In the yard, Amy took a few uncertain steps towards him, the rolling gait caused by her weak lower spinal muscles very marked. He didn't even slow down as he walked to and fro, just said, 'I'm busy, Amy.'

Ella put her arm round her daughter. 'Let's go into the house, love. Your father's in a hurry to leave.'

Inside, she went round bolting all the external doors so that he couldn't come back in. She'd have the locks changed tomorrow. Well, the house locks, anyway. The barn locks were centuries old and would have to stay, but she didn't think he had keys to them. Why would he?

After his first tour of the group of outbuildings, he'd hardly ever gone inside again.

'Why is Daddy so angry?'

'Because he's not going to live with us any more.'

Amy frowned. 'Never?'

'Never.'

'Nessa's old daddy went away. It's called a divorce. Are we going to have a divorce?'

So much for breaking the news gently! 'Yes.'

'Nessa's going to have a new daddy soon. Are we going to get a new daddy?'

Ella shuddered at the thought. She was done with men. 'No. There'll just be you and me.' She hugged the child and settled her with a glass of milk and a biscuit, keeping an eye on the barn through the kitchen window, watching Miles load his possessions into his car. When he'd finished he stood for a minute or two, studying the jumble of outbuildings, turning slowly round in a circle, staring for a few minutes at the picturesque eighteenth-century farmhouse then staring at the line of willow trees along one side, where the stream ran into the lake.

Taking out a camera, he snapped a few photos then climbed on a nearby wall and turned his attention to the chalets. The outsides were fully clad in timber now, waiting for the insides to be finished, and the buildings looked pretty, even without being painted.

That raised her suspicions again. She could only suppose he'd not given up hope of making money from Willowbrook. *Well, I'm not going to sell it, whatever you do!* she thought as he put the camera back into his briefcase. *You'll get nothing from knowing this place exists.*

It was a relief when he got into the car and drove away, but sounds carried clearly in the still air and she heard the car stop again on the other side of the house. She ran upstairs and watched him get out of the vehicle near the end of the long dirt drive. Once again he took photos.

Surely he didn't think he could still get his hands on the farm?

She'd see him in hell first.

⋆   ⋆   ⋆

After lunch the next day, Ella went up to the bedroom to change out of her old jeans ready for her trip into the village to see Ian Hannow and discuss the divorce plus Miles's suggested financial agreement.

Sitting down at the dressing table she tidied her hair then opened her jewellery box. Tears came into her eyes as she took out three eighteenth-century pieces she knew to be valuable. They were family heirlooms, but she'd have to sell them now to finish fitting out the chalets. Perhaps Ian would be able to advise her on how best to do that.

'Georgina's set' was named after the jewels' original owner. The small gold brooch was in the form of a circle bridged by a bar studded with pearls and it was one of her favourite pieces. She held it up against herself one final time, admiring it in the mirror, then put it resolutely into the padded bag, together with the matching necklace and bracelet.

She couldn't afford to get sentimental. Keeping Willowbrook was more important than keeping the jewels and anyway, there were still one or two other pieces of jewellery left, so she could at least pass on part of the family inheritance to Amy.

Closing the drawers, she locked them carefully, something she didn't usually bother doing, then studied the battered old box, which held her last objects of real value.

Perhaps Miles was right, about this at least, and it wasn't safe to leave the box on her dressing table. She hadn't bothered much about security before, because she was two miles out of the village and could see or hear if anyone drove up the track to the house.

But now . . . She couldn't be too careful of what few treasures she had left.

So she put the box in the safest place she knew. The old house could still keep its secrets, she thought with a smile as she went back downstairs afterwards.

*   *   *

Ten days later, having sold Georgina's set with Ian Hannow's help, Ella went into the village to look at paint colours for the inside of the first three chalets. She'd thought about it a lot and had decided not to press for child maintenance because it might push Miles into demanding his money back. Anyway, Amy was hers, had always been hers and she didn't want Miles to have any reason for interfering in how she brought the child up.

Ian had tried very hard to change her mind about that, but she'd stuck to her guns. She wanted Miles to leave his money invested in Willowbrook.

It'd take all the money from the sale of Georgina's jewels to finish the chalets. She'd got slightly less money than she'd expected, but if she managed it carefully, it would be enough. She was considering giving each chalet a colour theme, so in the end she left the shop with a handful of sample colour cards. She'd get her cousin to come over and help her decide. Rose was the artistic one of the family. They'd grown up together, been inseparable till her cousin went away to art college, were still close friends.

When Ella got back to Willowbrook there was no sign of Porgy and she noticed the broken kitchen window straight away. Instantly on the alert, she told Amy to stay in the car and locked it after she got out.

From the barn came the sound of hysterical barking. Porgy. She ran over there first. As she opened the door, he came out growling and sniffing the ground, but he didn't run round as usual. In fact, he was walking gingerly as if it hurt him to move. When he stopped beside her she saw that he had a cut over one eye. The blood was matted, so it must have happened some time ago.

Picking up a piece of wood for protection, she gestured to Amy to stay where she was and went inside the house, with Porgy limping along behind her. She stood listening carefully but even without the dog she could sense that whoever had broken in had left. She'd always been able to sense whether a building was empty or not, had been surprised as a child to find that others didn't have the same ability.

She went out to fetch her daughter, keeping watch for anyone coming out of the outbuildings, but again, she could sense no human presence, only feel the wind blowing her hair gently across her face and making the flowers bow their heads to her as she passed.

Together she and Amy inspected the house.

The intruder had trashed the sitting room, but hadn't stolen anything that she could see — well, her TV, sound system and computer were elderly, worth nothing. He'd smashed them, though. Perhaps he'd been disappointed by the lack of valuables.

'Some bad people have been here,' Ella told her daughter by way of explanation.

'Why did they break our things?'

'I don't know. Some people are like that.' She led the way up the stairs, waiting for Amy's slower pace. Porgy didn't even try to come with them, just stood at the bottom, whining in his throat.

'Ooh, mummy! Look at that! The bad people have been in here too.'

Amy's drawers and toy cupboard had been emptied out, but a quick glance showed the toys hadn't been damaged.

Ella gave her a quick cuddle. 'I'm sorry about all this, darling, but I don't think anything's broken. Don't put them away until the police have seen the mess.'

'Can I pick up teddy?'

'Yes.'

Amy picked up the elderly teddy which had once been her mother's and was her favourite toy, cradling it against her. 'It's all right now, Teddy. I've got you safe.'

Ella looked towards the chalets from the bedroom window. Thank goodness the electricians were working there today. The chalets should be untouched, at least. 'Let's look in my bedroom now,' she said, speaking as cheerfully as she could manage.

The burglar had clearly concentrated his upstairs efforts on this room, trashing it thoroughly. It was as if he'd been searching for something. What?

'Don't cry, Mummy. I'll help you to put your things away afterwards.' Amy took hold of her hand.

Ella hadn't realized tears were running down her face until then, tears of relief as well as pain. Thank goodness she'd hidden her jewel box!

'Let's go downstairs and call the police.' She settled Amy and the dog in the kitchen, then slipped back upstairs to check the hiding place, which her daughter was too young yet to be told about.

Her heart was thudding in her chest as she opened the panel, but the box was safe, its contents untouched. She leaned against the wall for a moment, shuddering in relief, then closed the panel again. The old house had indeed kept its secrets.

Why had the intruder concentrated on her

bedroom, though? He couldn't have known about the jewellery, surely? In fact, why had anyone come to Willowbrook at all? Everyone in the neighbourhood knew she wasn't rich. All her spare money had been sunk into the tourist chalets and she couldn't even afford to finish all of them.

But perhaps someone passing by had seen the size of the house and assumed rich people lived there. Who knew what made people break into others' homes and steal their possessions?

Picking up the phone she called the police, hesitated afterwards, then rang her cousin Rose. 'The farm's been broken into. Can you come round?' Her voice broke on the last word, try as she would to stay calm.

'Of course I can. Poor you. Did they take much?'

'There's not much of value to take, but they certainly made a mess.'

'I'll be there as soon as I can.'

Ella walked slowly down the stairs, as always getting a sense of something — or someone — on the half landing. Today, she paused at the turn of the stairs, feeling comforted by that shadowy presence. It might sound foolish and certainly Miles had always laughed at her, saying the family ghosts were figments of her imagination. But she'd seen them since she was a tiny child, too young to know what ghosts were.

Her father had sensed them too. He'd told her the apparitions were real but nothing to be scared of, since they were members of the family who were still keeping an eye on their old home.

Her mother had downplayed this side of life at Willowbrook, saying *she* had never seen anything. But then, Mum was more into practical stuff — and she wasn't a Turner by birth.

Recently Amy had started talking about the lady in the long dress who came to say goodnight to her and sometimes about the man in funny clothes she'd seen on the stairs. Ella had had to try and explain what ghosts were. Not easy with a four-year-old. Since then Amy had taken to calling the main ghost *the Lady*, using a special tone of voice to say the words.

Ella looked round before she moved on down the stairs. The house was shabby, full of awkwardly shaped rooms, but she loved it, most especially this crooked set of stairs with a cupboard on the landing.

Miles had always said it was no wonder the heritage people weren't interested in listing the farm, it was such a shambles. She'd been surprised that they didn't want it, but Miles was right. The place was very run down and was indeed a mish-mash of styles.

At first he'd made a joke of its condition, but even those remarks had been enough to make her keep quiet about the secret places in both the house and outbuildings. Some of them were accidents, nooks and crannies created during the various waves of rebuilding and modernizing that had taken place over the centuries. Others had definitely been put there on purpose, perhaps to hide people in the early days, as well as treasured possessions. The rooms and floors were so uneven you'd not notice that walls didn't match exactly unless you were shown or took extremely careful measurements.

To her, Willowbrook was beautiful, a rambling place perfect for raising a family. She'd always intended to have several children, but after producing one child with SMA3, Miles had been adamant about not having any others, even though they could have got tested to make sure it didn't happen again.

A vehicle drew up outside, an old van with a loud exhaust. She didn't have to see it to know who it was and ran out to her cousin. Rose, taller than her by three inches, swept her into a big hug, as if she understood Ella needed the comfort.

'Auntie Rose! Auntie Rose!'

Ella stepped aside to give Amy a turn at being hugged by the woman she called auntie, for lack of any actual aunts or uncles, then the two women went inside, slowing down automatically to keep pace with the slower-moving child.

'Porgy's very quiet today, not like himself at all,' Rose said. 'He didn't come running to meet me.'

'He's been hurt. I think they hit him with something. I'll have to take him to the vet's as soon as I can get away.'

'Once the police arrive, I'll do that for you. But I'll wait with you till then. There you are, you old scamp.' As they entered the kitchen Rose bent to caress the dog, who sighed and leaned against her.

'Thanks. I really need your support after this.'

Ella gestured to the mess.

The police arrived half an hour later and soon afterwards Rose left with the dog.

The two officers examined the house carefully, but once it had been established that nothing had been taken, they put it all down to vandalism and asked if she'd upset anyone lately.

'Only my husband,' she said, intending it as a joke. 'We've just split up.'

'Could you give me his name and address, please, Ms Turner?'

'You're not taking that remark seriously? Miles would never — '

'People can do nasty things when marriages end. It won't hurt to check where he was when this happened.'

When they'd gone, she brewed a pot of tea and sat in the kitchen, trying to seem cheerful for Amy's sake, but jumping at sudden noises, nerves on edge.

It couldn't be Miles. He wouldn't steal Amy's inheritance. He'd trick it out of them but not take it in a way that made him liable for imprisonment if caught. She was sure of that.

The police were probably right and it had been casual vandals looking for something to smash. It was just bad luck that they'd picked on her.

★ ★ ★

After she left Willowbrook, Rose drove carefully along the narrow lane, worrying about her cousin, who had been looking strained for a

23

while now, and no wonder. Ella was working inhumanly long hours to get Willowbrook's chalets up and running.

How she could have fallen for that . . . that *con man*, Rose had never understood. Oh, Miles Parnell was quite good-looking, but he'd never fooled her and he knew it. After he moved in, he'd not encouraged her to visit them at the farm.

She grinned. He'd never known how often she and Ella met in the village or at her house for a quick cup of coffee or just a chat. He hadn't realized how strong the bond was between them. They were more like sisters than cousins.

The van jolted in and out of a particularly bad rut and there was a whimper from the back.

'Soon be there, Porgy!' she called

The vet was new in town, young, giving her the glad eye until he started examining the dog, then becoming serious and forgetting her completely.

'I'd like to X-ray him. I think he's been kicked. He's probably got broken ribs.'

'Will it cost much?' She winced at the amount. 'Is it absolutely necessary to X-ray him? Much as we love the dog, neither my cousin nor I are exactly overflowing with money.'

He pursed his lips. 'Well, I'm pretty certain that's what's wrong. How did it happen?'

She explained about the break-in. 'What's the treatment for broken ribs?'

'Just rest, really, if they're not too badly damaged. He'll heal on his own.' He sighed. 'Look, I'll let you have the X-rays at cost. We really ought to check that there are no chips of bone, or other internal damage.'

'I'll pay for it then and we won't say anything to my cousin unless we have to.' She knew how short of money Ella was now. Paying would max out Rose's credit card and mean holding off buying a new exhaust system for a little longer, but she was getting good at wrapping that special tape round the hole in the tail pipe.

To her relief, Porgy only had a couple of fractures and the cut, which needed four stitches.

She hesitated, then seized the moment and told the new vet about one of her moneymaking ventures, taking him to see the small poster she'd put up, which was now partly obscured by other notices in the waiting room.

He grinned at the little sketches of the dog and cat on the notice. 'Do you get many clients?'

'Some. Enough to help keep the wolf from the door.'

'I must come and look at your paintings one day.'

She looked at his hopeful expression. She didn't want to upset him, but she didn't fancy him in the slightest. 'I'll bring some in to show you next time I'm passing. I do wildlife paintings as well. They're my favourite, really. Thanks.'

She took the dog back to Willowbrook and helped clear up the worst of the damage. She and Ella hugged wordlessly before she left. They didn't see as much of one another as they'd like because they were both working every minute they could manage, but they were always there for one another.

Back at her own cottage Rose worked for a while on her latest commission, a portrait of a fat and wheezy boxer dog, who looked particularly dopey to her in the photos. But you didn't say no to a cash offer. She'd done enough pet paintings to know she needed to make the poor old fellow prettier than he was, because that was how the owner saw him.

She'd tried realism the first time she did one of these paintings and smiled at the memory of the elderly corgi, whose owner had thrown a huff and refused to accept the painting until she'd 'shown the twinkle in Fluffy's eye'. The final result had been more like a cartoon, but it'd earned Rose some much-needed money.

She signed paintings like that *R. Marr*, shortening her surname, keeping her full name, Rose Marwood, for work she was proud of.

What she was really passionate about was painting the smaller wild animals and plants of her native county, Wiltshire. Passionate!

It was an obsession. She'd be the first to admit that. She made only the occasional sale from by-products of that, paintings that didn't quite meet her rigorous standards but were good enough to hang on walls. She left them on commission in two or three nearby galleries. She didn't even try to offer her other nature paintings for sale because she was working up a collection which she hoped to see published as an art/nature book. It had been a passion of hers for years and a few months ago had come between her and a guy she'd loved, because she wouldn't move away from Wiltshire and he had to. The thought of him still hurt and she'd not dated since.

Last year she'd spent what was to her a fortune on a special metal security box to keep the finished products in. The need for that was non-negotiable, like Ella's fire extinguishers at Willowbrook, which had cost her cousin a lot of money she could ill afford. Bottom line was: you didn't leave your most precious things vulnerable to fire and theft.

Rose smiled at the box and reached out to pat it. Her friends and regular customers at the pub had teased her about buying it. It had a secure lock and was supposed to be water and everything-proof, even capable of withstanding house fires for a certain length of time. It was almost the right size to hold her paintings and she'd added a wad of bubble plastic round the edges to stop the pieces of card moving around. She just hoped she never needed to put the maker's claims to the test.

Her timer rang and with a sigh she put away her painting equipment and got ready for her work in the pub, where she spent two or three nights a week behind the bar, and did casual waitressing, cleaning, whatever they needed.

That evening they offered her a few extra evenings' work behind the bar, as one of the other staff had had to rush north because of a death in the family. Rose took the work gratefully. Maybe now she'd be able to afford that exhaust system as well as the X-rays.

As for her personal life, she would concentrate on her painting. She was clearly not the sort to get married.

* * *

It took Ella several days to remove all traces of the burglary, and it took several weeks for the insurance company to cough up the money for repairs and replacements of the things that had been smashed. She bought a new computer but waited to get a TV. She was too busy finishing the chalets to miss it and luckily, her daughter could always find something to play with, acting with her toys mainly, using her vivid imagination to dream up stories.

Ella was trying to get the chalets ready for occupation before the summer, sewing curtains, table runners and bedspreads in the evenings, doing the landscaping round each chalet in the daytime.

And since no one except herself knew about the farmhouse's secrets, she wrote a letter on her new computer to leave at the lawyer's, in case anything happened to her before she told Amy about the hidden places.

She also appointed Rose guardian to Amy, knowing Miles wouldn't want to look after the child. She didn't even inform him about that, but she made sure the lawyer knew that he'd not asked for access, hadn't tried to visit his daughter or even ask about her.

Her lawyer tried several times to persuade her to ask Miles for maintenance but she shook her head stubbornly. He was letting her keep the money he'd invested and that would have to do, whatever Ian said. She didn't want any more hassles, knew Miles would argue over every penny, or maybe call in her debt.

Anyway, she wasn't afraid of hard work. She'd pay him back and keep Willowbrook for Amy — whatever it took.

2

Three years later: April

Cameron O'Neal turned off the M4 motorway and headed south into Wiltshire with a sigh of relief. Traffic had been heavy all the way from London and he was hoping for a restful weekend once he'd done this small job. He hadn't wanted to take it on, but Ray Deare was a close friend of his father's and had helped Cameron when he was younger and eager to make something of himself in the business world. He owed a lot to the older man and this was the first time a favour had been asked in return.

He intended to get this over with quickly, though, then find somewhere peaceful to stay, so that he could take stock of his life and make constructive plans for the future. He was getting less and less satisfaction from his work as a financial consultant. There had to be more to life than sorting out the problems of rich idiots.

The place he was heading for, Chawton Bassett, turned out to be so picturesque he didn't go straight to the address he'd been given, but stopped in the main street to enjoy the village. In the middle of the long, vaguely triangular space stood an ancient market hall perched on stone columns. The village centre was edged by houses built from a variety of materials — narrow old bricks, uneven stones,

30

black and white plasterwork. Most butted on to one another, even though their upper stories didn't quite match in levels or styles. But that only added to the attraction.

Local planning regulations wouldn't allow that sort of nonconformity these days and most modern town centres looked like tidy, boring piles of boxes to him. But this village took his breath away with its quaint beauty.

As he strolled round, he felt a sense of homecoming that surprised him. Yet he'd never been here before, he was certain of that. He shook his head in bafflement. Strange.

He paused as he reached a black and white timbered pub prettied up with hanging baskets just coming into bloom. It was advertising rooms. Maybe he'd book one here later. He strolled on.

The ground floors were mostly given over to shops, but these had discreet signs outside and there were no garish notices in the windows screaming out about unbeatable special offers. Well, there was only one supermarket to be seen. Above the shops three or four storeys saluted the sky and he had a sudden fancy that the houses were begging the elements to be kind to their sagging roofs and walls.

It wasn't like him to be so fanciful.

Someone had been doing an excellent job of conservation, though, from the looks of it. Ray's informant was right: a pretty village set in beautiful countryside had excellent potential — well, it would have if the local council was prepared to be flexible — and the planners at DevRaCom were rather skilful at persuading town councils to look on their proposals favourably. But give Ray his due: his company did keep listed buildings and features intact. In fact, the PR staff used them to showcase how much they cared for the nation's heritage. As if! What they really cared about was the company's image — and the bottom line: making money. And they'd made plenty over the years.

The property Cameron had come to look at for Ray was some way out of the village, so at least a hotel/conference centre development there wouldn't impinge on this medieval-Georgian gem. Apparently some woman was blocking the whole scheme by refusing to sell the central and most essential piece of land. It had a few tumbledown buildings on it, which weren't even heritage listed. Ray wanted to know more about her and her farm buildings. Were they genuinely old? Did they have any value per se? Or were they fit for nothing but being demolished?

It was probably some old lady clinging to her family home, Cameron thought. The poor thing didn't want to move! She didn't stand a chance against DevRaCom, though, not if Ray decided he wanted something.

Cameron didn't intend to get any more involved in this project than taking a quick look at the farm and reporting back to Ray in person. Typical of Ray to check up privately on what his informant had told him! he thought with a smile. He wouldn't like to work for DevRaCom full time. Ray kept a tight rein on all those working for him.

Yawning suddenly and easing his aching

shoulders, Cameron wondered if there was a decent hotel round here. The pub was pretty, but it'd probably be noisy later on. He needed a good night's sleep, had no need to rush anywhere once he'd seen the old house, could do what he fancied.

When he got back to the car, he found a traffic warden standing next to it.

'Just in time, sir. Could you move on now, please? This is only a thirty-minute spot. There are longer-term car parks behind the shops.'

'Sorry. I was just enjoying the views. It's a very pretty village.'

She beamed at him. 'We like to think so.'

*   *   *

Ella drove into the village for groceries, mentally working out which tasks she'd manage to fit into what promised to be an even busier day than usual. She made a mental note that Amy was due for one of her regular check-ups quite soon. She'd have to look in the diary and see when exactly it was, some time in June, if she remembered correctly.

She couldn't settle to anything till she heard about her application for a loan, but to her disappointment, her mailbox was again empty. How could it possibly take so many weeks for a bank to decide whether to give her a second mortgage? If it was up to the bank manager in the village, it'd have been done already, but apparently head office had to okay this sort of thing nowadays.

If they didn't approve it, she'd lose the farm. It was as simple as that — and the mere thought was so gut-wrenching she stopped walking for a moment to brace herself.

It couldn't happen. It just — couldn't.

In the supermarket she selected the fruit and vegetables with her usual care, eyeing the grapes with brief longing. Too expensive. Especially as there was a two for one offer on apples. She picked up two packs, checking each one carefully for overripe fruit, then went on to hunt out other specials, making every penny count.

Damn Miles! She didn't need this extra worry just as the tourist season was getting started. He'd promised her five years before he tried to reclaim his money. If he'd kept his word, she wouldn't be so anxious.

She should have known better than to trust him.

★ ★ ★

When she went to buy some petrol, Ella faced yet again the problem of Brett Harding. Knowing his tricks of old, she tried to keep her distance from the counter, but he grabbed her hand as she was putting her credit card into the gadget and wouldn't let go.

'You need to loosen up a bit, girl.' He gave her a wink and squeezed her hand.

With a growl of exasperation she jerked it away from him. She'd known Brett since they were children and he hadn't improved with age. They'd called him 'the octopus' at school because of his roving hands and he still merited the nickname. He'd always been stupid and brutish, and his main idea of fun these days was getting blind drunk.

If it'd been anyone else but a Harding, she'd have made a complaint of sexual harassment against him, but Brett's father was on the area council, with a special interest in the planning committee, and it wouldn't be wise to offend him. She wondered sometimes whether he knew what a loser his only son was.

When Brett had finished taking her payment, he asked, as he'd been doing for the past year, 'How about coming out with me tonight? We could — '

'Will you please stop pestering me, Brett. I keep telling you I don't date.'

''Bout time you started again.' He winked. 'Aren't you missing it?'

'Not at all.' And even if she was, a man like him wouldn't tempt her, not in a billion years.

If only there was another service station on her side of the village! She didn't want to travel several miles to fill up her car each time. That cost money and she had to be so careful.

★ ★ ★

Cameron easily found his way out to the property he was to check. A big sign with beautifully executed flowers in each corner said:

WILLOWBROOK FARM
CHALETS TO RENT
SHORT OR LONG STAYS

35

* ★ ★

He slowed down to watch a magpie land near the hedgerow and start pecking at something.

'*One for sorrow*,' he murmured automatically, feeling irrationally pleased as a second magpie appeared and he could add, '*Two for joy*'. Silly to put any credence on his grandmother's old sayings, but still, he'd rather have joy than sorrow.

He turned through the gateway, stopping the car just before the end of the drive to whistle in amazement. He could see at once that Ray's informant was wrong. This wasn't a tumbledown place, just a very old house. It was sagging a little, sure, but was still beautiful, like a very old and stately dowager. And it was well cared for. Its paintwork was immaculate and the leaded windowpanes twinkled in the sun. Across the front of the building curled a fringe of bright flowers, and a hanging basket hung on either side of the front door.

Why the hell wasn't a house like this heritage listed?

He let the car roll slowly down the slope at the side of the house to settle in one of the marked parking bays. As he got out, he studied the outbuildings at the rear. The architecture was a mixture of styles, eighteenth century mainly at a guess. But one barn looked far older than the rest. He'd have a closer look later, perhaps get permission to go inside.

A place like this needed preserving, not demolishing, surely? He hated to think what

Ray's building development team would do with it.

From here he could see the glint of water at the foot of the slope behind the house. It wasn't a big lake, about a quarter of a mile long, at a guess, and quite narrow, but it was as pretty as the rest of this place. A line of willows led down to it from the left and its still, dark-green waters were fringed by more willows on the left half of the other side. Fields and woods patterned the slopes round it.

He could see why Ray wanted to build one of his exclusive tourist developments here. Only . . . the peace would be gone and probably the line of willows with the bulrushes in front of them. It wouldn't be the same place at all, he was quite sure of that. It wasn't his business what happened to it, but still, it would be a shame.

Cameron strolled back up to the front door and used the heavy lion's head doorknocker. He wielded it a second time, hearing it echoing inside the building. Just as he was raising it for a third and final assault, there was a sound from the side of the house, and he turned.

An elderly golden Labrador padded round the corner and stopped in front of him with a sleepy woof, its head on one side as if it was asking what he was doing here. He bent to let it smell his hand and it sniffed earnestly, then gave a tentative wag.

Only then did he notice a neat sign in a glass pane next to the door saying *Back in an hour*. If the owner was away, this might be a good opportunity to explore a little. He walked round to the rear of the house with his new companion. 'Fine watchdog you are!' he murmured and it wagged again.

The rear yard was immaculately neat with two wooden tables and benches to one side of an area edged by flowers and bushes. The owner must have very green fingers.

He strolled along the outsides of the outbuildings, seeing through the gaps between them the roofs of the six chalets — cheap, tatty places the informant had told Ray. Only they weren't. They were quite new, neatly painted, each with a small paved area in front of it containing a wooden table and benches looking out on to the lake.

It suddenly occurred to him that these chalets would be a far better place than a hotel for his own needs. He could imagine sitting outside one in the evening, sipping a glass of wine and enjoying the peace.

He walked all the way round the outbuildings, marvelling at how solid they were still, built of stone, roofed with narrow slabs of the same stone. He found himself stroking the oldest barn, but he didn't feel it right to go inside, so he went back to the front of the house to wait.

The dog was there already. Cameron sat on the steps beside it, enjoying the light breeze ruffling his hair and the gentle English sunlight on his skin. When the dog nudged him, he caressed its head and with a sigh it relaxed against his leg. Golden hairs attached themselves to his neat, charcoal grey slacks and he didn't give a damn.

I'll get myself a dog, he thought. Once I've found somewhere to settle, I'll definitely get a dog. He'd had one as a lad, still missed old Rusty.

*   *   *

Ella drove out of town along the highway, noticing a kestrel hovering to one side. Cow parsley was just coming into bloom along the sides of the road, the white, mop-like heads swaying in the breeze. She smiled at a memory of herself and Rose using the hollow stems as pea shooters. She must remember to teach Amy how to do that — only her daughter would have difficulty creeping along hedgerows and climbing over walls.

She banished that painful thought quickly. She had vowed years ago only to focus on what was possible, not what was impossible. In every other way but one Amy was a normal child — a lively, attractive and sometimes naughty little girl.

Spring was in the air and perhaps that was what was making her feel so restless today. Brett's words had touched a sore spot. It was three years now since her marriage had ended and yes, she did miss a man's company, in and out of bed. She was only thirty-three, after all, not ninety.

Five minutes later she turned up her own lane, smiling as she passed the sign Rose had painted for her. Sign painting was a bit beneath an artist of Rose's skill, but since they were both struggling to make ends meet, they helped one another whenever and however they could. Some of Rose's paintings were displayed in the chalets at Willowbrook, with discreet little price tags. A few had sold. It all helped.

Ella was proud that her chalets were now making a steady profit, with as much trade as she could handle in the summer. But this year's tourist season hadn't really started yet and she'd had to use up a large chunk of her repayment savings because one of the outbuildings had been damaged in a particularly bad winter storm and the insurance company refused to authorize heritage standard work on an unlisted building. She hadn't been willing to do a cheap repair that would stick out like a sore thumb.

If only she could sell off a little of her land! That would solve the problem about repaying Miles once and for all. But local zoning didn't allow her to subdivide her farm. It was all or nothing as far as Willowbrook was concerned.

As she swung round the final curve of the long drive, she saw a white convertible parked outside the house. People who drove expensive vehicles like that didn't usually rent her chalets. Still, it'd be nice to make a bit of money this early in the season.

The owner of the vehicle was lounging on the steps leading to the front door, looking as if he belonged there. He'd taken off his jacket, rolled up his shirt sleeves and was petting her dog. And Porgy, usually suspicious of strangers, was lying beside him looking contented. As she came to a stop, the stranger stood up and moved down the steps towards her. Porgy stayed where he was at the top, tail beating out a greeting.

'I hope you don't mind me having a chat with your dog. He's a fine old fellow, isn't he? I'm a sucker for Labradors, had one myself when I was a boy.'

The man's voice was low and smooth as dark chocolate. He wasn't tall, only a couple of inches above her own medium height, but he was extremely attractive, with strong features, sun-gilded brown hair and bright blue eyes fanned by laughter lines at the corners.

Goodness, how long was it since she'd found a man so instantly attractive? Not since she'd met Miles. She found herself hoping her face wasn't too flushed or her hair tangled. When she was a child, she'd desperately wanted straight blond hair, not curly auburn, but that was only one of many wishes that had never been fulfilled — like a happy marriage and a large family.

She got annoyed with the way her thoughts were going. What did it matter what she looked like? She was running a business here.

'Can I help you?' she asked crisply.

'I'm looking for somewhere to stay.' He held out his hand. 'Cameron O'Neal.'

'Ella Turner.' She took the hand briefly, thinking how different it was from Brett Harding's meaty fist.

Behind the stranger, Porgy heaved himself to his feet, stretched carefully, then padded down the steps to swipe a quick lick over Ella's hand.

'I see my ferocious watchdog's been keeping an eye on you.' She bent to pat the dog who was getting so old and stiff now that she was relieved every day just to see him wake up.

'He did come over to ask what my business was. But when I said I wanted to rent a chalet, he gave me permission to wait.' Cameron bent to caress the old dog again.

'How long do you want to stay for?'

'Tonight and possibly the night after, I'm not sure of my schedule yet.' He hesitated, then added, 'I'm here for another reason as well. I've been asked to take a quick look at your property.'

She stiffened. 'You're here to value Willowbrook?'

'Just informally. Not a detailed valuation, just a general assessment. It's a beautiful place.'

'I think so. My family's lived here since the seventeenth century.'

He looked startled. 'That long? I wasn't sure the house would be genuinely old, because it's not listed.'

'The main building is eighteenth century — well, most of it, though we think the cellars are older. But there are other buildings even older, like the barn.'

'I'd love to see over it.'

'For the valuation?'

'No. For myself. I can give an approximate valuation of your property and its potential without a detailed inspection, but I happen to like old buildings.'

Her heart sank. 'So the bank hasn't come to a decision yet?'

He didn't want to be specific about who had sent him here, but he found it left a sour taste in his mouth to deceive her, even by omitting to set her straight. She had such an open, vivid face, though she looked tired today.

He compromised with 'These things take time.'

★ ★ ★

'I see.' Ella pulled herself together. It'd not do her case any good if she seemed desperate. 'I'll just have to put some things in the freezer then I'll show you to a chalet.' She went to get her shopping from the car and found him there beside her ready to help carry the bags in. Gold star for manners, if nothing else. 'Thank you.'

As they walked inside she wondered why a man like him, a man who drove an expensive car and looked so affluent, would want to rent a chalet when there were several excellent country hotels in the vicinity. And what sort of valuation didn't require a detailed inspection of the property? Weren't they interested in the house? Was it just the land that had value? To her it was the house that mattered most.

She dumped the bags of shopping on the long preparation surface in the kitchen, asking automatically, 'Would you care for a cup of coffee, Mr O'Neal?'

'Do call me Cameron.' He hesitated, then smiled ruefully. 'I'd love one, if it's not too much trouble. I've not had anything to eat or drink since I left London.'

'It's no trouble at all.'

He moved over to the window. 'That's a beautiful view. So peaceful.'

'I love it.' She allowed herself a minute to look at the lake, trying to see it through his eyes. A light breeze was ruffling the surface of the water and around it trees were swaying gently, birds darting to and fro. Even as she watched, a fish broke the surface, then splashed its tail and vanished again.

She got out a mug and some home-made biscuits.

'Won't you join me?' he asked.

'Well . . . all right. Just for a few minutes.' She didn't usually sit with clients, but it'd been a hectically busy morning and ten minutes' rest would set her up for her next round of jobs.

When the coffee was ready, she led the way out to the conservatory, which she used as a dining room, and sat down with him at a table. It was looking very attractive, she decided, with its red checked tablecloths and dried flower arrangements.

She took a biscuit, gesturing to him to help himself. Inevitably her thoughts drifted back to the bank as she took a bite. If they refused the loan, she had one last fallback: selling Jane Turner's rubies. They were beautiful, though old-fashioned, a necklace with a pendant that could be removed and used as a brooch, plus matching earrings. She knew they were worth a good deal of money, though not exactly how much. When she'd shown them to Miles, he'd offered to sell them for her, but had warned that the rubies weren't of the first quality.

Would the jewels be good enough to save her family home or would she be throwing good money after bad, as well as losing one of the last family heirlooms?

She hoped desperately that she wouldn't be driven to selling them. Family lore said if the rubies left the family, then the Turners' luck would go with them. She wasn't superstitious, not exactly, but she'd hate to be the one who tested the truth of the myth.

★   ★   ★

Cameron stirred his coffee, studying her covertly. She was frowning and seemed to have forgotten his presence. She looked tired and strained. Surely she didn't run this place on her own?

After enjoying some of the excellent coffee, he bit into a biscuit. Home-made, no less. Delicious! He stared out at the water and found himself enjoying the silence so didn't force any conversation.

When he'd finished, he set his mug down. 'That was delicious, thank you. It's a long time since I've had home-made biscuits. May I see the chalet now?'

'What? Oh, yes, of course. Sorry. My thoughts were miles away.'

'Good thoughts, I hope.'

She shrugged. 'Financial thoughts.'

'It must be expensive maintaining a house like this.'

'What isn't expensive these days?'

She went to unhook a key from a rack in the kitchen and he watched her get milk from the refrigerator, together with tea and coffee sachets.

45

'This was one of the original pantries, but I use it as my linen store.' She opened a rough door made of upright planks, bound together by a z-shape of smaller planks. It had a big old-fashioned latch. 'This is the earliest part of the building. It dates from the early seventeenth century, we think.'

He took a closer look. 'Is that the original door?'

'Yes. I can't bear to replace it. A modern panel door would look ghastly here.'

He watched, intrigued, as she picked up some towels from sturdy shelves made of solid wood. 'The original shelves too?'

'Yes. Oak, I think. Though this one's stone, for keeping things cool originally.'

'Is the house heritage listed?' Ray had told him it wasn't, but after seeing it, admiring it, he wanted to hear her version.

'No. My ex looked into that, but it wasn't well enough preserved or of a coherent enough architectural style to be of interest.'

Cameron frowned, puzzled by this. From what he'd seen of the place, that surprised him. He might check that later.

'I'll give you chalet six. It's my favourite, on the very edge of the lake.'

He followed her along the lakeshore, then stopped on the tiny patio of the chalet to nod approval of the view. 'I shall enjoy sitting out here. And the weather forecast is good.'

As she switched on the small refrigerator inside, she went through what was obviously a well-rehearsed speech, 'Drinks and a few snack foods are on sale at the farm. We don't sell alcohol. There's a microwave here if you want to cook anything.' She went to hang the towels in the bathroom, still talking. 'If there's anything else you need, you've only to let me know.'

'Do you do meals?'

'Yes. Only simple ones, though. Home cooking rather than gourmet dining.'

'I'd appreciate a meal tonight, if that's possible?'

'Certainly. Meals are served in the conservatory. Will seven o'clock suit you?'

'I think everything about this place suits me.'

She led the way out again and pointed to a dirt track. 'You can drive your car round the dirt track on the far side of the barn and park it right next to your chalet.'

He watched her walk back to the house, striding energetically, completely oblivious to him now, he'd guess.

He'd known she was in financial trouble when he took on this assignment. Now that he'd seen Willowbrook, he suspected she was in more trouble than she realized.

Cameron didn't like underhand dealing, but Ray was working with an outside consultant who had advised strict secrecy about the project at this stage. Ray must have some concerns about this fellow or he'd not have asked Cameron to check Willowbrook out. The trouble was, unless DevRaCom acquired this central piece of land, the whole project would be in jeopardy, so Ray didn't want Ms Turner finding out she could ask what she wanted for the old place.

Before he brought his car round to the chalet, Cameron couldn't resist going for a stroll along the edge of the lake. He stopped several times to listen to birds chirping and twittering, once to watch a hare race across a nearby field. Then he stopped in delight to watch two small deer moving slowly through the trees.

By the time he got back to the chalet, he'd decided it'd be a great pity to spoil this delightful spot by building a DevRaCom Hotel and Conference Centre on it.

He clicked his tongue in exasperation at himself as he went to fetch his car, telling himself yet again that what happened here was none of his business. Yes, it was beautiful. But he also had a significant number of shares in DevRaCom. The money they brought in was one of the reasons he didn't need to do any more consulting work and could take his time in finding a new way of life, one less stressful.

A man didn't have to do the same thing all his life. Not this man, anyway. He wasn't going down the same track as his father, who lived for his job, and trailed his wife all over the world. Why his mother put up with it, Cameron had never understood. As a child he'd seen her in tears several times about having to move on from somewhere she'd made friends and a good life, had been upset himself for the same reasons.

What he really wanted was somewhere to settle down and *stay*. He envied Ms Turner with Willowbrook as a home.

And he was beginning to wonder if Ray's adviser on this project had some hidden agenda.

The fellow was certainly sparing with the truth.

All in all, it would be a good thing to stay here a while and investigate further.

And he wouldn't mind getting to know Ms Turner better. She was a very attractive woman.

3

In the kitchen, Ella caught sight of the clock. 'Oops! Come on, Porgy! Let's go and meet Amy.'

She waited for the old dog to haul himself to his feet and lumber off towards the car. As she matched her steps to his, she bent to pat his head. 'I think I'd better cut down your food, old fellow. Yes, I know you enjoy my cooking, but I also know for a fact that you haven't been chasing your quota of rabbits lately.' It had been a while since he'd actually caught anything, poor love. And he probably never would again.

She looked up to see Cameron standing by his car, watching her and grinning. She could feel herself blushing at being caught talking to Porgy like that.

Cameron nodded towards the dog. 'Was he a good rabbiter once?'

'The best. The very best.' Her voice came out choked, as she remembered Porgy the puppy, the young dog, the protector. He'd once ripped the leg of Brett Harding's trousers when Brett tried to force a kiss on her. She'd given the dog a juicy bone as a reward afterwards.

She should definitely have paid more attention to Porgy when choosing a husband. He'd known instinctively what it had taken her years to find out, and had never gone to Miles for petting. Indeed, he had often bared his teeth and growled during that last fraught year they'd been together.

Miles had once threatened to have him put down. That was when she'd lost it completely and told him that if he harmed her dog, she'd slice up all his fancy business suits and shirts, every last one. She'd meant it, too. Miles knew that. He'd never threatened her dog again. He was more vain about his clothes than any woman she'd ever met.

Unfortunately Amy had heard the quarrel and burst into tears, pushing her father away when he tried to reassure her that he'd only been joking.

Ella drew a deep breath. She was doing it again, wandering off into her memories, had to stop doing this. Surprised, she watched as Porgy ambled over to butt his head against Cameron's leg because he didn't usually treat strangers like this. 'I'm sorry if he's bothering you.'

'He's not bothering me at all.' He was caressing Porgy's ear now, sending the dog's back leg into an ecstasy of twitches.

She glanced at her watch and clicked her tongue in annoyance at herself. 'Sorry. I can't stay to chat. Porgy and I have to meet my daughter off the school bus. Won't be long. Come on, boy! Come and meet Amy.' She helped Porgy up into the back of her station wagon and drove down the lane to the main road.

★ ★ ★

Amy got down awkwardly from the bus, schoolbag on her back, clutching a sheet of

51

paper. Ella knew better than to offer any assistance. Amy hated being helped, even when she was tired and more wobbly on her feet than usual.

Her red-gold hair, several shades lighter than her mother's but equally curly, was an untidy tangle, as usual by this time of day. Her white socks were filthy, her blue checked school dress was crumpled and stained where she'd probably fallen. She fell a lot, inevitably, but never let that stop her trying to do things. And she was definitely growing again. The dress was getting too short and there was no hem left to let down. Time to buy some new clothes. Ella prayed they'd have something to fit Amy in the school's clothing exchange.

She couldn't remember the last time she'd had a new outfit herself, apart from the jeans and tee shirts she wore most of the time, and she got those at charity shops when she could. If it made a difference to keeping her home, she didn't care if she never had another new outfit as long as she lived.

She forgot her worries for a few minutes as she stood smiling at her daughter's afternoon ritual. Unless it was raining Amy always dropped everything to lean into the back of the car and cuddle Porgy, assuring him that he was the 'most handsomest dog in the whole world'.

Lately, Amy had stopped flinging herself into her mother's arms when she got off the bus. That wasn't a cool thing to do in front of her friends, it seemed, but once the bus had driven off, Ella usually got a hug. Amy was growing up so quickly. Seven already, and very mature for her age. Already the child accepted that as she grew older, she'd find it more difficult to walk and might prefer to use a wheelchair, though that would be her own choice and wasn't inevitable.

Miles had hated to see Amy's awkward, rolling walk, hated a child of his being 'crippled'. His use of that old-fashioned and derogatory word had caused another huge row and his lack of real affection for his daughter had helped accelerate the process of alienation between him and Ella.

'Did you have a good day, darling?' she asked as the cuddles with Porgy came to an end.

'Wicked. We had sport this afternoon. I played rounders and guess what — I hit the ball right to the edge of the field. My running partner got to third base.'

'Who was your running partner today?'

'Louise. She's terrible at hitting the ball, with her bad eyes, so we make a perfect team, Miss Baker says.'

Thank heavens for understanding teachers, Ella thought as she drove back to the house and parked at the rear.

'Oh, wow! Look at this car!' Amy hurried over to examine it. 'I'd love a ride in it. Wouldn't the other kids stare?'

'You are not to ask Mr O'Neal for a ride. He's a guest.'

'But if *he* asked me to go for a ride, you'd let me, wouldn't you?'

'He won't ask if you don't hint.'

Amy hunched one shoulder and scowled, understanding the hidden warning. 'Who is he, anyway?'

'Mr O'Neal is from the bank.'

'Oh.' Amy wrinkled her brow in thought. 'But you said they'd send us a letter or phone us.'

'Well, they sent this man to see us instead.'

But the child's innocent words had added to the worry lurking at the back of Ella's mind. Why had Cameron O'Neal decided to stay at Willowbrook? A quick inspection of the property wouldn't have taken more than an hour or two, surely? And now she came to think of it, he didn't seem like a bank minion. He looked too affluent, too confident. What sort of job did he hold there? Her heart lurched and a leaden feeling settled in her stomach and set up camp there. Was he here to prepare the ground for a forced sale?

What other reason could he have for staying on?

As she prepared the meal, still puzzling over that mystery, she watched a mature rabbit and two young ones move slowly along the nearer edge of the lake.

Lately these everyday sights and sounds had seemed more charged with emotion because if Miles pushed things too far, she might not be here for much longer. Her worries swirled inside her in a black flood and she rubbed her aching head. If she lost the farm, where would she go? Jobs weren't easy to find in Chawton Bassett and she didn't have very marketable skills. Worst of all, if she had to find employment elsewhere, how would she bear living in a town?

'Mummy, there's a man coming to the house. Is he the one with the car?'

Ella jerked to attention and peeped out of the

window to see Cameron strolling towards them. Gone was the business suit, the crisp white shirt, the immaculately styled hair. Instead, his hair was damp, his skin rosy from a shower and he was wearing a tight-fitting pair of jeans and casual sweater.

He'd looked good before, but now he looked absolutely gorgeous. She deliberately finished rinsing two mugs before turning to nod to him casually as he stood in the open doorway.

'This is Mr O'Neal — my daughter Amy.'

The child limped across to give him a wide, gap-toothed smile and hold out her hand. 'My name's Amy Parnell, but I'm changing it to Turner like Mum when I grow up. My dad won't let me change it now, though.'

'Pleased to meet you, Miss Parnell.'

Amy giggled at this formal way of addressing her and shook the hand he was offering.

'Have you hurt your foot?'

She gave him another of her sunny smiles. 'No. I've got SMA, so I can't walk properly.'

He didn't move away, either mentally or physically. Ella always watched carefully to see how people took her daughter's frankness about her disability.

'I don't know what that is, exactly.'

'Mummy can tell you about it best.'

Ella explained briefly about the faulty cells in the spinal cord, which meant that messages from the brain didn't get through properly to the muscles in her daughter's body, and how this would have more effect on mobility as Amy grew bigger.

She was pleased when he continued to talk normally to her daughter afterwards. So many people behaved as if the child was slow mentally as well as physically, when actually this disability had no effect on intelligence.

'Must be a nuisance for you,' he said.

Amy considered this, head on one side. 'Sometimes. But it's a nuisance to wear glasses all the time, like Ruth Makerby does. They mist up on hot days or when she's doing sport. And Colin Seeble has to use a spray for his asthma. He has to carry it everywhere and sometimes he can hardly breathe.' She imitated the wheezing sound her friend made with a fair degree of accuracy, then added philosophically, 'Most people have some problem or other, Mum says.'

Cameron nodded gravely. 'I guess you're right. I'm allergic to cats. Being near one makes me itch and sneeze.'

Amy nodded. 'I like dogs better anyway.'

'So do I.'

Ella judged it time to intervene. 'How can I help you, Mr O'Neal?'

'You said you sold snack foods.'

'Yes, we do.' Ella turned to her daughter. 'Amy, can you deal with it for me? I have to start making the tea.'

The child came forward, very self-important, and indicated the display area. 'What would you like, Mr O'Neal?'

'I'll have some lemonade, I think. A couple of cans. A packet of nuts — and are those chocolate bars on sale, too?'

'Uh-huh. And I get to have one every Saturday

after I've finished my jobs. They're yummy.'

'Then as you recommend them so strongly, Miss Parnell, I'll take one as well.' He hesitated, looked at Ella and when she shook her head as if guessing he was going to offer to buy one for her daughter, he said nothing more. Not slow on the uptake, Ms Turner.

Amy opened the glass door of the display cabinet, reached up to get the things he wanted then shut the door carefully. She took a printed list from the nearby holder and a pencil stub from the drawer below it. 'Which chalet are you in, Mr O'Neal?'

'Number six.'

'And how do you spell your name?' Laboriously, she printed his name and chalet number on the paper, then ticked off the items he'd bought and showed the list to him, before putting it into the numbered slot of the bill holder.

'You did that very efficiently,' he told her gravely.

She nodded several times. 'I like to help my mummy. She works too hard, my Auntie Rose says. Hey, I love your car. It's — '

'Amy, don't gossip!' Ella warned. 'Can we get you anything else, Mr O'Neal?'

'No.' Sensing the dismissal in her tone, he turned towards the door. 'Seven o'clock, then.' He strolled off, whistling softly.

'He's nice, isn't he?' Amy put her head on one side. 'And quite good-looking for someone so old. He's probably even older than you.'

'Yes.' Ella watched him walk back to the

57

chalet, wishing there were some other guests to interrupt the strange sensations that swirled between her and Cameron O'Neal. What was there about the man that attracted her so strongly? Maybe his aura of confidence or the twinkle in his eyes. And of course, the kind way he'd dealt with both her daughter and her dog.

Amy's indignant voice interrupted her thoughts. 'Mummy? I just asked you a question twice and you didn't answer!'

'Sorry, love. What did you want?'

★ ★ ★

By six o'clock, Ella had heard Amy read, fed her, supervised the nightly shower and made sure everything was ready for school next day. She switched on the TV in their private sitting room and left Amy watching it with Porgy sprawled on the carpet beside her, then went to set the table for her guest.

When someone knocked on the door just before seven, she called 'Come in!' assuming it was Mr O'Neal.

Brett Harding appeared instead, beefy face red, brandishing a bottle of wine. 'Surprise!' He moved forward, dumping it on the nearest surface and eyeing her up and down in a way she detested.

She dropped the lettuce back into the colander. 'What the hell are *you* doing here?'

'Thought you might be lonely t'night, Ella.'

'Well, I'm not, so go away!'

'Well, I'm very lonely.'

He was swaying on his feet and she could smell his beery breath from right across the room. Not liking the look on his face, she moved quickly to put the table between them. 'Look, just go home and sleep it off, will you?'

Strange. She had never been afraid of Brett before, not after going to school with him, even though he was a big man. But tonight he had a dangerous gleam in his eyes and he was so drunk she doubted she could reason with him.

He ignored her request to leave and moved forward quickly, shoving the central table towards her. That caught her by surprise and he crowed gleefully as it banged against her thighs and pushed her back towards the sink. A plate slid dangerously close to the edge of the table.

'Ouch! Stop that!' She kept her voice low, not wanting to alarm Amy.

'Aw, loosen up. I c'n give you a real good time, Ella.'

'Will you stop this!'

'*Stop this!*' he mimicked. 'Why stop? It's been three years since Miles left. You must be missing it, Ella. Wouldn't you like someone to warm your bed?'

She abandoned reason and picked up the nearest heavy implement, which happened to be a meat tenderizing mallet. 'Get out of my house, Brett Harding. *At once!*'

In response, he shoved the table backwards again, trapping her against the workbench.

'I'll call the police,' she threatened, trying to push the table away and failing.

He sniggered. 'I'll tell them you were begging for it. Only your word against mine.'

'Not quite!' snapped a voice behind them. 'There's my word, too. And all I heard her begging for was that you go away.'

To be discovered in this embarrassing situation was the final straw that lit Ella's temper to white heat. Hefting the meat mallet, she took advantage of Brett's surprise to shove the table away, making him yelp as it hit his thighs. She started round it purposefully.

'I'll deal with this.' Cameron moved in front of her, grabbing Brett's shoulders and spinning him away from Ella. When Brett made a flailing attempt to punch him, he countered the blow easily, even though he wasn't as big, then twisted the other man's right arm behind his back. Ignoring Brett's bellows of helpless rage, he frog-marched him out of the back door.

Ella let her weapon drop, rage still humming through her. She could have dealt with this herself, she thought angrily. Brett had caught her by surprise, that was all. She could damn well look after herself.

There was the sound of shouting from outside, so she ran to the door and watched as Brett broke away from Cameron and tried to punch him. The blow didn't land and Cameron was clearly refraining from decking his drunken opponent. This restraint gave Brett the chance to grab him and both men fell to the ground. Behind her, Porgy growled and she said, 'Shh, boy!' without turning her head.

In the parking area, the two men rolled away

from one another and got to their feet in a crouching position.

'Get away home, you drunken fool!' Cameron yelled.

'Don't you tell me what to do! That bitch has been askin' for it for months.'

When Brett took another clumsy swing at him, Cameron moved swiftly out of reach, circling the drunken man and clipping him sharply with a quick counter-punch to the jaw. Brett reeled back against his van, shook his head in a vain attempt to clear it and swung his fist again, missing completely and falling to his knees.

'You aren't going to win, you know.'

'Oh, aren't I? I will if you'll stand still an' fight like a man.'

Cameron sighed and as Brett jerked forward again, punched him even harder on the chin. 'Just go home and sleep it off.'

This time Brett stayed down on all fours, groaning.

Behind Ella, a voice said, 'Mummy, what's happening? Why is Mr Harding fighting Mr O'Neal?' Clad only in her pyjamas, Amy stood beside her, goggling at the two dishevelled men, holding a still growling Porgy by the collar.

'Mr Harding is drunk. He was being very silly. Mr O'Neal had to throw him out.'

'Oh, wow! Like on the TV. Can I stay and watch them fight?'

'No, you can take yourself back inside, Amy. Ten minutes more and it's time for bed.'

'But I — '

'*Go inside now!*'

Amy stamped away indignantly, dragging Porgy with her. The sitting room door banged shut and the volume went up on the television.

Brett dragged himself to his feet and stood for a moment, swaying, fists still clenched. He took out his keys, dropped them and scrabbled for them, unable to find them till he saw the lucky figurine attached to them poking out from behind the car tyre. He'd carried that figurine about with him since school, an ugly little creature with glass eyes that glittered in the light. Ella had always disliked it.

Muttering something under his breath, he opened the van door. There he stopped and turned to look back at Ella. 'I'll be back. Fancy boy won't be here for long. If you're giving it out, I'll get my turn later.'

'Then I'll be sure to keep the meat mallet handy from now on,' she called back.

Cameron remained where he was, arms folded, a cold expression on his face, as Brett closed the van door.

She wouldn't like to be on the receiving end of that icy stare, Ella decided, watching her guest. Goodness, how different he looked at the moment to when he'd been talking to Amy earlier! Dangerous and powerful.

Only when the van had bumped off down the drive did Cameron turn and come back towards the house, the icy look softening. As he reached her, he flourished a bow and said with a wry grin, 'Sir Galahad at your service.'

Dropping him a curtsey, she clasped her hands together and replied in a breathless, girlish voice,

'Oh, my lord knight, you've driven away the evil dragon. How can I ever repay you?'

His hearty laughter took away some of the nasty taste the incident had left.

But she was still worried about Brett's parting words. He'd not looked like a buffoon then, but like an angry and brutal man.

4

As the light began to soften and colours lose their vibrancy, Rose put down her paintbrush and rolled her shoulders to ease the stiffness. She'd been painting from early afternoon, enjoying what she was doing too much to stop. Yawning, she released her hair from its bonds, shaking her head as it fell about her shoulders. At least she didn't have to work tonight. She was fed up of serving behind the bar in the Green Man pub, nice as people were there, but she needed the money.

What she really wanted to do at this time of year was go out to Willowbrook with her camera. The place was teeming with wild flowers, birds and small animals like hares, rabbits and frogs. She loved to listen to the bird calls, to watch the changing patterns of flowers as the seasons changed and slid into one another. And then she'd take her photographs home and use them as the basis of wildlife paintings.

Was she fooling herself? she wondered. Was she really good enough to make a living as a painter? She'd been trying for years now and still hadn't managed more than half a living. And was her special project the most foolish dream of all? Who knew?

She sometimes thought the whole village knew about her project because of her working in the pub. There had been considerable interest from customers she chatted to there in the secure box she'd bought to protect and store her finished paintings, and of course in her ongoing progress. Occasionally one of them would buy a painting from her. She was never certain whether that was from kindness or because they liked what she did.

All she was certain of was that she couldn't stop painting. Something in her would die if she did.

She studied her work, her spirits lifting a little. It was good, one of her best ever, and it was commissioned, so would earn her some much-needed money.

Putting the wet canvas carefully on the high shelf at the rear of the room, she began to clear up her painting equipment. She worked in the larger of the two bedrooms in the tiny one-storey cottage, which stood right on the main road into the village and was very cheap to rent. She made do with the smaller bedroom to sleep in, didn't care about fancy furnishings as long as the place was clean and she had a bed. But she couldn't bear her studio to be untidy, or her equipment to be left lying around, so had bought a huge old mahogany wardrobe in a junk shop. It not only held her paints, brushes, rags and stores, but some of her finished canvases. Beside it stood her precious metal box.

Suddenly she heard the screech of brakes outside, followed by the unmistakable sound of cars colliding. Before she could move, something slammed into the side of the cottage, the window shattered and one wall of her studio caved in.

The open door of the wardrobe protected her from most of the flying glass and she cowered back among the equipment, one arm flung up protectively across her face, praying the vehicle wouldn't come any further inside.

When silence fell, she peered out from behind the door, to see the nose of a large van poking through the wall. Pieces of glass were still falling with a faint tinkling sound, the air was full of dust and the metal of the vehicle was settling and protesting about being twisted out of shape.

The driver of the van was motionless, slumped over the steering wheel, but she recognized him at once. Brett Harding! Anger filled her. She'd bet he was drunk again.

On the thought that he'd destroyed her home, she turned to scrabble among the dusty debris for her precious box. There was a shallow dent in one corner, but it was otherwise intact. She looked up at the shelf where she'd put her new painting and although it was dusty, it was safe. It was in oils, so she could clean that. Groaning in relief, she tried to work out what to do next.

Voices came closer and she rubbed her forehead in an attempt to banish the spaced-out feeling and think clearly. Shock, she told herself, but even that understanding didn't make her brain function properly.

Someone opened the front door and a voice called out. 'Anyone there?'

'Yes. I'm here.'

'You all right?' Footsteps came towards her. The handle turned but the bedroom door was stuck and even when the catch gave, there was rubble behind it. Whoever it was grunted with the effort of moving the door back against the rubble.

She watched, still feeling as if she was moving under water.

A man edged himself through the gap and paused. He was tall with dark hair greying very slightly at the temples, and blue eyes that were still as bright as ever. He scanned the room quickly, eyes moving from one pile of debris or broken furniture to another till they settled on her.

They didn't speak for a moment or two, just stared at one another, then she found her voice. 'Oliver Paige. What are *you* doing back in Chawton?'

'How delightful to see you again, Rosie — and to get such a warm welcome.' He stared round. 'You've not changed at all, still getting into trouble.'

She stiffened as he came towards her. She didn't want him to touch her, hadn't wanted to see him again ever. Then she glanced back at the van and reaction set her shaking.

The sarcasm left his voice as he folded her in his arms. 'It's all right. Shh now, Rose, it's all right. You're safe.'

She let herself relax against the familiar shelter of his chest. Just for a moment or two, she told herself. She wasn't going down that path again.

★   ★   ★

It wasn't until Cameron came into the brighter light of the kitchen that Ella saw the blood.

67

'You're hurt!' She grabbed a clean tea-towel, dampened it under the tap and gently wiped his face.

'It's only a graze.' He rubbed his thigh and grinned ruefully. 'I've probably got one or two bruises as well from tumbling around with that idiot.'

'Sit down and I'll see to that cut.' She pulled out a chair and grabbed the medical kit, trying to stay calm. But being so close to him affected her and she guessed it was affecting him, too. She saw his eyes flicker towards her, heard him suck in a breath. It hadn't happened to her for a long time, but you couldn't mistake the invisible sparks of a mutual attraction.

She said the first thing that came into her head, anything to break the tension. 'I — um — I'm grateful you came to my rescue.'

He smiled. 'I wasn't sure at first who needed rescuing. That meat tenderiser could have done considerable damage to your intruder.'

'It'd have served him right.'

'I might agree with that, but I think the police would take a different view. Who is he, by the way?'

'Brett Harding. Son of our local service station and garage owner. I was at school with him. He was a pest then, too.'

'Sexual harassment is against the law. I could act as your witness to what happened.'

'Don't I wish! Trouble is, his father's a well-known figure in town and he's rescued Brett from trouble many times. Mr Harding is a member of the local council and chairman of the planning committee. I need his good will.'

'Nuisance, that.'

She nodded. 'Let me see to your face.'

'It's nothing much. I'll just wash it and — '

'I prefer to be certain you're all right. I don't want you suing me for injuries received on my property. Sit on this stool, please.'

He spread his hands wide in a gesture of surrender and sat down.

She dampened a piece of cotton wool in water and antiseptic, pressing it gently on his injured cheek. 'It's more a graze than a cut. I don't think it'll leave a scar.'

When she'd finished, she wrapped some ice in a tea towel. 'Here. If you hold this against your face, it should stop any swelling.'

'Thanks!'

As she put the things away, she began to worry. What if she'd been alone? Brett was a big man. Could she really have fought him off on her own? Would he come back again, as he'd threatened?

'Are you all right, Ella?'

'Just wondering what got into him, whether he'll . . . '

' . . . do it again?'

She nodded.

'You could have a quiet word with his father.'

'I suppose so. But Mr Harding doesn't take kindly to criticism of his family.' She didn't want to think about Brett again tonight. To her relief, the timer on the cooker went ping. Moving towards it, she said briskly, 'There! Dinner's almost ready. If you'd like to come through to

69

the dining room, Mr O'Neal?' She led the way, indicating a place near the window.

He eyed the table set for one with disapproval. 'Have you eaten already?'

'Well, no, but I don't usually eat with guests.'

'There's only one guest tonight. You mean you're going to sit alone in the kitchen while I sit by myself out here? That's ridiculous. Join me for dinner, Ella? Please. And use my first name, as I asked.'

'Well, I — ' she took a deep, slow breath ' — Oh, all right. I'll — um, just go and see Amy to bed, then I'll get the food and set another place.'

But when he'd gone to sit down, she fled first to the sink, where she could splash her hot face with cool water and tell herself she could handle this.

* * *

For a few moments Rose gave in to the temptation to lean against Oliver. But then suddenly she remembered the way he'd left her without a word. Pulling away, she stiffened her spine. 'Sorry. Just a momentary weakness.' She turned to check the metal box again.

'You're still too independent, Rose.' He watched what she was doing, lip curling scornfully. 'And you always were more concerned about your painting project than about anything else.'

She couldn't find the energy to argue.

Then people began clambering over the van

and someone called, 'You all right, Rose?'

'I'm fine.' But she stayed where she was, too wobbly still to risk clambering out across the rubble. She watched as they used the jaws of life to cut open the van door, rubbing her forehead, which was hurting.

Oliver pried her hand away and said in his doctor's voice, 'Let me see.'

Still feeling weak and boneless, she let him.

'Just a small gash. No need for stitches, but we'll make sure it's clean as soon as we can get you out of here.'

By then Brett was stirring. He looked round the van, bleary-eyed. 'What happened?'

'Stay where you are, sir. Don't move.'

But being Brett, he ignored that and tried to get out of his vehicle. He had to wait until they'd pulled away the pieces of his door, then found himself facing a policeman.

'Would you blow into this, please, sir?'

He reared back. 'No way! I'm injured. I need to go to hospital.'

'Are you refusing to take a breathalyser test?'

Brett tried to push past him, but the policeman caught his arm in a firm grip.

'If you don't blow into this, we'll have to take a blood sample. I can smell beer on your breath.'

For a moment all hung in the balance then, with a growl of anger, Brett did as he was asked.

'You didn't do that properly, sir. We'll have to do it again. Now, continue to blow until I tell you to stop and make sure your breath goes into the tube properly.'

When that was over, the police officer shook

71

his head over the results and Brett insisted on seeing them.

'It's wrong!' he yelled, snatched the kit out of his hand and hurled it across the road.

It took them a couple of minutes to subdue him and put him into the police car.

'He'll go to the station, take a blood test, willingly or not, and be charged with driving under the influence,' Rose said with relish.

'He doesn't seem to have improved with keeping.'

'No, he hasn't.'

One of the policemen came over to Oliver. 'You were driving the second car, sir, I believe?' Then he smiled. 'Oliver Paige. I thought you'd left Chawton for good.'

'No, just for a few years. Nice to see you again, Chad.'

'I have to ask you to take a breathalyser test, I'm afraid.'

'Sure. Happy to oblige.'

Rose watched as Oliver complied and was cleared of drinking. He had the faintest of American accents now, after his years in the States. She'd not heard that he was coming back, and she usually picked up all the gossip at the pub. What was he doing here? She hoped he'd not be staying long in Chawton.

She waited for him to leave but he didn't. He watched as they towed away the van and fastened a tarpaulin over the gaping hole in her wall, then turned to her. 'This is one of my father's cottages, isn't it?'

'You know it is.'

'You won't be able to stay here while it's being repaired.' He stared round. 'Was this your studio?'

She nodded. 'And I'd rather stay, so I'll manage. I can take my painting things into the living room while this room is being repaired.'

'Surely there's somewhere else you can go? Isn't your cousin still out at Willowbrook? She'll have room for you.'

'I'd rather stay here, where I can walk to my evening work at the pub.'

She decided to change the subject. 'Home for a visit?'

'No, home for a while. Dad's partner's resigned and the practice is too big for one person.'

'You, a GP?'

He smiled. 'Why not? A and E training is perfect for the job, and anyway, I need a change.'

His face took on that shuttered look she'd always hated. Oliver could conceal his feelings better than anyone she'd ever met. She should know. His wooden expression had been much in evidence during the time they were splitting up.

'If you're sure you can manage tonight, I'll come back tomorrow.'

She watched him walk away, got angry with herself for doing that and slammed the front door shut — which was a waste of time with a gaping hole in the corner of her house.

She looked round the studio, of which she'd been so proud, and tears welled in her eyes. This was a backward step.

So was the return of Oliver Paige. It'd taken

her years to get him out of her system — and he still crept into her dreams occasionally, damn him! Why did he have to come back to Chawton?

She couldn't imagine him as a GP. He definitely didn't have a bedside manner, or much tolerance of fools. Maybe his return was only temporary until his father found another partner. Maybe he was marking time between jobs.

She sighed as she started to clear up the mess. Worst of all, Oliver was just as good-looking as ever, damn his baby blue eyes and honey-coloured hair.

★   ★   ★

After the meal, Ella and Cameron lingered at the table, sipping her best cooking port in a companionable silence as they watched the moon's reflection in the lake. The conservatory was shadowed, apart from their small oasis of brightness, and when he went to switch the remaining light off, she made no protest.

'I often sit here in the dark in the evenings,' she admitted, her voice quiet, her body still and relaxed.

'The view is just as beautiful by moonlight as by day. Did you grow up here?'

'Yes. We Turners have lived here for centuries.'

She smiled at some memory and Cameron marvelled at how softly tender that smile was. There was something so very attractive about the quiet warmth of her, though she had been magnificent in her anger. She was too thin, though, and her clothes hung rather loosely on her. She looked as if she'd be the better for a good rest. 'Are your parents still alive?'

'Dad died a while ago. Mum's remarried. What about yours?'

'They're in Toronto. But only until next year. Then they'll move to London. Dad's nearing the end of his working life, but he'll probably continue to manage the occasional project for the company after he retires. I don't think he knows how to do anything else but work, actually.'

'Where did you grow up? I can't quite place your accent.'

'That's because there's a bit of everything in it. When I was a kid, my parents hauled me all over the world, wherever Dad happened to be based. I've spent most of the last decade based in the UK, but doing projects in other countries.'

'Do you enjoy moving around?'

'I used to.'

'But not now?'

'No, not any more.' He cocked one eyebrow at her and grinned. 'You haven't asked me if I'm married?'

She'd been dying to. 'And are you?'

'No. Never have been, either. But I've cohabited a couple of times, one of them for two years. My lifestyle didn't help. Nothing acrimonious about the break-ups, there just wasn't enough to keep us together.'

'What exactly do you do at the bank?'

Should he confess? No, not yet. Not everything, anyway. 'I'm not actually employed by the bank. I just work on projects here and there.'

Something to do with her property? She didn't want to think about that now, didn't want to spoil the evening. 'And when the current projects are finished?'

He shrugged. 'Who knows? I certainly don't. I'm at one of those crisis points in life.' He smiled, but it faded quickly. 'I'd call it a mid-life crisis, except I'm only thirty-five.'

Silence fell between them. She wondered whether to get up and clear the table, but felt exhausted, so sat on, nursing her wine glass, sipping occasionally and watching the moonlight play on the gently moving water of the lake. The conservatory was one of her favourite places to sit.

'I can see why you love your home,' he said after another few moments of comfortable silence. 'Have you ever thought of expanding this place into a larger operation?'

She jerked upright at that, feeling suddenly tense. What had made him ask that? 'I've got as much on my plate as I can manage at the moment.'

'If this is a one-woman operation, I'd say you're managing more than most people could, and the place is a credit to you.'

She inclined her head in acknowledgement of this compliment. 'Anyway, I don't have the capital to develop anything else or I'd not have had to apply for a loan to pay out my ex. Once that's done, I shall need to consolidate for a year or two. You're a business consultant. You should understand that.'

'But would you expand, if you could?'

'Yes, I would. I'd like to keep the history of the farm alive, have staff wearing old-fashioned clothing and perhaps keep some period costumes to loan to guests. People love dressing up if you give them a good enough excuse. I'd conserve the land, offer small animals and birds an asylum, and give the townies and foreign tourists the chance to appreciate the natural beauty of Wiltshire. There's a local nature society that would help me set up nature walks and observation points.'

She'd dreamed of it so many times, lain in bed picturing it, studied old history books. She realized she was betraying her most cherished dreams, dreams she hadn't told anyone else about, and cut the conversation short, surprised at herself. 'Well, you get the picture. I definitely wouldn't want to offer guests a noisy resort full of expensive restaurants, shops and bars that could be found anywhere in the world. A large company made me an offer a few years ago, but I turned it down. And now another company is interested. I'm not selling, though, not unless I'm forced to. It's my family home. I want to go on living here and hand it to my daughter one day, just as my father handed it to me.'

'I know what you mean about resort hotels. I've stayed in enough of them to last me the rest of my life. And when there were conventions going on, I kept mostly to my room. I'm not a party animal, I'm afraid.'

How lonely his life sounded! She kept the conversation firmly on him, feeling she'd already betrayed too much about herself. 'You must have seen quite a bit of the world, though? Which countries did you like best?'

He spoke for a while about some of his favourite places — Vancouver, Sydney — then the talk drifted to a standstill again. It had been a long time since she'd enjoyed a man's company so much, a long time since anyone had listened to her as Cameron had, as if he was really interested in what she was saying.

Eventually she forced herself to break up the evening, nervous of how much she'd told him. 'If I don't go to bed, I'll never be up in time to get Amy off to school tomorrow.'

He stood up with that lazy confidence that was so much a part of him. 'I shouldn't have kept you up so late, but I enjoyed your company.'

'I enjoyed yours, too,' she said before she could work out if it was wise to admit that. The trouble was, she really liked him. He hadn't tried to score off her or prove anything as they chatted, just . . . well, acted like an old friend.

Only he wasn't an old friend. Or even a new one. He'd be gone in a day or two, would probably forget her before he even reached his next stopping place. She had to remember that. Her customers were birds of passage. She was, she hoped, here to stay.

He moved across to the door, then turned. 'Will you be all right on your own here, Ella?'

'Of course I will.'

'But you'll lock up carefully?'

'Yes. I'm sure Brett's safe in his bed by now, though. And I'd hear a vehicle coming up the drive.'

'What time is breakfast?'

'Just come across whenever you're ready. Since you're the only guest, it doesn't matter to me when you eat. I'll be gone for about five minutes just after eight, taking Amy to the bus, otherwise I'll be busy here.'

'Fine. I think I'll sleep well tonight. It's been a long day.'

She watched him walk along the path to the chalets then switched off the outside lights, except for the security light that guarded the approach from the lake and the other light at the front of the house. Miles had had those put in, ironically, because he said it was a dangerously isolated place. Then he'd left and she'd been glad of them, she admitted, though they did sometimes get triggered by animals.

When she went to bed, she lay awake for a while, reliving the evening, worrying about Brett Harding, about the loan, about her home . . . till eventually tiredness claimed her.

But she dreamed about Cameron O'Neal, dreamed of being held by him, kissed by him.

In the morning, remembering those dreams, she was angry with herself. How stupid could you get? *Act your age, Ella Turner*, she ordered. *Show a bit of sense. You're not a man-mad teenager.*

But she was so tired of being sensible. And she did miss having a man in her life, the companionship, the support, the fun — and the loving.

★ ★ ★

79

Brett Harding was charged with being in charge of a motor vehicle with excess alcohol and once the formalities were over, he rang his father to come and pick him up.

His father was furious and didn't spare him when he turned up. Brett knew better than to argue, so bowed his head and put up with the tirade in silence. This was all that bitch's fault, leading a man on.

'Are you still conscious?'

He realized his father had asked a question and was waiting for a reply. 'Sorry, what did you say?'

'I asked what the hell you were doing, driving one of my vans in that condition. It's a total write-off now. What was wrong with your own car?'

'Needs a new carburettor.'

'I didn't see it at the garage.'

'I forgot to book it in.'

'You'd forget your head if it wasn't nailed on, you would. And if you weren't my only son, heaven help me, you'd be out on your ear. I'm still tempted to fire you anyway, and I would if it weren't for your mother. Where had you been tonight?'

'I'd been out to Willowbrook, seeing Ella Turner.'

'I didn't know you two were involved.'

'Yeah. Sort of.'

'She's got encumbrances, that one, and the child's disabled.'

Brett snickered. 'It's not the child I'm interested in. And who's talking about marriage?'

'You should be. It's more than time you settled down and by hell, after this, you'll cut down on the drinking or you really will be out on your ear. Your mother's worried about you and no wonder. You're looking bloated and unhealthy. At your age, I was lean as a whippet, working all the hours God sent to build up my business and . . . '

Brett closed his eyes and let the words flow over him. He'd heard it all before. Too many times. There were more things in life than working and once he inherited the family business he'd leave others to do the dirty work and enjoy a very different lifestyle from his father's.

He didn't want marriage from Ella Turner, or from anyone else. Definitely not. He wasn't putting on the manacles.

Then they arrived home and he had to face his mother, who was furious with him and worried about what friends would say about their drunkard of a son.

He kept quiet and escaped to his bedroom as quickly as he could, flinging off his clothes and getting into bed with a sigh of relief.

But it was a long time before he got to sleep. He kept replaying the scene with Ella in his mind. It was her fault he'd had a few too many drinks, just to give himself confidence.

He'd get his own back on the bitch, though. He'd fancied her from the age of fifteen, when she got curvy and he got randy. She'd laughed at him then, so bright and sure of herself.

She shouldn't have married that fellow from London. Brett had known it wouldn't last.

But if she was starting to give out again, she should turn to people she knew, not strangers.

5

Ella had everything ready for Cameron's breakfast by seven o'clock, even before Amy left for school. At eight she drove her daughter to the main road and saw her on the bus. When she got home, she watched Porgy circle a couple of times then ease himself down in his favourite spot in the yard, a place which caught the sun all morning.

No sign of Cameron.

She fidgeted to and fro between kitchen and laundry. There was always something to do. She kept peering out of the window expecting to see him, then getting angry at herself for doing it.

At last, just before eight thirty, she heard footsteps on the gravel and saw him strolling towards the house.

He beamed at her. 'I can't remember the last time I slept so well. I hope I've not inconvenienced you by such a late start, Ella?'

'No, of course not. I was just getting on with the housework.'

He looked round. 'You keep the place immaculate. Cleanliness shines everywhere I look.'

That particular compliment pleased her. Keeping the place clean was something that didn't cost much money but added to the general attractiveness of Willowbrook. She'd achieved a three-star rating from the AA last year in the guest house category. She was proud of that, hoped to get a higher rating next year . . . if she was still here next year . . . if Miles didn't ruin her.

'What would you like to eat? Cereal? Bacon and eggs? Toast?' She handed him the menu.

'All of that sounds wonderful. I'll happily pay extra for a bigger breakfast. I haven't been this hungry for ages. Must be the country air.'

'Lots of people say that. And there's no extra charge.'

'Can I stay and watch you cook?'

'Wouldn't you rather sit in peace in the conservatory and sip some orange juice?'

'Nope. I'd rather sit on a stool at the breakfast bar and talk to you.' He suited the action to the words.

'Oh. Well. All right.' She poured him a juice and got on with her work. It didn't normally bother her to have people watching, but this morning she felt all fingers and thumbs. 'So you, um, slept well?'

'Like the proverbial log. When I woke, I went for a walk round the lake, simply couldn't resist it.'

She smiled. Few of her guests could resist strolling near the water or sitting on one of the benches she'd put in. But she'd have to do something about the weeds on the path soon. She moved across to her whiteboard and wrote it down. 'Just reminding myself to find time to weed the path round the lake.'

He looked at her in shock. 'You surely don't do the gardening as well as everything else?'

She continued preparing the rashers of local bacon. 'I get someone in to mow the lawns, but I do the rest. My cousin Rose helps me sometimes if I'm extra busy.'

'Where do you find the energy?'

'I'm pretty efficient and I prioritize. I don't do some things, like weeding, as often as I'd like.' Her eyes strayed to the window and she smiled then turned back to prepare the eggs and bacon. 'I like to keep things looking nice. Now, I've set out the fruit and cereals. By the time you've finished those, the rest will be ready.' She led the way out into the conservatory. 'I thought you'd like to sit by the window.'

'Lovely. It's nice being the only guest.' His smile gave his statement another meaning.

'In summer we're usually full at weekends and often during the week, too, in the school holidays. Even Amy helps then. She loves that.'

She was talking about herself again, she realized, should watch what she revealed. She picked up the empty tray. 'I'll just cook your bacon and eggs. Won't be long.'

He put out one hand to bar her way. 'When you've done that, how about joining me for a coffee, Ella? Surely you're ready to take a short break?'

And once again she couldn't resist spending time with him, so she made herself a cup and took it into the conservatory.

There was the same feeling as the evening before, a companionable mood. No need to fill the silence with empty chatter. Spring sunshine poured through the windows, birds sang and a

84

breeze wafted in the smell of earth and growing things.

'It isn't often I take a break during the day. It feels quite decadent.'

'You're a hard worker.'

'Two compliments in one morning,' she teased. 'Be careful or my head will swell.'

His eyes held hers for a moment, serious and very direct. 'I don't think so.' Then he turned his attention back to his plate, clearing every morsel. 'That was wonderful. I'm ready now to conquer the world.'

When she began to clear away, he immediately jumped up to help.

'I told you last night — guests shouldn't be doing that.'

'No trouble. Look, are you busy this morning, Ella?'

'Um — well — '

'Would you have time to show me round your property, tell me about its history? I walked round the outside of the barn this morning and was fascinated. You can see signs of old openings, half of an arch that must have been a window. Was it always a barn?'

'No. That barn's been many things in its lifetime.'

'But it's been repaired recently, and done well, too.'

She nodded. 'That's why I'm so short of money. The insurance wouldn't cover the right sort of stonework, let alone the woodwork in the roof, because the house isn't listed.'

Now that he'd seen more of the place, he was

surprised that it wasn't listed, but he didn't comment. There must be some reason, surely? Or perhaps she just hadn't wanted the authorities to interfere. 'Would you show me round?'

She looked across into his smiling eyes and was lost. 'Oh — all right.'

Could a man smile like that and mean you harm? Surely not?

★　★　★

Rose got up as soon as it was light and began clearing up the mess. To her surprise, Oliver joined her soon afterwards by the simple expedient of walking in through the gap in the wall.

'What woke you so early? I didn't think you exposed your eyeballs to light before eight o'clock.' She continued to work, piling up the broken wood and the bigger pieces of glass outside, her hands protected by some heavy duty gardening gloves.

He touched the back of one. 'Got any more of those? I don't want to cut my hands.'

'There's no need. I can manage.'

'Either you provide me with some or I'll go back and get Dad's.'

'Why? Surely it's best that we stay away from one another?'

He ignored her question, though his scowl deepened. 'Do you have some other protective gloves or not?'

For answer, she went to the big drawer at the

86

bottom of the storage wardrobe and pulled out an unused pair. She used them when she was making half-relief pieces from scraps of metal. She'd been playing with this in her spare time, because she believed in challenging and extending her skills. And it didn't cost much. She could pick up all sorts of bits and pieces of metal that people threw away.

'You always were a pack rat,' he said, staring down into the box where she stored her smaller pieces.

She didn't bother to answer, just shut the drawer and went back to her work.

They continued to clear up the mess and when that was done, she fetched her outdoor broom.

'Find me something to put the smaller rubble in.' He took the brush out of her hands and started sweeping. 'Dad says you can have the flat over the surgery for the next few weeks while this place is being repaired.'

'Surely you'll want the flat.'

'I may do later. For the present I can stay with Mum and Dad.'

That stopped her in her tracks. The last thing she wanted, the very last, was to live close to where he'd be working every day. 'I can manage here. I'm used to roughing it.'

'Very noble. But Dad wants you out of here while we check that the structure of the building hasn't been weakened. We don't want to put you in danger. He nearly came to get you out last night.'

'Oh.'

'What does that mean?'

'I'll think about the flat. I may find somewhere else to live.'

'Isn't that taking your antagonism towards me a bit far? Cutting off your nose to spite your face?'

He was right really, but she hated to admit it. 'What's the flat like now? I know your locums sometimes live there.'

'It's in good order. My parents renovated it a while ago.' He looked round with a grimace. 'The rooms are much bigger than those in this place. Dad said I was to show you round it.'

'Why you?'

'Because he's busy. Do you have to challenge everything I say?'

'It's safer.'

He finished sweeping the floor in silence, pulled off the gloves and threw them down, muttering something under his breath. Then he gave her a strange look. 'I'll meet you at the flat in half an hour.' He didn't give her time to reply, but strode off down the street.

She watched him go. He'd stormed off like that after their final quarrel. And the next thing she knew, he'd left Chawton without a word.

That was how their great love had ended. With a bang. Then she'd been left to whimper on her own. She'd wept a good few times. They'd had irreconcilable differences, life goals that diverged. He'd wanted to travel the world and specialize in emergency medicine. She'd wanted to stay — needed to stay, because she could only work on her project here.

A piece of loose stone fell off the edge of the battered outer wall, as if to emphasize that he was right. She did need to move out. The cottage was probably safe. It'd lasted over two centuries already, but if old Doc Paige wanted her out, she'd go.

Not because Oliver said so.

She could go to Ella, didn't need to ask to know she'd be welcome — only that was a long way out of town when you were working late at night and came home exhausted. It'd be more sensible to take the flat, as long as the rent wasn't any higher. Surely she'd be able to avoid seeing much of Oliver.

He brought back too many memories of a time she'd been young and optimistic about love and life.

She and her cousin had both been disappointed by their early choices in men. They were wiser now, knew better than to trust anyone.

★   ★   ★

Ella took the key off the hook and led the way out to the barn. Once she'd not have bothered to lock it, but since the break-in she'd become more careful. The incident had made her feel unsafe in her own home and she resented that bitterly.

It was a large key, black, made of iron, the circle at the end smooth to the touch. How many people had used that key over the centuries? she wondered as she fitted it into the lock.

She flung open one of the big doors and

Cameron followed suit with the other, then stood there looking round.

'It's a cruck barn!' he said in amazement. 'I wondered, but — wow, I can't believe it's so well preserved inside! What happened to the outside?'

'My ancestors made so many changes over the years, they covered a lot of the old building.'

He walked slowly round, his face alight with interest and excitement, reaching up to touch the old wood where he could and pacing the place out.

She stiffened. If you measured it inside and out, you'd find it didn't quite fit. No, he'd not bother to do that accurately, surely?

He turned to her from the other end. 'I walked along the outside when I was waiting for you. Unless I'm much mistaken, there's a difference of a couple of yards at this end. Did you realize that?'

She couldn't think what to say. Miles hadn't once thought to do this, not in all the years he'd lived here, and now this stranger had found one of the old place's secrets within a day of coming here.

He stared at her. 'You already knew, of course you did.'

Reluctantly she nodded.

'Is there a hiding place?'

She didn't know what to say.

A little of the excitement died from his face. 'Sorry. I'm probably intruding on something private. Of course you won't want to share your house's secrets with a stranger.'

'No one else has ever guessed.'

90

'Old houses are a bit of a hobby of mine. I love history.'

On a sudden impulse she said, 'I'll show you, then. A special treat.' She went to the wooden wall which separated two of the storage spaces and pressed one of the upright planks in a certain way, as her father had shown her when she was sixteen, a rite of passage into adulthood. It was a bit stiff. She'd need to oil it again.

The door opened slowly. 'Come inside.' She took the candle and matches her father had always insisted on keeping ready and lit it.

Cameron followed her inside, touching the rough wood of the door, then running his fingertips along the walls.

She pointed to the little bench. 'They even provided seating.' She didn't close the door because some people got claustrophobic.

When she sat down, he joined her, not speaking just studying their surroundings with a half-smile on his face.

'Did you play hide and seek here when you were a child?'

'We usually get shown the secrets of Willowbrook when we're about sixteen. Amy doesn't know about this place yet, because she's a bit young to keep a secret. I never even told my ex about it. Well, he wasn't interested in ancient monuments.' Miles had several times called this place an old ruin.

'Then I'm honoured that you trusted me. I'll keep your secret, I promise.'

She was surprised to realize she'd never doubted that. What was there about this man?

She looked sideways and found him watching her.

He leaned forward and pressed a gentle kiss on her cheek. 'Thank you for sharing this with me.'

After they'd closed the hidey-hole up, his mobile phone rang.

'Excuse me. I'm expecting an important call.'

He moved away, but she couldn't help overhearing.

'No, it's been switched on for the past hour. No, it definitely didn't ring before.' He sighed in exasperation. 'Look, I don't intend to be available twenty-four seven, Ray. I do have a life of my own, you know.'

She walked back to the kitchen, leaving him to his phone call. She had more than enough to do today, shouldn't have taken even an hour off. And she felt more tired than usual, having to force herself to keep going. Which wasn't like her.

When she got there, the phone was blinking and she checked who'd rung. Rose. She glanced out of the window. Cameron was still talking on his mobile, not looking best pleased, so she rang her cousin back.

The phone rang a few times and she was just going to put the handpiece down when the line crackled and she heard Rose's voice, a bit breathless as if she'd been running.

'Ella. Thanks for ringing back. I just wanted to tell you my news. Brett Harding had an accident last night and crashed into my cottage. He knocked the corner walls down.'

'He was drunk when he left here.'

'He's not been pestering you again?'

'Yes.'

'He's a sleaze. But never mind him . . . Oliver Paige is back!'

'I heard that he was coming. How do you feel about seeing him again?'

'Same way you'd feel if Miles came to live nearby.'

'Ha! There's no hope of that. He hates country life. Are you going to take the flat Doc Paige has offered? There's plenty of room here if you don't fancy that.'

Another silence, then, 'Thanks but the flat's more convenient for my work at the pub.'

'Well, if things change, you know you can come here.'

'Thanks, love.'

As Ella put the phone down, the door opened and Cameron came in, his expression serious. 'There's some sort of minor crisis concerning a project I've been working on. They won't discuss it over the phone. And I have a final few things to tidy up, so I'm going up to London to do everything at once.'

'You're leaving now?'

When he nodded, she was angry with herself for feeling disappointed. 'I'll make up your bill, then. I'll only charge you for the one night, of course.'

'I'm coming back, Ella. I love it here. I'll pay for three nights, to show willing.'

She looked across at him uncertainly.

'And when I come, I'd like to see more of *you*.

If you'd like it, that is.'

She stilled, shocked by the gladness welling up, remembering suddenly how quickly she and Miles had become an item. Too quickly. Far too quickly. 'I . . . don't know. It's a bit sudden, isn't it?'

'How long does it take to be attracted to someone?'

He looked as if he was going to draw her into his arms and she took an involuntary step backwards. 'I've not . . . I'm not sure I — '

He studied her, head on one side. 'He hurt you badly, that husband of yours, didn't he?'

She could only shrug. She hadn't discussed her feelings about the failure of her marriage with anyone except Rose.

'OK. We'll take it easy. Just give me a chance. I don't like the thought of you being on your own out here while I'm away, though.'

'I've got my ferocious guard dog.'

'You're more likely to have to rescue Porgy.'

'Well, I don't think Brett Harding will be troubling me again.' She explained about the accident.

'That might keep him away but it's very lonely out here and you said you'd had another break-in.'

Even as he was speaking, they heard a car coming along the drive. She moved away from him, straightened her clothes and ran a hand over her hair, which was always escaping from the scarf she used to tie it back. 'I'll — um — just go and see who that is.'

Two elderly couples emerged from a large

station wagon which had seen better days. Ella showed them the chalets then brought them back to the house to book them in, listening to the tales of their trip as if it was the most fascinating story she'd ever heard.

Cameron nodded to them and waited for her to finish.

'Is there anything else, Mr O'Neal?'

'I'd like a can of lemonade. Shall I help myself and put it on my account?'

'Yes, please do. And we'll settle the account after you get back.'

He smiled at her, then the two couples. 'I hope your stay here is as enjoyable as mine has been. Ms Turner is an excellent cook if you're thinking of eating here.'

'Well, that's nice to know.' One of the men came across to offer his hand. 'Joe Blake. We're only here for a couple of nights, but it'd be nice not to have to drive out again tonight, I must admit.'

Cameron went to pack his things, relieved that Ella wouldn't be on her own. When he'd put his bags in his car, he went to find her.

'Promise me you'll be careful.'

'I will.'

'I'll be gone for a couple of days, three at most. If they leave before I get back . . . '

'Cameron, I've lived here alone for the past two years. I'll be perfectly all right.'

Only when he'd driven off did she realize that he hadn't given her his mobile number, and the only address she had for him was a post office box.

He'll be back, she told herself as she began to defrost some food for her new guests. I can trust him.

I'm missing him already, she thought later as she and Porgy went to meet Amy after school. How stupid can you get?

He will come back, she thought again as she prepared a meal for her guests. Of course he will.

I'm worrying for nothing, she told herself as she got ready for bed.

But surely, if he'd meant what he said, he'd have arranged to keep in touch?

6

In the middle of the night the security lights switched on and the buzzer linked to them sounded next to Ella's bed. She woke with a start and sat up, her heart thumping madly. Quickly she dragged on her dressing gown before picking up the old rounders bat she now kept next to her bed for protection. Without switching on the lights, she crept from one side of the house to the other, peering out of the windows, but could see no signs of movement outside.

After the usual two-minute period, the lights automatically switched off again. She waited for a while longer, roaming the shadowy house, peering out of windows, then went back to bed. It was probably some animal that had strayed on to the farm. A deer, maybe. The fence must be down somewhere.

Just as she was dozing off, the lights came on again and the buzzer jerked her awake.

Another tour of the windows showed nothing.

This happened several times, then stopped. Only she kept expecting the lights to go on again and couldn't relax, let alone sleep.

She felt very angry. Someone was playing with her. Was it Brett Harding? Why would he bother? Wasn't he in enough trouble?

And if it wasn't him, who was it? What about the people who'd vandalized her home? She still worried about why they'd picked on her.

She returned to bed but tossed and turned for a long time before falling into an uneasy sleep.

In the morning, the alarm clock woke her at the usual time. Feeling heavy-headed, she went into Amy's room, lingering a moment or two to smile fondly at the child sleeping as usual in a tangle of covers and soft toys.

By the time she got into the car to drive Amy to the bus stop, she had everything ready for her guests, who had booked breakfast for half past eight.

'When is Mr O'Neal coming back, Mummy?'

'I'm not sure. In a day or two — if he can. It's not absolutely certain.'

'But he said he was coming back.'

'I know he did, darling, but people sometimes change their minds.'

'He won't break a promise. He's a nice man. Me and Porgy like him. Do you like him, Mummy?'

'Yes.'

'That's good.'

Ella didn't ask Amy to explain what she meant by that because she didn't want to get into a tangle of explanations. Some things were just too complicated for seven-year-olds.

When she got back, she checked the ground near the house and found several blurred footprints, the sort you got from cheap wellies like the ones she wore herself in winter. She stared at them, her breath catching in her throat. She'd guessed it hadn't been an animal, but this was proof that someone had been prowling round her house trying to spook her — and they'd succeeded, damn them.

Who would do that? Brett was the first name that came to mind. He'd been pestering her on and off for years, but why would he suddenly go off the rails like this?

'Good morning, Mrs Turner.'

She jumped in shock, then realized it was the new guests, ready for their breakfast.

'Sorry. Didn't mean to startle you.'

'I was miles away. Did you sleep well . . . ?'

They were a charming quartet, in their seventies, all seeming full of energy and with a young attitude to the world. They were very appreciative of her cooking and made arrangements to have dinner at Willowbrook again that night.

When they'd gone out for a day's sightseeing to Avebury, Marlborough and wherever chance took them, she cleared up quickly before going across to their chalets to tidy up. But everything was already immaculate, with beds made. They'd set out the card that said they were happy to reuse the towels, so she only had to put fresh milk in the fridge, and restock the biscuits, tea and coffee sachets. She wished all guests were as easy to look after.

She couldn't resist going into the chalet Cameron had used. He'd taken all his things. She stood there, wondering if he'd be back, then sat down for a minute on the bed, smoothing the duvet cover with her right hand. He'd talked about them getting to know one another. She'd really like that. Only . . . was she reading more into what he'd said than he'd meant? She'd rushed into a relationship once and look where that had led her.

She wasn't going to make that mistake again. Anyway, she'd only known Cameron for a couple of days. That was far too soon to talk about relationships.

Wasn't it?

But the dog liked him, and so did Amy. And he's said — *Oh, stop it!* she told herself. *You're being silly. He probably won't even come back.*

Back at the house the message light was blinking on the phone, showing two messages. She pressed the replay button.

Miles's voice. 'Ella, will you call me back as soon as possible, please? I need to sort out something with you.' There was silence for a moment, then he added, 'Now that I've got my life in order, I want to see more of my daughter. I can come down on Saturdays and take Amy out for the afternoon, starting this weekend.'

Ella stared at the phone in horror, ignoring the tinny voice still talking in her ear. Had she heard correctly? She replayed the message.

Yes, Miles really was saying he wanted to see Amy. Why? He had a very short span of both attention and patience where small children were concerned, so what on earth would someone like him do with a child for a whole afternoon?

Ella didn't want to give him any access at all. He'd hurt the child enough by not coming near her for three years. She remembered in the early days Amy asking where her daddy was. And one day, the child had suddenly asked if her daddy didn't like her because she couldn't walk properly.

100

A child shouldn't think that way. She hoped she'd convinced Amy that it wasn't because of the SMA. Whether she had succeeded or not, the subject hadn't been raised again.

Why this sudden interest from Miles?

It wasn't because he loved his daughter, Ella was quite sure of that. He could say the words of love, said them often and easily when he wanted something, but she'd found the hard way that he didn't really care about anyone but himself.

How was she to protect Amy from being hurt by him now?

Tears came into her eyes. She didn't think she had any choice about allowing access, was sure she remembered Ian Hannow saying her ex would still have the right to see his child, whatever they'd arranged.

Still holding the handpiece, Ella sat down on the ancient oak settle at one side of the kitchen. Miles would have some reason for doing this. She didn't know what, but she was quite sure there would be one.

She checked the other message and noted a booking for a few weeks' time, a couple who'd been here before.

Just as she was about to set the handpiece down, the phone rang. She stared at it, wondering whether to answer it or not. 'Don't be such a coward!' she told herself and said crisply, 'Willowbrook.'

'Ella? Ella, is that you?'

Cameron's voice. Joy flooded through her and suddenly the world felt brighter. 'Yes, of course it's me.'

'You sound strained. Are you all right?'

'I'm fine. I was just — um, lost in thought.'

'You've not had any other problems?'

She hesitated, not knowing whether to tell him or not. She hardly knew him, after all, however comfortable she felt with him.

'There is something. What's happened? Can I help?'

'The security lights kept going on and off last night. I'm sure it wasn't an animal. Whoever it was would wait ten minutes, then trip the lights again. This morning I found footprints near the house.'

'Hell! And I can't get back till late tomorrow at the earliest. Are those four people still staying there? Thank goodness. Look, you'll call me if anything else happens? Got something to write with? Good. Here's my mobile number. I forgot to give it you before I left.'

She scribbled it down, smiling. She'd been worrying about nothing.

'I'm missing you, Ella.'

'Are you?'

'I wouldn't say so otherwise. Aren't you missing me?'

'I've been busy with my new guests.'

He laughed softly. 'You're right to tread cautiously. You don't know me yet. But you will.' There was the sound of voices in the background. 'Oh, damn. I have to go now. I'll call again tonight. And Ella — be careful.'

The four guests came back mid-afternoon, teasing one another about their need for a rest.

Later Ella watched them walk round the lake,

one couple holding hands and the other two looking as if they belonged together, even though they weren't touching. It renewed her faith in marriage just to see them.

And it made her feel good that Cameron had called. She couldn't help hoping . . . just a little . . . that something might come of their . . . friendship.

But she would definitely tread carefully. There wasn't only herself to be hurt this time, there was Amy.

★ ★ ★

Later that afternoon two men turned up in a large four-wheel drive. They were wearing business suits and didn't look at all like tourists. Puzzled, she watched them get out of their vehicle and stand for a long time, gesturing towards various parts of her property.

They were obviously checking out Willowbrook. Who'd sent them? It couldn't be the bank, because they'd sent Cameron. Was it the developer who'd approached her about the property recently? What were they called? DevRaCom, that was it. Why would they think she'd changed her mind? She hadn't. She wouldn't.

She couldn't help wondering if Miles was again behind these efforts to get her to sell. Was it just a coincidence that he'd rung today, wanting to see Amy every Saturday? That would give him an excuse to come down regularly. She hated the thought of it, wished she need never see him again as long as she lived, didn't want him upsetting her life — or her daughter's.

When the men came back round the house to ring the front door bell, she waited a moment or two before answering. A flurry of rain made her feel obliged to invite them into the hall.

The older one held out a business card. 'We're from DevRaCom. Do you mind if we look round the property?'

'Why should you want to do that?'

He looked at her as if she was dull-witted. 'I just told you. We're here on behalf of DevRaCom, doing a preliminary survey. You know . . . the company that's buying this place.'

She heard the timer go and let out a puff of annoyance. 'Excuse me just one moment. I have to take something out of the oven.'

When she got back they were still standing there. The spokesman's expression suddenly brightened as he took in her dirty apron and the duster she'd stuffed into her pocket. 'Ah, you must be the cleaning lady. You won't know about DevRaCom, of course. Look, could you fetch the owner, please? Ella Turner.'

She folded her arms. 'I *am* the owner. And no one is buying this property that I know of.'

Silence. They exchanged puzzled glances, then one said, 'I think you'll find Mr Parnell has already started making the arrangements.'

'I think *you* will find that since I'm the owner, Mr Parnell, who is my very-much-ex-husband, has no authority here. I'm definitely — *not* — selling Willowbrook.'

Another silence, then the spokesman said, 'We'd still like to take a quick look around anyway, if that's all right.'

'Sorry, but this is private property. Only family and guests have the right to walk around it.'

'Then we'll book a chalet for the night, for heaven's sake. How much is it?' He pulled out a credit card.

'I don't have any vacancies. And I'm busy today, so I'd be glad if you'd leave.'

Their expressions grew ugly, but after another exchange of glances they walked back to their car, where they sat for ages talking on a mobile phone. Even when the call ended they still sat on for some time. It wasn't until they'd received another call, which involved some earnest talking and gesticulating, that they drove away.

She watched them go with a sick feeling in her stomach. They'd been so confident about the development. Why?

She'd guessed right. Miles was behind this and it was the second time he'd tried to sell her property against her wishes. Why did he think he'd succeed now, after a three-year break? Did he know something she didn't?

She had to get her loan, pay him back, get him out of her life for ever. If there was no financial benefit for him here, she could be pretty certain he'd leave Amy and her alone.

$\star$　$\star$　$\star$

Rose took off her painting overall and tidied herself up a bit, but didn't change into anything smart. She was going to look at the flat, not trying to attract a man, especially that man. He could take her as she was — or better still, not take her.

Oliver was waiting for her at the rear of the surgery, which had a second car park there for staff. He was leaning against the wall, face turned up to the sun with a half-smile. She'd expected him to be walking up and down impatiently, because she was a few minutes late. He always used to do that.

He didn't open his eyes for a moment, though he must have heard her footsteps.

She went right up to him. 'Well?'

He smiled at her. 'Impatient, aren't you?'

'I have a lot to do today.'

'Come upstairs, then.'

The flat was lovely, two large bedrooms and a huge living room, all with big wide windows that caught the light, and there was even a small storage room which would be perfect for her painting materials. She walked slowly round, hoping she was hiding her feelings, reluctant to admit that it was much better for her purpose than the cottage. Eighteenth-century cottages were not built to let in much light. But when they were as small and inconvenient as hers, when the owners had known her since she was a child, they came very cheaply.

He didn't say anything, just waited . . . and watched. 'It'll do,' she said in the end.

'Is it just me or have you turned grumpy in your old age?'

'*Grumpy!* What do you mean, grumpy?'

'You're not exactly chatty and cheerful today, Rosie baby.'

She didn't rise to that one. She'd always disliked being called Rosie and he knew it. 'I have to move out of my home. I'm a busy person. I can do without all these hassles.'

'Tell that to Brett Harding. He caused this trouble, not me.'

'I'd not give him the time of day. Do you know, he's been sexually harassing my cousin for a while now? He'd been out to Willowbrook pestering her just before he crashed into you.'

'Why hasn't she laid charges, then?'

'His father still runs the planning committee. Mr Harding isn't a man to cross when you're hoping to expand your tourist development.'

'Ah. Dad said Ella put up some chalets out there after she split with Parnell. How is the old place? I used to love the feeling of history you got there.'

'Willowbrook is fine. It'll outlast us because it's better built than most modern houses and — ' she realized he'd got her talking and clamped her lips shut ' — I'll go home and pack.'

'I've got the packing cases my stuff came in. I can borrow Dad's car and bring them across. My car will be out of commission for a while, unfortunately, until the bodywork is repaired.'

She turned to stare at him, arms akimbo. 'Why are you suddenly being so helpful? We didn't part on the best of terms.' And there'd been no word from him in five years. Not one lousy email, even.

His face took on a shuttered look. 'Do you object to me being helpful?'

She didn't answer. There had been a flash of

pain in his face before he hid behind that inner wall he could erect. Unless he'd changed totally, she knew his expressions nearly as well as she knew her own face in the mirror. No use being stupid about his offer, though. 'Thank you. You can use my van to fetch the stuff, if you like. It'll probably hold more than a car and it always behaves well for you.'

'You haven't still got the same old van?'

'Yes.' She handed him the keys.

'Seems we've both had our ambitions frustrated, doesn't it?'

She watched him stride away. What did he mean by that? How had his ambitions been frustrated? What exactly had brought Oliver Paige back to Chawton?

Whatever it was, she wished he hadn't come. He was yet another failure in her life.

⋆   ⋆   ⋆

In London, Cameron was greeted by Miss Bradley, Ray's secretary, who gave him one of her tight smiles. She'd been with DevRaCom for at least twenty years and was reputed to be willing to kill on her employer's behalf — though you wouldn't need to go as far as killing when you could make a man feel nervous and ten years old again simply by looking down your nose at him. Even Ray sometimes bent to her will.

'I'm afraid you'll have to wait for a few moments, Mr O'Neal. Mr Deare has someone with him.'

They'd changed the decor and he sat down gingerly in an angular modern chair, which might look trendy but was hell on a normal human's anatomy. After wriggling around a little, he gave up trying to get comfortable and went to stand by the window.

Central London lay beneath him, teeming like a grey ant heap in spite of the congestion charges. Not so different from other large cities from this viewpoint, it looked better when you walked round it on foot, because there were some magnificent old buildings in the City still.

He suddenly remembered the peace and lush greenery at Willowbrook, the delicate chorus of bird calls that not only greeted you in the morning but threaded through the day. He loved the smell of earth and plants, and his nose wrinkled involuntarily now, because canned air always felt stale to him. And as footsteps were muffled by the thick carpets in this part of the building, a blanket of heavy silence lay upon the senior executive floor. You didn't exactly tiptoe, but you had a sneaking suspicion that you ought to.

The door to the inner office opened and he swung round to see a good-looking guy of about his own age emerge. The man stopped by the desk. 'You have my mobile number?'

'I have all the necessary information, Mr Parnell.'

'Good.' The stranger cast a quick glance in Cameron's direction, as if to size him up, then turned his thousand megawatt smile back on Miss Bradley, whose cool expression didn't change one iota.

Cameron hoped his amusement hadn't shown. When she was on duty, Sonia Bradley was impervious to gestures of friendliness even from people who'd known her for years. This man was a stranger and his friendly manner wasn't genuine. Cameron wasn't sure how he sensed that, but he'd stake his life on it. Parnell. Now where had he heard that? . . .

He suddenly remembered little Amy telling him she was changing her name from Parnell to Turner when she grew up. Could this be her father? If so, it must be more than a coincidence that the fellow was here.

'You can go through now, Mr O'Neal.'

'Come in, Cameron lad.' Ray boomed from inside the office.

Out of the corner of his eye, Cameron saw that Parnell had paused to watch this.

Ray shut the door and gestured to some easy chairs set neatly round a low table. The floor to ceiling windows made for stunning views but Cameron sat with his back to them. He didn't need distracting.

'Let's make ourselves comfortable.' Ray leaned back in his big leather armchair and steepled his fingers as he studied his guest.

'I see you didn't get rid of your own furniture.'

Ray grinned. 'Hell, no. Who'd want to sit on those things out there.'

'Why buy them, then?'

'They look up-to-the-minute and more to the point, they discourage people from hanging around. Now, thanks for coming. Did you get to see this Willowbrook place?'

'Yes. But I didn't have time to look at anything in depth. What was the rush to see me today?'

'Got a glitch in the Parker project. I need someone I can trust to work on it.'

'Is that the one with Middle Eastern involvement?'

'Yeah. Big project. It'll take months to sort out. It'll pay extremely well, though.'

Cameron shook his head. 'I told you last time, Ray: I'm not taking on anything new. I'm burned out.'

'Not you.'

'Then let me put it another way: I've had enough of wheeling and dealing, and I'm looking for a quieter life. So thanks for the offer and the confidence you've shown in me, but no, thank you. I don't want the project.'

Ray frowned at him, opened his mouth to say something, then shut it again.

Cameron met the older man's eyes squarely and let the seconds tick by until he could see that Ray believed him. 'I only checked out Willowbrook as a special favour to you and because I was heading in that direction anyway.'

'Oh, that. It's not important now, though I always value your opinion, of course, and I'll pay you what we agreed. But the guy I just showed out is going to deliver it. The owner owes him quite a bit of money and I can make sure the bank doesn't give her the loan she's asked for.'

Cameron had no trouble keeping his expression calm. He'd had years of practice at that. But he was surprised and disappointed to hear what Ray was doing. 'You don't usually play dirty.

111

How did you get her account details?'

Ray looked pained. 'I didn't need them, just the name of her bank. I dropped a word in a friend's ear and there will be no loans available to her for any reason.'

Cameron stared down at his feet to hide his displeasure, wondering what was going on. He'd never heard Ray talking like this, or seen him behaving in quite such an underhand way. Why bother to do it with a relatively small project?

None of his business, since he wasn't intending to get involved in the business side of things, only he liked Ella, felt sorry for her. And if his feelings continued to grow, could he stay out of it? The farm obviously meant a lot to her and why should she have to give up her home? Why the hell did this have to happen now?

Ray snapped his fingers. 'You were miles away then.'

'Yeah. Keeps happening to me. I definitely need a rest.'

'You need something to focus your mind. I'm not going to take a no on the Parker project.'

Cameron frowned at the edge to the older man's voice. 'You'll have to.'

Ray leaned forward. 'I never have before. Don't cross me on this. It won't do you any good and you owe me.'

There was dead silence. Ray's stern gaze didn't change or soften.

Cameron hoped he hadn't let his astonishment show. 'I've more than paid you back for the help you gave me when I was starting out.'

'It formed a link between us, and I like to keep

my business connections — shall we say, *active?*'

'The answer is still no. My heart wouldn't be in it and I've things going on here, so I'd not be able to give you the commitment you need.'

Ray's expression was briefly ugly. 'You might find it affected your other jobs.'

'I told you: I intend to take it easy for a while. I'm not looking for other jobs.'

'What's changed you? Are you working for another company, one I should know about?'

Cameron sighed. 'Ray, I'm telling you the absolute truth: I'm not going to be working for anyone for a while. I'm going to take a sabbatical and consider my future. And it'll be very different from my past.'

'Let me give you lunch. We can discuss your future in more detail. A man can never have too much money and you're not exactly rich.'

Cameron was suddenly impatient. He'd had enough of being guarded about everything he said, more than enough of treading on the eggshells of upper corporate life and egos. 'Another time, if you don't mind. I've a few things to sort out in town, then I'm going to take a long holiday in the country.'

He didn't let himself frown until he was well away from the building.

What the hell had got into Ray? Why was he pushing so hard?

Cameron's thoughts turned inevitably to Ella, who had been wandering through his mind ever since he left. He wanted very much to see her again, wanted to see if this would lead anywhere.

They couldn't have met at a more inopportune

time, though. He hadn't the faintest idea yet of what exactly he wanted to do with his life. And she was struggling to keep her home.

He didn't like the thought that her ex was involved with DevRaCom, didn't like it at all.

Did she know about that? And he wished he hadn't deceived her about who he was representing at Willowbrook.

7

Ella didn't ring Miles back, was hoping he'd lose interest in seeing Amy. Only . . . he'd not been prone to sudden enthusiasms before, had always planned what he did with great care, so there must be more to it than appeared on the surface. Several times her hand hesitated over the phone, then she shook her head and walked away. If he was going to insist on doing this, let him make the running.

The phone rang the following morning after Amy had gone to school and Ella suppressed a sigh when she heard Miles's voice, mellow, persuasive, friendly . . . if you didn't know better.

'Long time no see. How are you, Ella?'

She couldn't bear to mess around with small talk. 'Not happy. Why do you suddenly want to see Amy?'

'She *is* my daughter, in case you'd forgotten.'

'That didn't seem to matter to you before. You've never even asked about how we manage her condition, what the prognosis is. Caring for a child with SMA takes a lot of effort, visits to doctors and physiotherapists, you know.'

'I don't want to argue about things, Ella, I just want to arrange regular visits from now on. As for the treatment, I'm sure you're doing everything possible. After all, you're with her all the time, I'm not.' When she didn't answer, he added, 'If we need to arrange visiting rights through our lawyers, then I'll contact mine today. I'm not going to change my mind about seeing her.'

She tried to breathe evenly, to reply calmly. 'What exactly do you want to do?'

'See her now and then, every week to start off with. Maybe it'd be best if I booked one of your chalets each Saturday.'

She bit back a hasty refusal. 'You said on the phone you wanted to see her for the afternoon. Why should you want to stay on here afterwards?'

'We could have dinner, talk. I don't want us to be enemies, for Amy's sake.'

'I don't want to have dinner with you, Miles, and I'd rather keep my chalets for real visitors. Besides, I work on Saturday evenings. Who do you think prepares the meals for the guests?'

'Well, at least book me in this first weekend. We have to discuss how soon you can pay the loan back. I need that money quickly. I've found a good investment and don't want to lose the chance of getting in on it.'

Ah, that was more like it, his real reason for coming. Was he intending to use Amy as a bargaining tool? She nearly asked if it was DevRaCom he wanted to invest in, but bit back the words. Why give him information if she didn't need to? 'Very well. You can stay on Saturday night, just this once. But I'll have to charge you the normal rate. I can't afford to lose money on your visit.'

'That's all right. And I gather you provide meals now? I'd like to book an evening meal.

Save me going into Chawton. Do you have Internet access?'

'I can give you a daily pass into our wireless network.'

'Good.'

'It'll cost you extra, though.' She didn't usually charge for this, but Miles was different. He was just using their daughter, she knew he was, so she'd use him in return. After all, Amy desperately needed a new school uniform. Maybe she'd suggest he bought it, for once. And maybe she'd ask him for maintenance from now on, back payment even. That would reduce her debt to him. Why hadn't she thought of that aspect before? Because she hadn't wanted anything to do with him, that was why, because she was frightened of him asking for his money back. Well, he'd done that now, so she'd consult her lawyer and have a good look at all her options.

Miles wasn't the only one with bargaining power. Maybe if she got maintenance from him and also sold the necklace, she could manage to pay back enough money to satisfy him for the time being?

His voice became sharper. 'Are you still there? Right then. I'll be down around two o'clock. I'll take Amy out for a drive.'

'I'd prefer it if you stayed on the farm with her.'

'What the hell are we going to do there?'

'Walk, talk, play, whatever fathers usually do with their children.'

Another silence, then, 'How is her walking?'

'The same as before, only she falls more often because she's getting taller. She doesn't like to be helped up, though. She's very independent. And she's not doing too badly. Some kids are much worse than her.'

'I see.'

'And academically, she's near the top of her age group, very intelligent and precocious.'

'She is?'

Ella was furious at the surprise in his voice. 'Do you think I'd lie about something like that?'

'Sorry. Of course you wouldn't. I hadn't realized that was — possible.'

'It'd not hurt you to read up on her condition before you come down to see her. Just search the Internet. There are several sites which explain it clearly.'

'Right. I will.'

She doubted that. It wasn't important enough to him, never had been. How could she have been so stupid as to be taken in by a man like that? She wasn't going to let any man fool her again.

His voice interrupted her thoughts. 'Is that all? I've got a call waiting, I'm afraid.'

Was he still using that old excuse to end a phone conversation? He used to boast about it. She wanted to say *No, it's not all, I don't want you to come. I know you're going to hurt Amy.* But she couldn't. 'It's all for the moment.'

'I'll see you on Saturday, then.'

She put the phone into its cradle, adjusting the notepad next to it till it was exactly in line, and setting the guest book in place beside them. Even after she stood up, she couldn't carry on with her chores for a few moments because she was still trying to work out what was going on.

She'd have to prepare Amy for spending time with the father whose existence they mostly ignored, and who until now had completely ignored them.

That wouldn't be easy. Her daughter was no fool.

★ ★ ★

Ella waited until Amy was sitting down with a glass of milk and a home-made biscuit, and the flow of talk about the day had died down. 'I've got something to tell you.'

'Oh?' Amy looked at her expectantly.

'Your father wants to see you. He's coming down on Saturday.'

Amy frowned and began to trace a pattern in the crumbs on her plate, moving them into a pile, then scattering them instead of dabbing them up with a wet finger.

Ella waited, allowing time for the news to sink in, waiting for the difficult questions to start.

'Why?'

'He says he wants to see you.' For the life of her, she couldn't say Miles did want to see Amy, because she was sure it'd be a lie.

'He didn't want to see me before, so I don't want to see him now. Tell him not to come.'

'I can't do that. Fathers have rights. The rule is that they can see their children if they want to.'

An even longer silence, then, 'Don't children have rights too?'

'I can ask Mr Hannow, but I think you'll have to give your father a chance.'

'I don't want to.'

'I don't want him to come, either, but sometimes we have to do things we don't want, you know that.'

'There was a father on the television who killed his children because he was mad at their mother. Is my father mad at you?'

She blinked in shock. Had Amy remembered that old news item all these months? 'No, of course he isn't. And *your* father would never do something like that. The man you heard about on TV was sick in the head, wasn't thinking properly. I told you so at the time.'

'My father was mad at you that day he came back for his clothes. I can remember him shouting at you.'

'Do you remember all that time ago?'

Amy nodded vigorously.

'Well, he's not mad at me now, not like that anyway. He and I don't agree about things, but he's not the sort to go round attacking people, I promise you.'

'I still don't want to go out with him.'

'You're not going anywhere. He's coming here. You can show him your room and your cubby house in the barn, and walk round the lake with him.'

Amy scowled and shoved her plate suddenly sideways, sending crumbs scattering. 'We'd invited Nessa over to play on Saturday.'

'I'd forgotten. But she can come on Sunday instead.'

'He's spoiling things already. Me an' Nessa were going to play fairies.' After a moment's thought, she added, 'I'm not going to speak to him, whatever you say.'

And no matter how much Ella tried to reason with her, the child stuck to this. Hopefully Miles's charm would work on his daughter. Almost immediately, Ella hoped it wouldn't.

And she still hadn't heard from the bank, so couldn't tell him anything definite about repaying the loan. Trust him to change his mind and want his money back before the agreed date! Well, he'd have to wait. Surely he'd not sell out his daughter's home from under her?

She'd made an appointment to see Ian Hannow the next day, couldn't decide anything till she knew where she stood.

How badly did Miles need the money?

⋆　⋆　⋆

Oliver went into the surgery on Friday morning to start getting used to how things were run. It was such a small practice they only had a part-time office manager, and it was one of Jackie's days for working. He wasn't sure he was ready for this, but he had to get back to work again sometime, and being a doctor was all he knew, all he'd ever wanted. Being any sort of doctor was better than nothing.

The counsellor Oliver had seen in the States had said it was up to him when he started work again and if he'd had the choice, he'd have taken a few more weeks off. But his father had made it plain that he was needed as soon as possible, because the locum who'd been filling in had had to leave early.

The trouble was, Oliver hadn't told his family the full details of what had happened or how badly he'd been affected by the incident.

Well, he'd manage somehow. How hard could it be after A&E work? The traumas, violence, drug misuse and accidents he'd seen daily would be rare occurrences in a small country practice, he was sure. There was a much bigger practice on the other side of the village, but some people preferred the old-fashioned personal care that his father still offered. Not that his father didn't keep up to date with medical developments and the way services were offered. He did.

So, Oliver thought as he walked into the surgery, gun-toting customers would be non-existent here, surely? He would manage.

Jackie was the same as ever, permanently middle-aged, not seeming to have changed at all physically in the past decade. She treated him like the youth he had been when he first met her, but she could answer everything he asked about the practice, speaking as quietly as ever. He'd forgotten how soothing her voice was.

'I hope you're starting next week,' she said. 'Dr Paige is too old to work that hard and really needs your help.'

Oliver hesitated, then said, 'I suppose I can start then.'

She began to fiddle with her pencil, avoiding his eyes. 'Your father told me what happened.

No one else knows, but he thought I should be aware of it.'

'Oh.' Oliver hadn't wanted anyone outside the family to know, which was irrational. It wasn't as if it had been his fault, just bad luck, so why he felt so guilty about it, he didn't know — except he'd always managed to control situations with difficult patients before.

'Shall we give you a few simple cases tomorrow morning, so that you can get used to our system?' She grinned. 'I'll pick out some of our repeat offenders for you. As for the rest, we may be small but we're quite up-to-date as regards computerized records and prescriptions.'

He took a deep breath. 'Yes. Whatever you think best.'

'I'll come in tomorrow morning to help you get started.'

'There's no need. You don't usually work on Saturdays.'

She smiled. 'This practice is my baby as well as your father's, so bear with me on that, Oliver. If you're half as good a doctor as your father, you'll be a big asset to the place. This locum was — a minimalist.'

After Oliver had gone into the consulting room which was to be his, he sat and worked through the notes and practised on the computer program. It wasn't hard to deal with, had been well designed. What was hard for him was the feeling of being shut in. It was a small room, too small for him, especially with the door closed.

He held on for as long as he could, then had to get outside, just . . . had to. He took refuge underneath the old oak tree at the back, which he'd played in as a lad, hoping no one had seen him rush out. Crossing his arms around himself, he took deep, gulping breaths of fresh air and waited for the panic to subside.

Oh hell, he thought, what if this happens when I'm with a patient?

★ ★ ★

On Friday morning, Ella went into Chawton to do her weekly shopping and see her lawyer.

Ian listened with his usual intense concentration as she explained what had happened.

'We can set things in train to claim maintenance payments from him, if that'll help. Back payments are rather iffy. Is he earning good money?'

'I should think so. He usually does.'

'Then you should get a decent amount. Tell me more about your daughter and what she needs at this stage.'

She tried to explain, got upset and shed a few rare tears as he probed about the medical details: physiotherapy, walking aids, specialist appointments which cost quite a lot, money for travel. Afterwards she sat staring down at her hands, feeling gutted. She didn't usually let herself give in to her feelings, tried to concentrate on the positive things in life, but no mother of a child with disabilities could help being upset by it sometimes.

Only, other mothers usually had husbands to share the pain.

Ian shoved a tissue across the desk at her. 'You really should have asked your husband for maintenance when he left you. Amy was and is entitled to financial support from him.'

'We agreed that I'd not make a claim if he didn't ask for repayment of the loan.'

'An official agreement?'

'No.'

'Not wise.'

Ella sighed and fumbled in her bag, holding out the soft leather pouch. 'There's this. You helped me sell some things before. Can you find out what this is worth, do you think? I can't see how I'll avoid selling it and I don't know where to start to get the best price. You were so helpful last time . . .'

'Comes of having a cousin who owns a jeweller's shop.' He held out his hand and took Jane Turner's necklace from her, whistling softly at the size of the stones. 'Rich colour and I can't see any flaws. If these are as good as they look, the necklace could be quite valuable. Given its age, you might be better offering it for sale at a specialist auction for antique jewellery. I'm sure my cousin will give us the best advice on that, especially when I explain the circumstances.'

She was sure 'the circumstances' would include Amy's problems and that pity would help her case. She hated people feeling sorry for her, but couldn't afford to let her pride stand in the way of a solution, not now. 'Whatever you think best.'

She felt upset as she walked away from his rooms. She didn't want to claim money from

Miles and she didn't want to sell the necklace, didn't even like taking it away from Willowbrook.

And most of all, she didn't want her ex in their lives again.

★ ★ ★

On Friday afternoon Cameron returned and Ella felt a thrill of pleasure at the sight of his car. He looked healthy, sane and confident, which weren't the adjectives she'd normally have applied as measures of a man's attractiveness, but they seemed intrinsic to this man. And those qualities pleased her.

He opened the boot and took out something bulky that was carefully wrapped, stopping on the way to the house to speak to Amy. He made the child laugh as he bent to look at her toys, even examining the new pink fairy wings which she wore at every opportunity, incongruous as they were with a pair of sturdy jeans and the missing front teeth. Then he leaned closer to give her a peep under the wrapping paper and they both beamed at one another.

If only Miles was like that with his daughter. Ella cut off that thought abruptly.

The kitchen door was open so she called out to come in and was suddenly taken by a fit of shyness. What to say? What to expect?

As Cameron smiled at her from across the room, her anxiety faded. Such a warm smile, he had. Oh, dear! He was altogether too attractive.

'Ta da!' He removed the covering with a flourish and presented her with a huge hanging basket of flowers just coming into bloom.

'I thought you'd prefer this to a bouquet. It'll last much longer and I saw you had a hook on the wall just outside the kitchen door.'

For a moment she had trouble speaking. How long was it since a man gave her a present? 'It's beautiful. And yes, I do prefer it to a bouquet. But you shouldn't have.'

'I couldn't resist it. Shall we hang it up?'

She followed him outside and Amy got up to join them, watching solemnly as Cameron hung the basket near the kitchen door.

'It's pretty. I like the pink flowers best.'

'Pink's her favourite colour,' Ella explained. 'And the basket is really beautiful, perfect for that spot. Thank you so much.'

Amy nodded several times in agreement, her eyes on Cameron not the basket. Then she said suddenly, 'Did Daddy ever buy you flowers, Mummy?'

Ella could feel herself flushing. 'Er — no.' Not after their first few weeks together, anyway.

'Nessa's new daddy buys her mummy flowers all the time. Her mummy's face goes all red when he gives them to her.'

'Ladies like flowers,' Cameron said solemnly. 'Perhaps your father didn't know that.'

'Other daddies know. Mine is coming to see me on Saturday, but I'm not going to speak to him. I don't like him. He hasn't been to see us since I was little and we don't want him here now.'

Ella could feel herself blushing. 'Amy, Mr O'Neal doesn't want to hear about that.'

Cameron grinned at her. 'It's all right. I have a niece who is similarly frank.' He turned back to the child. 'I have something for you, too. It's a little parcel wrapped in pink paper on the back seat of the car. Why don't you fetch it?'

Amy hurried off and they went back inside.

'You shouldn't have,' Ella said softly.

'I wanted to. It's only a box of chocolates. I remember her saying she gets a bar of chocolate every Saturday for a treat. I hope you don't mind me buying it for her?'

'Not at all.' Mind! She was touched by it. He was far too kind for her peace of mind.

Amy came back clutching the parcel and got out the scissors, cutting the sticky tape carefully. Tongue sticking out slightly from one corner of her mouth, she unwrapped the package. 'I'm going to keep this paper, it's so pretty. Oh! Chocolates! A proper box.' She beamed at him. 'Thank you very much, Mr O'Neal. I'm going to save them to share with my friend Nessa on Sunday. Can I ring her and tell her about my present, Mummy?'

'Five minutes. Put the timer on.'

She nodded and hurried away.

Ella felt obliged to explain. 'We can't have the phone tied up in case someone is trying to ring and book a chalet.'

He nodded. 'Can you do me a meal tonight? I know it's short notice, but — '

'Yes, of course I can.'

'You're very efficient.'

'It's my job.'

'I've brought a bottle of wine. I hope you'll

share it with me, and eat with me too?'

She felt breathless, so contented herself with a nod.

'Same chalet as before?'

'Yes, but come up to the house whenever you like.'

Feeling warm and happy, she watched him drive his car round the far side of the outbuildings.

He had come back. And he'd not only brought her a present — exactly the sort of present she liked best — but he'd brought something for Amy too. Maybe . . .

She put a stop to such thoughts. It wasn't safe to hope for too much. And this was a bad time to meet someone, with Miles coming down tomorrow.

Now, she'd better start cooking and stop daydreaming.

★ ★ ★

Rose happened to be looking out of her living room window when Oliver came out of the staff door at the rear of the surgery below — ran out would be a more apt description for the way he erupted from the building as if it were on fire. Surprised, she stood behind the net curtains, unashamedly spying on him.

He looked as if — no, he couldn't be. But he *was*, he was shaking! What had happened to him? She watched in shock as he put his arms round himself in a protective gesture and began breathing deeply. She could see his chest rise and fall, see how white his face was.

She'd never seen Oliver looking vulnerable before. He'd always been strong and determined, too determined sometimes. When he set his mind on something and felt it was the right thing to do, it was like trying to shovel away a mountain to get him to change his plans or ideas.

It was a long time before he moved and she continued to watch. After a while he sighed and let his arms fall, than rubbed his forehead as if it ached. He didn't go back inside the surgery, but strode off along the street, leaving his car behind.

She watched till he was out of sight then went back to her work. The flat was in chaos still, but the light was so good she couldn't resist starting a new painting.

Only she couldn't get back into the right mood because she kept seeing Oliver in her mind's eye. Was he ill or just upset? She hated to see anyone look that distressed. Even the man who'd hurt her so badly.

8

More guests turned up at Willowbrook that afternoon, a young couple who wanted only to hire a chalet and, if Ella was any judge, have a sexy weekend. The looks they kept exchanging positively sizzled, so she gave them a chalet that was a little apart from the others and left them to themselves, feeling rather envious of their closeness.

Next a slightly older couple with a baby turned up, wanting a chalet, a meal and to 'chill out'. The baby was a dear little thing who beamed at the world and reminded Ella of her own daughter at that age.

She had to get a cot for them and as she lugged it from the outhouse next to the old barn, she found Cameron by her side.

'Let me take that.'

She resisted. 'You're paying to stay here. This is my job and I'm quite used to it.'

'Spoilsport.' He tugged it gently out of her hands and carried it to the trolley. 'Anything else?'

'I need to get the bedding.'

She was pleased to have several customers so early in the season. But this put paid to her romantic meal with Cameron and for that she was sorry. It was safer, of course, not to be alone with him — but you didn't always want to be safe.

In spite of everything, she decided there was no need to look as if she'd been born wearing jeans, so after she'd given Amy her tea, she went up and changed into a pretty summer dress, studying herself in the mirror. The dress was rather old-fashioned, because she'd bought it at a charity shop, but she hoped he'd not notice that. It was a very pretty shade of dull green that went well with her hair. Today the dress felt a little loose. She'd lost a bit of weight lately. So she found a gold chain belt, bought in the same charity shop, a place where she bought clothes for Amy sometimes as well. She didn't put on make-up, because she had a good complexion and anyway, make-up would have been an unnecessary expense, so she'd stopped using it. He must take her as he found her.

She peeped into Amy's bedroom. 'Tidy up now, darling, then you can read in bed for a while.'

Amy pulled a face but knew better than to argue about bed time. She began to put her toys away, the furry animals into a big basket, the dressing up clothes (also courtesy of the charity shop) into their box, the books on the shelves.

Ella watched, not offering to help. She'd decided years ago that she didn't have time to clear up the mess that seemed to reign in most children's bedrooms, so had made it a rule that her daughter must put everything away herself before bedtime, except for one soft toy and one book.

'I think I'll let Teddy sleep with me again tonight.' Amy picked up her oldest toy, which had belonged to her mother as a child.

Ella looked at her in concern. The threadbare teddy always came out for comfort when something was worrying Amy. It had been out a few times lately.

'Mr O'Neal is nice, isn't he?' Amy cuddled the teddy close, tracing one finger round and round his ears.

'Very nice.'

'I wish *he* was my father.'

'Well, he isn't. However nice he is, he's a visitor and in a day or two he'll be gone.' She had to keep telling herself that, didn't dare hope for anything else.

Though he had come back.

'I'm going to make a spell with my magic wand tomorrow so Mr O'Neal won't go away again.'

What did you say to that? Ella wondered. She was never quite sure whether Amy believed in magic or not. 'You aren't — upset about anything?'

In answer Amy held out her arms for a hug and for a minute Ella cradled her close.

'Mr O'Neal doesn't mind my limp, does he?' the child asked in a muffled voice.

'Most people don't, darling.'

'Some of them do. I can always tell. Daddy used to look away when I walked. He made me feel stupid.' She sobbed suddenly. 'I don't want to see him. Do I really have to?'

'Yes, I'm afraid you do.' Ella swallowed hard to get rid of the lump in her own throat. What sort of man made a child feel like that? 'We've said before that there are people who don't like to see anyone limping or with other problems. Some people don't like red hair. I used to get teased a lot about mine at school. They called me Carrots.' They'd had this conversation many times, but Amy seemed to get comfort from the iterations, so Ella would go through it as many times as necessary.

Amy reached out to touch her mother's hair. 'It's not at all like carrots. I wish mine was the same colour as yours.'

'Sometimes red hair gets darker as you get older. We shan't know about yours for a few years yet. But I shall love you whatever happens to your hair.'

'And you won't mind if I have to use a wheelchair when I get bigger?'

'As long as you drive it carefully and don't run me down.'

That brought the usual soft gurgle of laughter. After she'd hugged her mother, Amy pulled away, quickly rubbing a hand across her eyes. Picking up the book, she positioned the teddy carefully and snuggled down. 'This is my mostest favourite story of all. I'm going to read it to Teddy. He always forgets the ending.'

'He'll enjoy that. Goodnight, darling.'

Thoughtful now, Ella went slowly down the stairs to finish cooking the evening meal for the guests. She tried never to react with pity to her daughter's questions, but to speak about the problems Amy faced in matter-of-fact tones and treat her as you would any child. But sometimes you couldn't help wondering what it'd be like to

134

have a child who could run freely, wondering why any child should be born with such a burden. Life could be so unfair.

Worry about things you can change! she told herself firmly. It was one of her mantras and usually helped.

The thought of her daughter's vivid face and loving nature cheered her up, as it always did. Amy was a delight and Ella was lucky to have a child like that.

★　★　★

Rose couldn't help noticing the various staff members at the practice finishing for the day and calling cheerful farewells as they got into their vehicles. Everyone wanted to get home early on Fridays. By seven o'clock the small car park contained only one car besides her own — Oliver's.

She'd sworn to ignore him but couldn't get the memory of his anguish out of her mind, kept seeing him standing just below her window, looking alone and upset.

Her painting had gone well today. She tidied up carefully, put a stew on to simmer and then started on the unpacking she ought to have done earlier.

It was a while before the sound registered. Someone was knocking at the back door. She went to peer out of the window and saw Oliver looking up at her. He gestured to the door, asking her to open it. After a quick wave to show she'd understood, she ran down the back stairs and opened the door for him, surprised at how tired he was looking.

'Are you all right?' she asked, forgetting for a moment that she didn't want to speak to him.

He shrugged. 'I went for a walk, probably overdid it a bit. I've not been well, so haven't been doing a lot of exercise lately.'

She knew him too well. It was more than tiredness; he was deeply upset about something. She hesitated, not wanting to be drawn in, but unable to leave anyone hurting like this without making an effort to help. 'Would you like a glass of wine? I was just about to celebrate moving in.'

He stared at her. 'I thought you wanted to ignore my existence.'

She shrugged. 'I can't. You'll be in and out of this building every day. Besides, life's too short to hold grudges. I'm used to the idea that you're back now. So what if you vanished without a word. I got on with my life.'

He grabbed hold of her arm and swung her round. 'Wait a minute. What do you mean, 'vanished without a word'? Since I had to go up to London suddenly and had only minutes to catch a train, I wrote you a letter and arranged for someone to leave it at your cottage.'

She stared. 'I never received any letter.'

He took hold of both her arms, so that she was facing him. 'Rose, I swear that I did write to you. After all we'd been to one another, I wouldn't just vanish. How could you even think that of me? In the letter I asked you to meet me at a London hotel, on neutral territory, to see if we could work something out. You know I didn't want us to break up.'

'Neither did I.'

'You didn't turn up at the hotel. I was sure the letter would have been delivered, so I took it for a refusal to compromise. That's why I didn't come back.'

She studied his face. Oliver wasn't lying. She'd swear to that.

'You believe me?'

She nodded. 'Who did you give it to?'

'Your cousin.'

She stared at him. 'Ella wouldn't forget something like that.'

'You can be sure I'll be asking her what happened to it.'

So would she. 'Come up and share a wine, then.' She felt shaky inside, didn't know what to do next, only knew she had to get to the bottom of this.

What could have happened to Oliver's letter?

What would have happened to her life if they'd found a way to compromise?

She took a deep breath. Best not go down that path. Water under the bridge.

★　★　★

Ella turned to see Cameron standing in the kitchen doorway. 'Hi. Shall I show you to your table?'

'I'd much rather stay here and lend a hand.'

'I've just about finished. It's only casseroled steak, which is my main standby and freezes well. I made a big batch today, so that I could freeze some. I don't claim to be a gourmet cook.'

'It smells wonderful.' He went to sit on a kitchen stool. 'I'll stay and chat, then.'

'I'll be moving to and fro, serving.'

He caught hold of her hand, forcing her to stop and look at him. 'Are you nervous about being alone with me? Surely not?'

She was going to deny it, out of sheer pride, but couldn't lie to him. 'I am a bit nervous.'

'So am I.'

'You are?'

'Yes. I don't want anything to go wrong between us. I want to — well, give us a chance. I know it's early days, but I really like you as well as finding you attractive. I love your hair. It's a glorious colour.' He raised one hand to touch it, and even that slight gesture sent warmth through her.

She really liked him too, but didn't dare go as far as to admit that.

While she was still trying to work out what to say to him, the guests with the baby turned up for their evening meal and the moment was lost. She forced a bright smile and showed them to their places, suggesting they park the buggy in which the baby was sleeping in a place where she could switch off the wall light. She then went to fetch their starters. It was only tomato and red pepper soup with cheese croutons, a soup that also froze well and was another of her standbys, but guests seemed to like it.

'You're at the other corner table,' she told Cameron as she came back into the kitchen. 'I'll serve your soup now as well and — '

'No. I'll eat here with you later and we'll take it in turns to keep an eye on your other guests. I can serve them for you. It's no fun eating on my own.'

He spoke firmly, as if he didn't intend to take no for an answer, so she didn't argue. She'd been looking forward to sharing a meal with him. 'Oh — well, all right. Amy and I usually eat at this table. I'll set it in a minute.'

'I'll do that.'

'The cutlery is in the top drawer.'

While she served the other guests, he quickly set two places, opened the bottle of wine he'd brought, found the glasses and poured them each a drink. Then he sat waiting for her, sipping the wine occasionally, not making her feel rushed.

But the silence in the kitchen was like no other that she'd experienced. It fairly hummed with . . . something, as if invisible energy was flowing around them. She'd never felt like this with Miles, was a little afraid of being swept away by it, so started work again, searching desperately for some innocuous topic of conversation. 'Um, if it's not too personal, tell me what you've been doing for the past few days.'

He gave her a knowing smile, as if he knew perfectly well what she was doing. 'I went to see an old client, who was trying to bribe me to do one more project for him. But I refused. I've been careful with my money and have no need to rush into another job, especially one I don't fancy.'

'You're lucky to have the choice.' She glanced

towards the conservatory and saw that the young couple had finished their first course. 'I'll just — '

He stood up and moved quickly in front of her. 'I'll get their dishes. You concentrate on plating up the next course.'

After chatting to the two guests and admiring the baby sleeping peacefully in its buggy, he returned with the empty soup bowls and side plates. 'They said it was lovely. I'll take those plates out, then you can serve our soup while they eat their main course.'

They ate slowly and he accepted a second bowlful, then collected the couple's empty plates while she got out the frozen desserts she kept in stock. She served them with fresh raspberries from her own garden and a ginger sauce.

By the time he'd taken the desserts out, she had their own main courses ready.

'Tell me about your family history,' he said, after making appreciative noises about the steak and its sauce.

So she told him the story of Jane Turner, her favourite ancestor, who had brought much of the land into the family as well as the rubies which had supposedly brought good luck.

'I envy you,' he said when she'd finished her tale. 'I know nothing about my ancestors. My father scorns the past and won't say anything much about his own childhood or youth, and my mother only knows up to her grandparents. It's one of the things I intend to do now that I have more time, research my family history.'

She went to glance out at the other guests, but

the baby was fast asleep and the couple both looked tired. Even as she watched, they stood up and the man wheeled the buggy gently towards the outer door. She went to wish them good night and find out what time they wanted breakfast, then returned to Cameron.

No avoiding him now — and she didn't want to.

★　★　★

Rose gestured to the elderly sofa, which was the only seat not loaded with bundles dumped as they were brought into the flat.

'I remember this,' Oliver said with a smile, running one finger over the frayed braid on one sofa arm. 'And I recognize that old wardrobe too.'

'It's perfect for keeping my supplies in,' she said defensively. 'I'll need it when I go back to the cottage, though I don't really need it here.'

He abandoned small talk abruptly. 'Haven't you changed *anything* about your life, Rose?'

She shrugged and poured him a glass of cheap red wine, then got one for herself. After a moment's hesitation she sat down next to him. On a two-seater sofa that was too close, far too close, but it was the only other seat free. 'I've changed in myself, I think. I'm older and wiser, but — ' she raised her chin defiantly ' — I'm just as stubborn about what I want from life. And I'm still working on my main project.'

He looked up at a painting she'd hung on the wall. 'Your style's matured. I like that one. It

141

draws the eyes, lets you understand the animals on their own terms.'

'Thank you.' She took a quick sip of wine to hide her pleasure at that compliment. Oliver never gave compliments that he didn't mean. 'And you? How have you changed?' To her dismay, that haunted look instantly returned to his face, even though he tried to smile at her. 'Don't.' She laid one hand on his. 'Don't pretend with me. We know each other too well. What is it, Oliver? What's happened to you?'

He took another gulp of wine, stared down into the nearly empty glass, then said tightly, 'Don't encourage me to let the demons out. They're better locked away, believe me.'

'Not if they're causing you so much pain.'

'Does that show?'

'To me — and probably to anyone who knows you well.'

He drained the glass and set it down. 'I'd better go before I make a fool of myself.'

She set her own half-full glass down and caught his arm. 'Don't go. Talk to me, Oliver. Tell me.' He tried to pull away, but she kept hold of him and he capitulated suddenly.

'I was involved in an — incident. A patient on drugs. He was stronger than he looked and I was careless. He hit me over the head. When I came to, I found he'd taken me prisoner. It . . . wasn't pleasant. He locked me in a chiller unit and kept the police and everyone at bay for quite some time. There wasn't a lot of oxygen. It was dark. I thought I was going to suffocate, or freeze to death. It's left me a bit . . . claustrophobic.'

'That's why you ran out of the building earlier today.'

'Mmm.'

'It must have been dreadful.'

'Mmm.' He had never been able to put into words how bad it had been, not even to the counsellor.

He wasn't quite sure how her arms got round him, how his head came to be resting on her shoulder, but it felt good. She didn't urge him to speak, which he didn't want to do. With a sigh he gave himself up to the sheer pleasure of being held.

He'd missed her so much.

★ ★ ★

In a large, luxurious house on the outskirts of Chawton, Brett Harding lingered at table waiting for his parents to finish eating, putting up with their chit-chat, fuming inside. What he wanted to do was go out with the lads. What his father had made clear was that if he did, he'd better not come back again, and he'd be out of a job as well as a home.

He might be over thirty, but he couldn't afford that and wasn't stupid enough to alienate his wealthy father. As the only son, he expected to inherit, had been banking on that as the basis of a very comfortable future.

'Your mother just spoke to you,' his father snapped.

Brett turned to her. 'Sorry, Mum. What did you say?'

143

'I asked if you'd like to watch a film with us. There's nothing on TV tonight.'

He judged it best to nod. 'That'd be nice. What movie were you thinking of?'

'An oldie, I'm afraid. Probably not to your taste but it'll pass an hour or two. Or maybe you and your father would like to play billiards for a while. That table is hardly ever used and you were the one who was so keen to get it.'

He did *not* want a tête-à-tête with his father, had already been lectured several times about his appalling behaviour and how much it was going to cost to hire a good lawyer. 'I'm a bit tired. I think I'd rather watch the movie.'

'Film,' his father corrected. 'This is England not America.'

He took a deep breath. 'Film, then. Can I get you something to drink, Dad?'

'Not tonight. And you're not having anything, either, not till I'm sure you're not an alcoholic.'

Looking distressed, his mother stood up. 'I'll just clear the table.'

Brett stood up. 'I'll help you.'

Those bloody Turners! he thought as he obediently carried crockery to the kitchen. It was all their fault. Ella had been asking for it. If it wasn't for her leading him on, he'd not have been so drunk. And her cousin was just as bad, even if she was a Marwood by name. She had Turner blood in her, didn't she? He was sure Rose's van had been badly parked. If he hadn't had to swerve to miss it, he'd not have ploughed into that stupid old cottage. She'd had time to move the van after the accident, so he could

144

prove nothing. But he knew he'd seen the van looming up in front of him, in the wrong place.

Uppity bitches, the pair of them, thinking they were better than anyone else. They always had been, even at school.

He smiled. He still had friends, good friends, who were prepared to pick him up when he crept out of the house after his parents had gone to bed. Fancy having to do that at his age! Only he didn't intend to be disinherited.

Well, he'd already put the wind up Ella Bloody Turner tripping the outside security lights out at that dump she lived in. He'd seen her outline at the windows, going from one to the other, seen the curtains move. He'd go back and do that again when he felt like a good laugh.

He hadn't decided yet what to do about Rose. He'd think of something though.

⋆　⋆　⋆

Ella turned to find Cameron watching her from the kitchen doorway. Feeling self-conscious, she walked across to join him, not protesting when he pulled her into his arms and kissed her.

'I've been dying to do that.'

It was the gentlest of kisses, and yet it sent another storm of response through her body.

He didn't kiss her again, just held her close. She could feel his heart beating, his soft breaths against her temples. It seemed so right to be held by him she was suddenly terrified and pushed him away.

'What is it?' he asked in bewilderment.

145

'We shouldn't. I'm not — not into chance encounters.'

'I thought I'd made it plain that I don't consider this a chance encounter.'

'How can it be anything else? We barely know one another.'

'There's a simple remedy for that. I have all sorts of things to sort out, either online or by phone. If I stay here, we could spend the evenings together, maybe an occasional half day if you have the time. I'm not trying to rush you, but it seems so simple to me — and so right.'

She stared at him, one hand across her mouth, afraid to speak in case she said yes.

'You've been hurt, I know.'

She nodded.

'I won't hurt you, Ella.'

No one could promise that, she thought bleakly, even with the best will in the world.

He gave her a hug and said into her hair, 'I'm enjoying your company but you look exhausted. Go to bed now. I'll see you in the morning.'

After she'd locked the door on him, she watched through a window as he strolled away towards the chalets. He looked so relaxed, so attractive, and he hadn't pressured her for more than she was willing to give. She liked that about him as well.

But did she dare trust him? Or rather, did she dare trust her own judgement where men were concerned?

When she went upstairs, she looked in on Amy and stood for a moment staring fondly down. She tucked the covers in more securely, picked up the book which had slid to the floor and went out, still thoughtful.

It wasn't just her who stood to be hurt, it was Amy. So she had to be doubly careful.

But perhaps this man wouldn't upset the child? He certainly spoke to her in a sensible, normal way, and Amy liked him.

How did you tell for sure whether you could trust someone?

Well, you couldn't be sure of anything or anyone. Life was chancy at best. So she'd take it one day at a time, give him a chance.

She went back out on to the landing and could have sworn she saw a shimmer at one corner. Was it Jane Turner, keeping watch on her descendants? At times Ella felt she could see a woman's outline, even her face. At others, just a shimmer of light.

Or was that too an illusion?

9

On Saturday morning Amy was grumpy from the minute she woke up.

'What's the matter with you today?' Ella asked in exasperation, though she'd already guessed the reason.

'I don't want to see Daddy.'

Ella was busy getting things ready for the guests and had no time to stop work and go over it all again. 'We've talked about that, darling. You don't have a choice. And it's only for an hour or two.'

Out of the corner of her eye she saw something move and turned to find Cameron at the door, just as her daughter spoke again.

'Well, I'm not going to speak to him. I don't care if he is my daddy, I don't like him. He makes you cry.'

Ella could feel herself blushing.

'Good morning,' Cameron said as if nothing was wrong, though he must have overheard.

Amy looked at him unsmilingly, head slightly cocked, as if considering. 'I wish *you* were my daddy, not *him*.'

'He's a lucky man to have a daughter like you.'

Ella shot an embarrassed glance at Cameron, and he shrugged and gave her a quick half-smile, as if to say he understood.

'I have to get on. I've set a table for one in the far corner.'

'Perhaps this young lady would like to show me where?'

Amy nodded and led the way, talking earnestly as he took his place. Ella wondered what they were saying, but then the toaster shot bread out and a timer pinged, so she turned back to dealing with breakfast.

When Amy returned, she slumped down at the table, picking at her breakfast in silence, where normally she'd have been wolfing down food and chattering non-stop.

Ella sighed and said nothing.

⋆ ⋆ ⋆

Miles woke late. He'd allowed himself a night out and hadn't got home till four o'clock, after meeting an old friend who'd invited him back to her place. He enjoyed her company and they shared a bed from time to time, satisfying their needs without the hassles of getting involved, which she wanted as little as he did.

When he'd eaten, the phone rang. He glanced at the sender ID. 'Hi, Mum.' He chatted for three minutes, deemed that long enough for tact and asked her advice about what he should do with Amy that afternoon.

'You're going to see her?'

'Yes.'

Silence then, 'I could come with you.'

'Not this time, Mum, but it might be a good idea later, if I can persuade Ella to allow it.'

'I don't know why she's so obstinate about letting me see Amy. It wasn't me she divorced and you know how I'd love to see my granddaughter again now that I'm living in the UK permanently.'

'Funny. I hadn't got you picked for the grandmotherly type!' He smiled at the mere thought of a successful, elegant business-woman like Stephanie Parnell cuddling a child.

'You've been too busy to have me picked for anything, Miles. I'm more or less retired now, you know, just doing the odd bit of work here and there.'

'Well, you didn't pay much attention to *me* when I was a lad, so I don't know why you want to bother with Amy. She's not your responsibility, after all.' He heard her sigh but she didn't answer that one. He might have known she'd make an issue of seeing his daughter. She'd always had a knack of doing exactly what you didn't want.

'Just give me some hints about what to do with her, Mum.'

'That'd be easier if I knew her. Take a present with you. All children like getting presents. I'm out of touch with what seven-year-old girls want, but any decent toyshop would help you pick something out. As for talking, get her to talk about herself and what she does. Children enjoy doing that just as much as adults do.'

He listened, jotted down a few notes and ended the call as quickly as he could without upsetting her.

Feeling irritated, he went online and found where the nearest toyshop was, then went there. He wasn't looking forward to this afternoon, not at all. What did he know about little girls? But this was the only way he could keep a close eye on Willowbrook and what Ella was doing.

Surely if he went out of his way to charm her, one small girl wouldn't be too hard to look after?

He wondered how far Amy could walk now and if she still had that ugly rolling gait. He didn't care what Ella or the specialists said, there was nothing like that in his side of the family.

★　★　★

'Why is Amy so upset about her father coming?' Cameron asked idly as he wiped some pans. He'd had a bit of difficulty persuading Ella to let him help clear up the kitchen after breakfast, but had refused to go away.

He saw her worried expression as she looked out of the window at her daughter, who was sitting on a bench talking away to her teddy. 'Her father hasn't been to see her since he left three years ago.'

He whistled. 'Not a doting parent, then.'

'No. He wasn't good with Amy before we split up, either. I daren't try to stop him seeing her, because fathers have rights, but she says she's not going to speak to him and that child can be very determined once she's set her mind on something.'

He grinned and picked up another pan. 'I believe you. I'd love to be a fly on the wall when they're together. What time is he coming?'

'This afternoon around two. I've told him they're to stay here at the farm until she's more used to him.'

151

'Will he do that?'

'He'd better.'

'So there's no hope of me tempting you and your daughter out for a drive later, then.'

'I'd not be able to go out on a Saturday, anyway. It's the day guests are most likely to turn up. We're on a main tourist route here, which is very useful. In the summer we get plenty of drop-ins.' She hesitated before adding, 'Another time, maybe. Amy would love a ride in your car.'

'What about Amy's mother?'

'She'd like it too.'

Their glances tangled and caught. He loved the way she'd blushed. She seemed so open, not a sneaky bone in her body. It pleased him that it took her a few moments to answer calmly. He liked to see her reacting to him, because he certainly kept reacting to her. And not just physically. For a moment neither spoke, then he said lightly, 'It's quite a tying job, isn't it, letting out chalets?'

'Especially in the summer. But it fits in well with raising a young child, so I don't mind.'

He saw her expression soften as she glanced again towards Amy, who was now busy with a sketch pad and some coloured pencils, the teddy still sitting beside her on the bench, still the recipient of her confidences.

He followed her glance. It was clear how much she loved her daughter. 'If I can't tempt you out, I think I'll go and have a look at a property I've heard about near Marlborough.'

Her attention was suddenly back on him, her mouth open in shock. 'You're thinking of buying a place in Wiltshire?'

'Yes. I like it here. And I'm only considering buying a place here at this stage. I'm not sure where I want to settle yet, but I have to start looking somewhere, and my first impressions of Wiltshire are very positive. The property I've heard about isn't on the market officially yet, but a friend recommended this local guy who's handling it.'

'Who is it?'

'His name's Julian Walkley.'

'I've heard of him. He's well thought of.'

'Good. Sounds like I've got the right guy, then.'

Cameron spent the rest of the morning helping her, refusing to take no for an answer, amazed at how much work she got through in a day and rather worried by how tired she was looking. She did too much. Far too much.

He accepted her offer of lunch in return for his help, but her mind was clearly on other things, probably her ex's visit, and although she sat opposite him, she hardly said a word.

After that he got ready to go out. There was a property to see, he hadn't been lying about that, but he hadn't intended to bother viewing it yet. He definitely wasn't at the stage of buying a permanent home. But house hunting would give him a good excuse for staying in the neighbourhood. And also for getting away today.

He didn't want Parnell to see him and say something to Ella about him being associated with DevRaCom, which he wasn't now. He'd explain the situation to her when he could make

153

her sit still for more than five minutes.

He stared out of the window towards the farm, saw her come out to sit next to Amy and felt a warmth at the mere sight of them. More than a warmth. You couldn't fall for a woman so quickly. It didn't make sense.

But he had done. Coming back after his visit to London, he'd seen her and felt his spirits lift at once.

He even liked her daughter. Well, who wouldn't? What a great kid Amy was!

He wasn't going away till he'd given this a chance.

★ ★ ★

Oliver went into the surgery on the Saturday morning to find a painting hanging on the wall of his consulting room. It was a view of north Wiltshire seen from a slight elevation, with a solitary bird wheeling overhead. It made him feel as if he could go walking across that wonderful space. It made the whole office feel . . . better . . . less closed in.

He stared at it in amazement. No doubt about who had painted it. How did Rose know him so well?

He was about to nip upstairs to thank her, when the buzzer went.

'Doctor Paige, there's a woman out here who's cut herself rather badly.'

Now that he could deal with.

★ ★ ★

Miles didn't arrive at Willowbrook till three o'clock, by which time Ella was angry that he hadn't bothered to let her know he'd been delayed. She'd seen Amy come in several times to look at the kitchen clock, then trail out again, shoulders drooping.

When she went to look for her daughter, she found that Amy had vanished, wasn't outside, in the bedroom or anywhere in the house. Uh-oh!

Miles got out of the car, brandishing a big bouquet of flowers.

Ella didn't go out to greet him, but waited for him to come and knock on the back door — twice.

Reluctantly she went to open it then and he thrust the bouquet into her hands. She thrust it straight back. 'I don't want it. You can put these in your chalet. I'll bring you a vase. Then you can take them back to London with you.'

For a moment his expression turned ugly, then he forced a smile.

Anyone who didn't know him might have thought it was genuine. She wasn't fooled.

'Can't we let bygones be bygones, Ella?'

'Anything between us is long gone, if that's what you mean. You're in the nearest chalet. It's open. You can come back for Amy after you've settled in — unless you've changed your mind about staying?'

'I've not changed my mind. You and I need to talk.'

He waited for her to answer so she gave him a glassy, uncomprehending stare, one she'd per-fected for dealing with awkward clients.

'Amy's playing somewhere. I'll go and find her.'

* * *

Cameron was surprised at how late Parnell was. He wanted to see the fellow arrive, so he waited, ringing to tell Walkley he was running late. He stayed out of sight inside his own chalet, from where he could hear cars coming.

When he heard the sound of a motor, he couldn't resist going out to have a look. From behind the corner of another chalet he saw a showy BMW come down the side of the house. He watched Parnell get out, spend a moment or two staring round, then walk into the kitchen with a big bouquet.

There was no sign of Amy or the teddy now, but the drawing materials were still lying on the bench.

A short time later Parnell returned, still carrying the bouquet, which he hurled into the back of the car. He drove round the side of the barn, which took him out of Cameron's sight for a few moments. Hell, he wasn't going to be next door, was he? That'd be very awkward. Cameron slipped back into his own chalet. To his relief, Parnell stopped at the building nearest the house.

He watched the fellow take out a small suitcase and laptop, turning after he'd locked the car to scowl at the groups of chalets. The flowers must still be inside the vehicle.

Cameron grinned suddenly. Had that expensive bouquet been intended to soften up Ella?

Even after a short acquaintance, he knew she wasn't the sort to be taken in by empty gestures like that from a man who'd hurt her and neglected their daughter for years.

From here he could see the upper floors of the farm. A face appeared at an upstairs window. It must be Ella. She seemed to be looking for something outside. Something or someone? Amy!

He'd better get going, Cameron decided. He was already late for his appointment to view the house. He'd moved his convertible so that he could get into it without being seen if he bent down behind the bushes as he crossed to it from the chalet. He felt a fool doing this and hoped Ella hadn't seen him.

As he eased the car round the side track, he saw Ella dragging a reluctant Amy back to the house. He couldn't help grinning. He'd bet a lot of money that child was going to be very uncooperative today. He'd place an equally large bet on Parnell having little if any experience of dealing with young children.

★ ★ ★

Ella found Amy in the barn, but had to speak very sternly to get her back to the house. She washed Amy's hands and face and bent down to give her a hug. 'Be a good girl, darling. It's only for a couple of hours.'

They waited for Miles to come to the house and when he didn't, Ella debated briefly whether to leave him where he was till he realized he

157

needed to get his daughter. But the waiting was so fraught in the end she took a scowling Amy to him and knocked on the chalet door. 'Here she is.'

Miles gave the child one of his best smiles. 'How nice to see you. Come in.'

Amy stayed where she was, lower lip jutting. 'Don't want to.'

'I have a present for you.'

She gave him a long stare, a curiously adult look that assessed him and found him wanting. 'Don't want it.'

He looked helplessly at Ella.

'I did my best. You can lead a horse to water . . .'

'Come in, both of you.'

'I have the evening meal to prepare. If you bring Amy back to the house at five, she can have her tea before the guests.'

'Where will we be eating?'

'You will be eating in the conservatory. I shall be working. I have guests coming who spend the weekend here regularly and I always make them a meal. And there may be some drop-ins. It's that time of year.'

'We could eat our meals later?' he offered.

She was tempted to echo her daughter and say, 'Don't want to,' but contented herself by repeating that she would be too busy then clearing up.

'What's the point of my staying if we can't talk?' His voice had that edge she recognized all too well. He was angry but trying not to let it out.

'I've nothing to say to you. And you were never any good at listening. All you're good at is talking about yourself and your needs.' She noticed Amy watching her closely and wished she'd bitten her tongue on those words.

Giving her daughter a quick hug, she murmured, 'Be good!' then turned and walked away.

★　★　★

Miles stared down at the sullen child. What had Ella been saying to her? He tried to speak gently. 'Come in and look at your present. If you don't like it, I can change it for something you do like.'

She stared at him, her expression not changing. He waited but she didn't move.

Exasperated, he took her hand and pulled her inside, but she shook him off and didn't sit down till he propelled her forward and pressed her into a chair.

When he put the present into her lap, she folded her arms and let it slide off.

'Don't be st — silly! It's a present.'

'I don't want a present from you.'

'What has your mother been saying to you?'

'*She* says I have to talk to you, but I don't want to.' She paused to glare at him. 'And *you* don't want to talk to me, neither. You don't look at me nice.'

After that, she refused to answer his questions and when he unwrapped the present the shop had assured him she'd love, she barely glanced at it.

159

In desperation, he said, 'Let's go for a walk round the lake.'

She shook her head.

He yanked her to her feet and she burst into tears.

'You're a bad man. I don't want to be with you.'

She was out of the door before he could stop her, running with that ungainly gait he hated to see. He hesitated for a minute, wondering whether to give chase. Then she fell and didn't get up. Without thinking, he ran along the path after her.

'Are you all right?'

She was sobbing in a despairing, heartbroken way, and he gathered her in his arms instinctively, annoyed with himself for managing her so badly and to his surprise, upset by her distress. 'Oh, Amy, I didn't mean to hurt you. Give me a chance. I'm trying to be a better father.'

She lay unresponsive in his arms and he became aware of how small she was, how vulnerable her slender arms and legs.

'Shh now, shh.'

Gradually the crying stopped, but when he helped her to her feet, her voice caught on a sob. 'I want my m — mummy.'

'I'll carry you back to the farm.'

She pulled away at once. 'I don't need carrying. I can walk. It doesn't matter if I fall down. I can get up again.'

She had a bruise on her wrist, and her eyes were still brimming with tears. He didn't want to admit defeat but didn't know what to do except say, 'I'll walk back with you, then.'

'I know the way.'

'It's only polite to walk a visitor home.'

'*You're* the visitor, not me. This is *my* home.' She set off, ignoring him.

He went with her, feeling like a louse.

★　★　★

Ella saw them coming, realized that Amy had been crying and rushed out of the kitchen. 'What's the matter?'

Amy went to cling to her, something she didn't normally do.

'She ran away and fell. I didn't mean to upset her. I'd bought her a present, only she didn't want it.'

'You can't buy a child's love.' She gave Amy a hug.

Suddenly the child let out a wail. 'I left my teddy behind!'

'I'll go and fetch it,' he volunteered. 'I can buy you a new teddy if you like. That one looked old and worn.'

Two pairs of eyes regarded him scornfully.

'He's *my* teddy,' Amy said. 'He's very special and I love him. He was Mummy's teddy when she was little, too.'

'Oh. Sorry. I was only trying to help.'

'Fetch the teddy,' Ella said quietly. 'I'll calm her down then we'll all have a drink of lemonade.'

He nodded, relieved to get away from the

fraught atmosphere for a few moments. Who'd have thought a child could make you feel like that?

★ ★ ★

After morning surgery Oliver went to find Rose. She wasn't at home and her door was locked.

As he was walking back down the outer stairs, his father came out to the car park and called, 'She'll probably be in the pub. She works there at lunchtime some weekends.'

'Oh. Yes, of course.'

His father stopped to eye him. 'You look tired. Something wrong?'

Oliver shrugged. 'I didn't sleep well last night.'

'Worried about the work?'

'Not exactly. I just — don't like being shut in.'

'Oh. I didn't realize you still — '

'It's all right. I coped. Things are — getting better.'

'Tell me if I've pushed you too hard. I can get another locum.'

'I had to start work again sometime.'

'You did a good job with that cut this morning.'

'That sort of thing's easy, compared to what you can see after a road accident or a shooting.'

'It must be hard working in such a — front-line position.'

'Great experience.'

'For what?' He held up his hand. 'Don't answer that. I'm being pushy again. You coming home for lunch?'

'No. I think I'll go for a walk.'

Of course his walk took him past the Green Man and then he couldn't help going inside the pub. After all, he had to thank Rose for the picture!

She was behind the bar, leaning on the counter, laughing with a very old man. Oliver stopped in the doorway and as easily as that, fell in love again with her wonderful smile and vivid personality. Too plump for modern standards, his Rose, but undernourished women never had turned him on.

Oh, hell! He still fancied her like crazy. As if he needed a further complication in his life.

She turned to wipe the bar surface, saw him and stilled, studying him gravely as if waiting for him to make the running.

He couldn't talk to her in front of all these people, so raised one hand in greeting and walked out again.

★   ★   ★

Rose watched him leave. Had he been coming to see her? Or just popping in to see if the place where he used to drink had changed?

He looked tense and drawn, much thinner than he had been. She'd never seen him like that. He'd always been brimming with confidence and energy.

But he was still the most attractive man she'd ever met, damn him!

She wondered if he'd seen the painting she'd put in his office early that morning and realized

163

why she'd done it. Would he send it back with a no, thank you? Would it do what she hoped and help him not to feel so shut in?

He wasn't a liar, so he must have sent her a letter before he left. She could weep for the years of needless pain she'd experienced at the thought of him abandoning her without a word.

Had he been upset about their break-up, too?

She'd not rest till she knew what had happened to the letter and what it had said. Tomorrow morning she was going out to Willowbrook to speak to Ella. Surely her cousin hadn't kept it back on purpose? No, not Ella.

So what could have happened to it? And why had Ella not mentioned it?

10

Ella calmed Amy down, but refused to let her go up to her bedroom. 'Darling, we've talked about this before. You have to spend time with your daddy.'

'But I don't like him.' She began to sob again. 'And he doesn't like me.'

Ella was horrified. 'Of course he likes you. He's your father.' She pulled the child on to her lap, even though Amy, who was tall for her age, had for a while been declaring herself too old to be treated in such a babyish way. The fact that Amy didn't protest only emphasized how upset she was. 'Shh, now. Shh.'

There was a knock on the door and they turned to see Miles standing there holding the teddy by one foot.

With a squeak of anger, Amy slid off Ella's lap and snatched her toy from him. 'Teddy doesn't like being held upside down.'

'Er — sorry.'

With awful scorn, Amy added, 'You don't know anything about teddies!'

'Er — no.' When he looked at Ella for help, she gestured to a chair, though only for Amy's sake. If it were up to her, she'd simply tell him to leave. But Amy was now even more upset about her father and that wasn't a good thing. 'I'll get you that coffee I promised, Miles. You must be thirsty.'

He looked at her in puzzlement.

Sit down, she mouthed, then turned to her daughter. 'Amy, you can get your weekend bar of chocolate now and your daddy is going to buy you a can of fizzy drink to go with it as a special treat.'

He had always been quick on the uptake. 'Choose whichever sort you want.'

For a moment Amy hesitated, then said a stiff thank you and took out a can of ginger beer. She hesitated again, but her mother beckoned so she brought it across to the table. Was she exaggerating her limp? It certainly seemed like it. And Miles was definitely looking away.

'We always have our drinks sitting down, because I don't like wiping up spills,' Ella said brightly. As if he cared! She took out some of her home-made biscuits and brought them across on a pretty plate. 'The coffee will only be a few minutes.'

'It smells heavenly. You always did have a weakness for good coffee.'

'It's more than a weakness here. I have some very discerning customers and the hotel inspectors approve of such touches. I'm aiming to get a four-star rating next time. Try one of my home-made biscuits.'

He took one, bit it without even looking at it, then chewed slowly, staring down before he took another bite. 'This is brilliant,' he said through a mouthful of crumbs. 'I've never tasted anything quite like it.'

'I pride myself on my biscuits. That's my own recipe.'

'Have you ever thought of selling the recipe?'

'Could I really do that?'

'Yes. And I probably know someone who'd be interested. I'd only charge you twenty per cent for brokering the deal.'

She looked at him in exasperation. He could never give you anything, could he, always had to profit from you. The meanness of this offer made up her mind: she was definitely going to claim maintenance from him.

Amy started eating her chocolate slowly, piece by piece, with the single-minded attention she always gave to her favourite treat. When she'd eaten half, she wrapped the rest up carefully.

'I'll save that for tomorrow, to share with Nessa. We'll have lots of chocolates this time, won't we?'

Miles looked questioningly at Ella.

'Nessa's her best friend. She's coming over to play tomorrow.'

'Oh. I see. Is she in your class at school?'

Amy nodded.

'What do you play at?'

She looked at him, shut her mouth firmly, then her mother nudged her and nodded towards the can of ginger beer her father had bought her. 'We play hidey in the barn.'

He frowned at Ella. 'Is that old place safe?'

'Safer than most modern houses. They knew how to build houses in those days.'

'It wasn't good enough to be listed.'

Trust him to point that out yet again. 'It'll outlast you,' she said, annoyed that her voice came out thin with annoyance.

After a moment's bristling silence, the conversation limped along. Give him his due, he was trying to talk to the child, using all the normal conversational tricks. But Amy answered mostly in monosyllables, sometimes not at all.

Ella decided she'd done enough to help him. 'I want to speak to your daddy. Why don't you go and play outside for a few minutes, darling? Don't go away from the yard, though.'

When the child had gone without even a glance in her father's direction, Ella said bluntly, 'It takes time to win over a child. She doesn't know you. If you come back next time, you can buy her another can of drink and maybe bring a bar of chocolate — a small bar, and she likes milk chocolate best. As she gets to know you, she'll soften up a little.'

'I brought her an expensive fairy outfit,' he said in an aggrieved tone. 'The best in the shop. I can't believe how much they charge for a bit of net and sparkle! They assured me that little girls of that age love them but she wouldn't even touch it.'

'She's no fool, knows you're just trying to buy her affections. I have to wonder why you're even bothering. You never did like children.'

'Amy is my daughter, that's why I'm bothering. And if you must know, my mother's been nagging me too. She wants to see her only grandchild.'

'How is Stephanie? I was always sorry when she cut Amy and me off after you left us.'

'She was busy then. She's retired now, got out early with a fat redundancy payment, so she's got more time.'

'Why don't you bring her down with you next weekend?'

He stared at the ceiling for a minute, eyes narrowed, then shrugged. 'Good idea. I'll see if she's free.'

'Tell her no expensive presents. I've not brought Amy up to expect such things. Now, I think that's enough father and daughter togetherness for one weekend — or do you really want more punishment?'

He shook his head, not even needing a minute to think about it.

'Right then. *I* don't have any more time to chat. I've guests arriving shortly and eight dinners to prepare for tonight. There's really no point in your staying the night.'

'I'll vacate the cabin then.'

'Good idea.'

She watched him go and as she'd expected, he did no more than wave goodbye to his daughter.

When he'd gone, Amy trailed back inside. 'I still don't like him.'

It was out before Ella could stop it. 'Neither do I.'

'Is he coming again next week?'

'He says so. And he may bring your grandmother. Do you remember her?'

Amy shook her head.

'Well, I remember her well and I liked her very much, so don't decide in advance how you feel about *her*.'

'Nessa has a grandma. She takes them out for burgers.'

Ella stifled a sigh. It was a long-running battle

between them. She refused to spend her hard-earned money on commercial burgers and fries. She made better burgers herself and chips were a rare treat at Willowbrook, because she was a firm believer in a healthy diet.

'If my grandma wants to take me out for burgers, will you let her?'

'Maybe. But not more than once a month.'

Amy's face lit up at this concession. 'I don't mind seeing *her*, then.'

★ ★ ★

Cameron met Julian Walkley, the real estate agent, and was shown round a huge and expensive modern 'executive residence'. It would give him something to report back on to Ella later, but he didn't like the feel of it at all. Soulless was the word that came into his mind.

He frowned round. 'I'm coming to the conclusion that I like older places.'

'How much older?'

An image of Willowbrook came into his mind. 'Really old.'

'Even if they're listed properties?'

'I know that term, but what exactly does it mean?'

'Buildings of special interest, with special architectural or historic features. Once they're listed, you can't do anything to alter them without permission — though the authorities aren't usually unreasonable as long as you stay in period.'

Cameron listened carefully and heard the

enthusiasm in the other man's voice. Maybe this afternoon's meeting could be helpful, instead of merely filling in time. 'I have a friend with an old farm which has several period outbuildings. If I'm not mistaken, part of the barn is a medieval cruck construction, and the house itself is mainly eighteenth century.'

Julian's face lit up. 'Cruck? You're sure of that?'

'I do know what cruck means: trees sawn up with strategic branches left on them for supporting cross beams.'

The other nodded eagerly. 'Is the farm near here?'

'Just outside Chawton Bassett. But I was told the owner's ex had made enquiries a few years ago and found the farm wasn't special enough to be listed.'

'I've not heard of anyone trying to list a property like that, and I would have done. Are you sure he made an official application?'

'No, I'm not sure. But he stated categorically that he'd been told the place wasn't worth listing.'

'When was this, do you know?'

'Three or four years ago.'

'I think you must be mistaken. I'd have been called in for a preliminary visit if someone had tried to list a place on my patch, especially with a cruck barn. Bit of a passion of mine, actually, old houses.'

Cameron looked at him thoughtfully. 'You wouldn't consider coming to look at this one unofficially and giving me your opinion as to whether we should try to list it? I don't want to raise any false hopes.'

'Be glad to. If it really has medieval parts remaining, I'd be particularly interested. Buildings erected before 1700 are more likely to be worth listing and preserving.'

'Who does this listing?'

'The conservation officer at the local council in the first place. He'd have a fair idea whether it'd be worth making an application. But I'm pretty good at spotting national treasures. I've brought a few to the attention of my local authority already.' He grinned. 'I see a lot of buildings in my job and they're not all like this one.' He made a scornful gesture at their surroundings.

'How about coming over tomorrow?'

'I'm afraid Sunday's my busy day. And I have meetings in Swindon all day Monday. How about Tuesday?'

Rashly, Cameron committed Ella to showing Julian round on Tuesday morning, then took his leave and drove back.

To his relief the car had gone from the chalet Parnell had been occupying but he was conscious the man might return at any minute, so kept his eyes and ears open for approaching cars as he hurried across to the house.

★ ★ ★

Through the window he could see Ella working in the kitchen — when was she not working? He'd not met anyone quite like her, never still

172

for a moment, always preparing food, doing the laundry, tidying up or caring for her daughter.

But did she always look so tired? Even as he looked, she rubbed her forehead as if it was aching. He turned to go in, but Amy was sitting outside, looking so unhappy he slowed down again.

'Hi there.'

She stared up at him bleakly.

'Is something wrong?' It obviously was. What had Parnell been doing to the child?

'My daddy came to see me today and I don't like him, whatever anyone says. I'm *glad* he's gone back to London early.'

Cameron blinked at the vehemence in her voice. 'Maybe when you get to know him better — '

'I don't want to know him better!' Amy clutched the teddy more closely. 'He's not nice. He brought me a fairy dress, but I'm not going to wear it. I wish I hadn't drunk the ginger beer he gave me. He didn't even say goodbye to me.'

'What does your mummy say?'

'She says I have to see him if he comes again. If I had a real fairy wand, I'd make a spell so he'd never come back.'

A voice interrupted them.

'Amy! Time for you to get your shower.'

With a long-suffering sigh the child stood up, gathered together her drawing things and walked back to the house with dragging feet.

Cameron waited a moment to give Ella time to speak to her daughter, then went into the kitchen. 'Need a helping hand?'

She turned. 'I can't keep expecting you to — '

'We had this argument before. You don't expect anything. I'm offering of my own free will.' He caught hold of her hand and asked gently, 'Bad day?'

She held back as he tried to pull her into his arms, then with a sigh she let him hold her close and rested her head against his shoulder.

'Very bad,' she admitted.

'The visit didn't go well?'

'I didn't expect it to. He tried to buy her affection.'

He could hear the scorn in her voice, could imagine how she'd have looked as she dealt with her ex. A strong woman, Ella. He liked that, had never been turned on by clinging, helpless females.

As she looked up at him, he couldn't help himself. He'd been longing to kiss her lips and find out if they were as soft as they looked.

After a murmur of surprise and a slight stiffening, she relaxed against him and returned his kiss.

'I've been wanting to do that for days.' He was about to pull her closer when a car turned into the back yard, tyres crunching on the gravel. 'Damn!' He planted a quick kiss on her nose. 'To be continued.'

She stepped back, face flushed, hands going up to smooth her hair. 'It's my first guests. They've been before, so I won't be long.'

'I'll finish the washing up.'

'Thanks. And would you just keep an ear open for Amy? I don't like to leave her on her own in the bathroom.'

He started scrubbing out the baking equipment she'd used, but watched as she greeted the guests, talked for a moment or two, then stood back and let them find their own way to the chalet. She had a natural charm and warmth which made people feel welcome. He'd noticed it himself the first time.

'It's always easier when people have been here before,' she said as she came back into the kitchen.

A voice from upstairs called, 'Mummy!'

'I'll just see what Amy wants.'

When she came down, he had the kitchen clear.

'Thank you so much!'

He gave a mock bow. 'At your service, m'lady. What next?'

'Once Amy's out of the shower, I want to check that the chalet my ex was going to stay in hasn't been messed up.' She hesitated.

'Go on. Give me a task, more than one. I mean it.'

'Could you set two tables for four people each? And you — '

'Will be eating with you in here.'

A smile slowly lit up her face. 'You're very determined.'

'When I want something.'

The smile vanished and was replaced by a wary look.

He was puzzled. 'What did I say wrong?'

'Want something. Sorry. It was one of Miles's favourite phrases. He *wanted* a lot of things.'

'I'll change that, then. Take your pick: desire,

175

wish for, hope and pray for. I'm not Miles, you know.'

Her smile returned. 'I shouldn't blame you for how he treated me, should I? Only seeing him today brought it all back — what it was like to live with him, I mean. I was angry with myself. I must have been utterly stupid and naïve to be taken in by his charm. What he wanted was this place and the money it could generate, not me as a person. He tried to hide it but I could tell he was angry when I insisted on a pre-nuptial contract, listing what we had each brought to the marriage.'

'And what you'd mainly brought was Willow-brook.'

'Yes.'

The sound of water gurgling upstairs stopped. He gave her a quick hug before she could stop him. 'It sounds as if Amy has finished her shower. Go and check that chalet. I'll keep an ear open in case she needs anything.'

★ ★ ★

Ella sighed with relief when the guests had eaten and gone back to their chalets. She turned to find Cameron looking at her thoughtfully. He poured her a glass of wine, which she'd refused until then.

'Thanks for your help tonight, Cameron.'

'It was my pleasure. I'm finding it very interesting watching you work. You're not only efficient, you provide a wonderful personal touch to your service.'

176

'Fussing over guests costs very little and makes a big difference. I'd not have got the three stars without it, especially as some of our furnishings are not top class. And if I'm to get four stars . . . '

'The furnishings seem all right to me.'

'They're not top quality.'

He could see her frowning again. 'Come and sit down a minute. We'll clear up together afterwards. I need to discuss something with you.' He waited till she was seated. 'The guy who showed me the house today is a local expert on listed buildings. I was telling him about Willowbrook.'

'Been there, done that. It's not special enough.'

'But have you really been there? He says he'd have heard if there had been any enquiries, even casual ones, about listing this farm. He hadn't realized parts of the structure were medieval.'

She stared at him as this sank in. 'Are you sure?'

'Not a hundred per cent, but it's his guess that no effort has ever been made to list Willowbrook.'

'But Miles said . . . ' Colour flared in her cheeks. 'Why would he — ' She broke off.

Cameron waited patiently, not interrupting her thoughts. It was obvious why her ex hadn't wanted the place listed: he'd wanted to sell it for development.

'I'll look into it — properly this time. Willowbrook deserves preserving — and having an officially historic property won't hurt when

177

people are looking for somewhere to stay.'

'I agree. I've arranged for Julian to come and look round on Tuesday, if that's all right with you, just to have a preliminary squiz at things, nothing official. He'll be able to give you a better idea of where you stand.'

'That's fine by me, as long as he comes during school hours. I don't want Amy saying anything about this to her father.'

'Ten o'clock in the morning suit you?'

'That's fine.' She couldn't hold back a yawn.

He stood up. 'Let's clear up, then I'll go to bed.'

When they'd finished, he hugged her and ran one finger down her cheek. 'One day, and not too far from now, I hope, we won't say goodnight with a mere hug.'

Warmth ran through her body and she couldn't move for a moment.

It was he who took a step backwards. 'I never take advantage of exhausted women, though. Do you ever get a real rest, Ella? Take a holiday?'

She shook her head, hesitated, then moved across to kiss his cheek, lingering for a moment, eye to eye, then stepping back with a tired sigh. 'Thank you, Cameron.'

'For what in particular?'

'For everything. Just being there for me. I've been alone for a long time.'

She marvelled as she locked the outer door behind him and walked slowly up the stairs. She felt as if she'd known him for years and she trusted him as she hadn't trusted a man since Miles. What was there about Cameron O'Neal

178

that did this to her?

She was still trying to work that out when she fell asleep.

* * *

The phone rang soon after Miles got back to his flat that evening. He stared round sourly as he went to pick it up, hating the contrast with Willowbrook. His place was small because that was all he could afford — tiny was a more accurate word, because it was only a studio apartment. It was a decent address, which was what mattered, but he never brought people back there.

And there Ella was in that rambling old house, with space for several families, just wasting a valuable resource. Well, he was more determined than ever after his visit. He was going to get some benefit from the years he'd spent commuting to the wilds of Wiltshire, putting up with the inconveniences of a house that was well past its use-by date and a wife who was so naïve a baby could have stolen candy from her.

'Miles? Is that you? All I can hear down the phone is breathing?'

He realized he was holding the receiver near his mouth but hadn't spoken. 'Mother. Sorry. I was miles away. How are you?'

'The same as I was when you rang me a few days ago. Did you go down to Willowbrook? How's my granddaughter? Will Ella allow me to visit?'

He definitely didn't want his mother to see

how his daughter reacted to him, he decided. She'd never let him live it down. 'Ella's thinking about it.'

'I thought better of your powers of persuasion.'

'She always was a stubborn bitch. Look, I have to go out. I'm meeting someone for dinner. I'll ring you next week after I get back from Willowbrook. I'll do my best to persuade her.'

★ ★ ★

Stephanie Parnell put down the phone, feeling desperately disappointed. She'd guess Miles hadn't really tried to persuade Ella to allow her to visit her only grandchild. Other people's needs were never a high priority with him. He was her younger son but her second husband's only child, and the lad had been spoiled, no doubt about that. Not by her — she wasn't stupid enough — but by her ex, who had believed money solved everything. It hadn't got him very far with Miles, though. Fred now saw even less of his son than she did.

What was she going to do? If this was an important business deal, she'd be taking care of things herself, not leaving it to an underling. And it was important to her. Very. She had only one grandchild, because her older son was gay. Lately she'd felt a desperate hunger to be part of Amy's life.

She went to switch on her computer and see if Willowbrook had a website. It did. Pretty but very simple, rather amateurish actually. But there

180

were some good photos that reminded her of how pretty the place was.

She wasn't going to wait for Miles to do something, she decided suddenly. She'd book a chalet and spend a few days there. She now had plenty of time for trips or for anything else she wanted to do.

But would Ella allow her to visit?

11

Rose didn't bother to call Ella first, simply drove out to Willowbrook on the Sunday, determined to find out what had happened to Oliver's letter. She'd spent a restless night, dreaming of what ifs and maybes. Could the two of them have found a way to compromise? She still didn't feel that would have been possible. She'd needed to stay in Wiltshire, had been immersed in painting its wildlife for years; he had needed to gain experience overseas in emergency medicine, the area in which he was determined to specialize.

She parked her car and as she was walking towards the house, saw Amy come out of the old barn with her friend. At the sight of her favourite aunt, Amy let out a shriek of delight and dragged Nessa across to greet her.

'Me an' Nessa have found a new hidey hole. Come an' see it!'

Rose resisted the enthusiastic tug. 'Later, darling. I need to see your mummy about something first. Where is she?'

'She and Mr O'Neal are in the kitchen. She's been talking to him for *hours* already.'

'Who's Mr O'Neal?'

'He's a guest, but I wish *he* was my father, 'cos he's nice. My real father came to visit us yesterday and he isn't nice. It's not fair! I have to see him when he comes, even though I don't like him.'

Rose stared at her in shock. Miles was back! Ella was crazy to let him come here. It was like inviting a man-eating tiger into your parlour. What did he want now? He'd not have come purely to visit, that was sure. He must see a chance of making money out of the place. Money was the only thing he really cared about.

She realized Amy was looking at her pleadingly. 'I'll come and see your hiding place in a little while, darling.' She walked to the house and rapped on the kitchen door by way of a warning, but could see at once that all her cousin was doing was sitting chatting.

Rose gave the guy a quick once-over as she went in and admitted to herself that Amy had a point. Mr O'Neal was extremely attractive, a man with class, presence and a very warm smile. From the way he was looking at her cousin, he found her attractive. *Don't push this one away, Ella*, Rose prayed. She knew how lonely her cousin felt sometimes. Well, she'd felt the same way herself since Oliver left.

After introductions, Cameron said he had some phone calls to make and left the two women alone.

Rose waited till he was out of earshot to speak. 'Sorry to interrupt your tête-à-tête.' To her amusement, Ella blushed.

'It's not — we weren't . . . I'll put some more coffee on and — '

'Who is he?'

'Just a guest.'

'From the hungry way he was looking at you, he's more than 'just a guest', surely?' She grasped her cousin's hand. 'It's about time you dipped a toe in the water again and started dating, don't you think, love?'

'I — we'll see.'

Rose knew that flat, determined tone so didn't pursue the point. She waited until the mug of coffee was in front of her to say, 'I've seen Oliver.'

'And? Is he upsetting you?'

'Not exactly. He says he's only here for a few months.'

Ella looked at her in surprise. 'I thought you were never going to speak to him again.'

'That was when I thought he'd gone away without a word and . . . Ella, he's insisting he gave you a letter for me just before he left. Do you remember that?'

'He definitely didn't give me a letter.'

'Oh.' She stirred the coffee, though there was no need. 'He seems pretty certain he did and he doesn't usually lie.' She held up one hand to prevent her cousin speaking. 'I know you don't lie, either, so . . . I must admit I'm a bit puzzled. I'll get back to him for the details.'

The coffee slopped over the edge of her cup and she stared down at it, her thoughts churning. Surely she couldn't be wrong? Oliver wouldn't lie to her about something so important, would he? No. He definitely hadn't been lying. She knew him too well to be fooled about that. She'd seen real pain in his eyes, pain that matched her own at his desertion.

She changed the subject and started telling Ella how light and airy her new flat was, perfect for painting. She hoped the repairs to her old cottage would take a while.

Eventually she took her leave without further mention of the letter. She knew Ella was dying to find out more about her and Oliver, but she wasn't ready to talk about him, even to her cousin. Well, she didn't know where they stood yet, did she? They'd barely re-established communications.

The two children had obviously been keeping watch, because as Rose left the house, they came rushing out of the barn, moving so quickly Amy nearly fell over. Nessa steadied her friend in a way that showed she'd done it many times before. That brought tears to Rose's eyes. Amy took her disability in her stride, but those who loved her ached for her sometimes as she stubbornly struggled to act as normally as possible.

As Amy grabbed hold of her aunt's arm, Nessa hovered shyly behind her friend, nodding vigorously to support the repeated demand that she go and see their hiding place.

Rose hesitated. The last thing she wanted at the moment was to delay confronting Oliver. But she could never say no to Amy, so she followed them into the barn, saying, 'Only for a minute or two.'

'Stand in the doorway,' Amy ordered. 'Now, close your eyes and count to thirty slowly.'

Rose did as she was told, counting aloud, hearing muffled sounds as if something was being dragged along the floor. When she opened her eyes, she was alone. Light was slanting through the doorway behind her. Motes of dust were dancing along the sunbeams that criss-crossed the empty interior. But there was no sign of the two little girls.

'Where a — a — are you?' she called playfully.

Normally this would have been answered by muffled giggles, but this time there was silence. The barn seemed empty. Amy played here sometimes when the weather was bad. There was a swing suspended from one beam, a skipping rope lying on the ground and a pink fairy wand resting on top of a partition that separated three stall-like storage areas, one of which had a rug and cushions in it. Rose checked each of these but they were empty.

'Amy, where are you?' she called more sharply, frowning now. She hoped the children hadn't found somewhere dangerous to hide. 'Amy?'

Still only silence answered her.

Then suddenly there was a scraping sound to one side and as Rose swung round, a section of the wooden wall began to move outwards. She knew there were secret hiding places at Willowbrook, because Ella had told her that the details of these were with her lawyer, in case anything happened. This had to be one of the old farm's secrets, surely?

She was quite certain Ella wouldn't have told the children about it because she'd never have let a stranger into the secret. Why, she hadn't even told her own cousin. And were such places safe for little girls to play in? What if they'd got trapped inside? Would their cries for help have been heard?

She hurried forward as the secret panel swung fully open, but her niece's face was so gleeful, Rose bit back a scolding and contented herself by asking, 'Does your mother know you play here?'

Amy shrugged. 'She's been busy. Me an' Nessa only found it last time she came here to play with me. Isn't it cool?'

'Yes. Will you show me how it works?'

They demonstrated how to open it from outside, then urged her to step inside. Before she could stop her, Amy had closed the panel again, standing on tiptoe to do it.

To Rose's relief, some light filtered down from above their heads because she didn't like dark, enclosed spaces, could fully understand Oliver's problem with them. The hidey hole wasn't large, but it had room for the three of them and there was even a narrow wooden bench to sit on.

'How did you find it?'

'The lady comes in here. Only *she* walks through the wall. Ghosts can do that, you know.' Amy clapped one hand to her mouth. 'Mummy said not to talk about our ghosts, but I've only told Nessa and you know about them already, don't you, Auntie Rose?'

'Yes.' But it made her blood run cold to hear the child talk so casually about seeing a ghost. She had no doubt Amy was telling the truth. That child couldn't lie to save her life. She must have seen something, and Rose knew her cousin had too. The thought of that made goose flesh rise on her arms. 'Um — how do we get out of here?'

'Like this.' Amy went to press the wall in one corner with her right hand, and a little further down with her left. The panel swung open again with only the faintest of scraping sounds.

Rose left the hole quickly and told the children to close it up, watching to make sure it was securely fastened again, and reminding them to tell no one about it. Then she went back to the house. Talking to Oliver would have to wait a little longer.

Ella looked up in surprise. 'Something wrong with your car?'

'No. Amy wanted to show me a hidey-hole she and Nessa have found in the barn.' She saw comprehension dawn in her cousin's eyes. 'Behind a secret panel.'

'Oh, damn. I wanted to keep the hiding places secret till she's older. Now I'll have to phone Nessa's mother and ask her to make sure her daughter keeps quiet about this one. We don't usually tell outsiders at all, but those girls have been friends since they were three. They're more like twin sisters. Anything one knows the other soon finds out.'

'How many hiding places are there at Willowbrook? You never went into details.'

'I know of three, but in her diary one of my great-greats says there are four. Dad and I looked for the other one several times, but we never found it.'

'That many! Will you show me the others one day?' She didn't wait for an answer because she'd noticed the time. 'Oops! I have to go. I'm working this lunch time.'

'I'll show you one more hiding place next time you come, but there's another we keep absolutely quiet about. Sorry.'

'It's all right.'

Rose drove off thoughtfully. Talking to Oliver would have to wait till after work. If only thinking about him was as easily prevented.

★ ★ ★

When her cousin had left, Ella remained lost in thought for a while. It went against the grain to have an outsider like Nessa knowing about the hiding place in the barn. Children were notorious for giving away secrets. She'd try to impress on the two girls how important it was to tell no one, but she didn't feel the secret would be safe with them.

And yet, did it matter so much? There wasn't exactly a need for such hiding places these days.

She was going to show Cameron's friend round tomorrow. Should she mention the secret places to him? Perhaps she'd show him the one in the barn. Not the one in her bedroom, though. The jewels were still there, until she decided whether to accept Ian Hannow's friend's advice. It felt far safer than if she'd put them in the bank. Besides, they belonged at Willowbrook.

After some thought, she decided that if the children knew about the hiding place in the barn, there'd be no harm in showing it to Cameron's friend. She'd wait till she met him though first, see how she liked him.

Her thoughts came back to the puzzle of why

Oliver Paige was saying he'd given her a letter for Rose. He hadn't. She was quite certain of that. She hadn't even seen him the weekend he left, a weekend she could still remember clearly because it'd been filled with arguments and recriminations. Miles had been pressing her to sell the farm and she'd refused, not in the slightest bit moved by the money he said she'd make.

With an exasperated sigh at how little she'd done that morning, she banished those dark memories and went to peg out the first load of laundry for the day. Somehow the work seemed heavier today, and a long list of chores loomed after this one.

Maybe she did need a rest — but how to find the time for one was more than she could figure out.

⋆　⋆　⋆

Before she went to work, Rose left a message with Oliver's mother, asking him to give her a call at the flat after she got back from the pub. But his mother said he'd be away till the evening, so he might not call until the following day.

'It's nice to speak to you, Rose. It's been ages. Whether you and Oliver are together or not, don't be a stranger.'

'No. No, of course not.' She wasn't sure this was wise, wasn't sure about anything where Oliver and his family were concerned. She'd loved all the Paiges and had missed visiting them very much after he left. Only it hadn't seemed right.

She did her work automatically that day, chatting to regulars at the pub, tidying up as she went without realizing what her hands were doing, and all the time longing to get home and start painting. Reluctantly she accepted the chance to work the following evening. She needed the money, but oh, she grudged the time it took to earn it.

Just before she finished her shift, Oliver came into the pub and stood leaning against the wall near the door, obviously waiting for her. She waved, glanced at the clock and finished serving a final customer before handing over to the owner's wife.

She walked across the lounge and he held the door open with a half-smile, falling into place beside her as they walked down the street.

'Busy shift?'

'Just average for a lunchtime. I need to pick up some groceries on the way home.'

'I'll come with you.'

It reminded her of old times, the way they'd walked round the supermarket, arguing cheerfully over what to buy. Today she whizzed round at top speed, hardly saying a word. He was very quiet, too. Did he remember? Of course he did.

Not until they were in the flat did he ask the question that had been lying between them, 'What did your cousin say about the letter?'

'She said you never gave her one.'

He stared at her in shock. 'Why would she say that?'

'Because it's true.'

'I'm not lying to you.'

'Now there's the dilemma. I know you don't lie, Oliver but nor does she. So what exactly happened?'

He frowned into space and she began to put her groceries away to give him time to think.

'I put it into Miles's hands myself, and he laid it beside him on the car seat. He was waiting for Ella and then they were going straight back to the farm, where you were looking after Amy.'

'Whoa! What did you say? You gave the letter to Miles not Ella?'

Oliver blinked at her. 'Well, I didn't actually put it into Ella's hands, but she was just across the road and — '

'Miles hated me.'

'I know you weren't the best of friends, but — ' Oliver slumped in his chair ' — damn! He didn't give it to her, did he?'

'I'd say not. Though why he deliberately withheld it, I can't think. We hadn't had a big quarrel for a while. Petty spite, do you think? Must have been. He saw me himself when they got back from the village, so had no need to ask Ella to give the letter to me.'

'If only I'd waited and given it to her. But I'd an appointment in London and had to run to catch the train as it was.'

There was silence for a few moments, then he said softly, 'What a lot of time we've wasted, Rosie! We could have worked something out, I know we could.'

She shook her head. 'I've gone over it again

and again. We couldn't, you know. I was tied to Wiltshire; you needed to get away.'

'I'm back now.'

'For how long?'

Another pregnant silence, then he said, 'A few months, as I told you. After that I don't know. But surely you can be a little more flexible this time?'

'Not about leaving Wiltshire.'

'You're obsessed by that project.'

'Yes I am. And proud of it, too.'

'Will you show it to me?'

'Not yet.'

He stepped back. 'It's not worth it if it comes between us.'

She looked at him sadly. 'I've wondered about that. Especially after you left. But I couldn't stop then and I still can't. I've put years of my life into it and I'm nearing the end. It's the best thing I've ever done, I know it is.'

With the faintest of sighs, he turned to open the door.

'Oliver?'

'Yes.'

'We could have dinner one night.'

He looked at her steadily. 'If you're never going to leave Wiltshire, what's the point of fanning the embers?'

He was gone before she could find an answer.

Well, there was no new answer to their dilemma, was there?

The embers didn't need fanning, though. Her love for him had stopped her forming serious relationships since they split up, had burned up again when he came back — without any encouragement whatsoever — and was getting in the way of her special project now.

The urge to weep roughened her throat but she fought against it. She'd wept too many tears over him.

★ ★ ★

The phone rang early the next morning. Ella.

'Rose, there are fledglings everywhere today. I can see a row of four swallows sitting on the fence even as I speak. You said you wanted me to let you know.'

'Yes.'

'You all right? Your voice sounds strange.'

'I — um, had a mouth full of food. I'll drive out to Willowbrook straight away.' She left her bowl of cereal uneaten on the table, grabbed her camera bag and was out of the flat within seconds, glad to be leaving because it always felt as if Oliver were hovering nearby.

And the fledglings were wonderful, cheered her up. She'd never seen so many all at once. They were fluttering round in little groups, supervised by anxious parents. Most were fluffy and some still had straggly drifts of baby feathers marring their plumage.

A tiny swallow tried to land on the fence, missed and fluttered to the ground, from where it made a more successful attempt to fly. She took a couple of quick shots. The birds of prey would get some of them, no doubt about it. She smiled wryly as she continued to take photos.

194

Nature red in tooth and claw.

But they were beautiful and many of them would survive in this little oasis that Ella guarded so jealously. Rose would make several pages for her project from today's shots, she knew she would, and also a couple of paintings that would stand a good chance of selling.

She went home at teatime, eyes full of pictures, driving automatically.

It was only when she arrived at the surgery that her thoughts went back to Oliver.

Damn you, get out of my mind! she muttered. But he popped in and out of her thoughts as she transferred her photos to the computer and started doing some rough sketches from them.

And he was still in her thoughts when she went to work at the pub.

He hadn't contacted her, though.

⋆ ⋆ ⋆

On Monday there were no guests so that evening Ella cooked a simple evening meal for herself and Cameron. She didn't know whether she was glad to be alone with him or terrified. Both.

Amy ate with them, then went to bed, still wanting to keep the ancient teddy bear close by.

After she'd tucked her daughter in, Ella walked slowly down to the conservatory, where Cameron was staring into his half empty glass of wine. He'd produced a bottle of merlot, an expensive wine judging by the awards listed on the label, had drunk moderately, seeming to savour each mouthful and be in no hurry to finish it.

Automatically she started to clear the table, but he stood up and pulled her gently towards him.

'We'll do it together later.'

She felt suddenly young, vulnerable and hopeful, all at the same time, and went willingly into his arms, lifting her face for his kiss.

The world faded around them and there was only the warmth of him, the velvet touch of his lips, gentle at first then growing more demanding. This was too tempting. And oh, it had been a long time since a man had roused her.

The wind blew more strongly outside, making it feel as if they were beleaguered in their small island of light. She nestled closer, loving the warmth and strength of him.

But the memory of how foolishly she'd rushed into her relationship with Miles came back, jerking her out of her mood. She moved her head away with an inarticulate murmur.

Cameron kept his arms loosely laced behind her back, studying her with his head on one side. 'You're delicious.' Raising one hand he buried his fingers in her hair. 'I love auburn hair.'

She jerked away and Cameron let go of her at once, frowning.

'What's wrong?'

'I'm afraid,' she confessed in a shaky voice. 'I've not dated since I split up with him and I . . . I feel — nervous.'

'Then we'll take things at a pace which doesn't upset you.'

'I know. And thank you for being so understanding. I'm tired as well as everything else. You're right, I'll leave clearing up till later. Let's go and sit in the living room for a while.'

The big sofa was just right and she murmured in pleasure as they moved easily into a comfortable position with his arm round her shoulders. With a sigh of happiness she relaxed against him.

She woke to find him kissing her forehead.

'Time you went to bed, sleepyhead.'

She sat upright, horrified to realize that she'd fallen asleep on him almost as soon as she sat down.

He chuckled. 'You're beautiful when you're asleep and I'm not at all surprised you dozed off. You work far too hard. Leave me to clear up and you go to bed.'

'I'm sorry.'

'Don't be. It was a compliment that you relaxed so completely with me. And I intend to make sure that we have plenty of time to get to know one another.'

He pulled her to her feet, walked her to the foot of the stairs and kissed her lightly on each cheek. 'Go to bed. I'll lock up when I've finished.'

She was so tired tonight she let him clear up.

12

The next thing Ella knew, light was flooding into her bedroom and Amy was tugging at her sheets.

'Mummy! Mummy, it's time to get up. I have to go to school.'

She dragged on some clothes and rushed downstairs. Everything in the kitchen was immaculate. She couldn't remember Miles ever clearing up on his own, though he'd made a show of helping her at first. Cameron's practical help seemed a far better gift than even the most enormous bunch of flowers.

Fine romantic I am, she thought ruefully. Was she too prosaic? Would that put him off?

She hoped not.

Her spirits rose at the thought of seeing him again at breakfast, perhaps being with him during the day while Amy was at school.

She smiled. Rose would approve but say she was a hopeless case when it came to romance. Perhaps she was. But she dare do nothing except take things slowly.

★ ★ ★

Cameron was up early too. He stopped on the way to the house to marvel at a fluttering group of fledglings, to admire the way the early morning light glinted on the water, and to smell an old-fashioned rose tumbling riotously along the side of the house.

'I'll help make breakfast,' he offered at once. It felt so right to be with her, to help, tease her daughter, smile at her and catch a smile in return.

As they ate together, Amy chattered away about her school and her friends, then it was time for her mother to take her to the end of the drive so that she could catch the school bus. The child looked a little flushed and he saw Ella studying her with a frown. But Amy was clearly eager to go to school, so as soon as the kitchen timer rang, she hurried off to get her things.

'I have to use the timer,' Ella explained, 'or she gets ready too soon.'

By the time Ella got back, Cameron had the kitchen immaculate once again. Strange, he thought as he hung up the tea towel, how much satisfaction you could get from these jobs when they were shared. He couldn't ever remember taking pleasure in washing up before.

'A guest shouldn't be doing this,' Ella scolded when she returned.

'Stop saying that. I hope I'm more than a guest here, though I do intend to pay for the chalet. In fact, let's sort it out now. I can pay for the days I've had this chalet and how about a week's payment in advance on top of that?' He chuckled. 'You're blushing. Ella, my love, don't be foolish about this. That chalet is far cheaper than a luxury hotel and far more comfortable. To me, it's an inexpensive alternative.'

'If you're sure?'

'I am. I don't have a permanent home in the

UK, only a serviced bedsitter in London, which I don't want to go back to. I'd be enjoying my stay at Willowbrook and feeling it well worth the money even if I hadn't met you. Now, sort this out!' He slapped his credit card down on the surface, glancing up at the tariff card near the desk in one corner of the huge kitchen.

★ ★ ★

Ella could only do as he asked. But she hated charging him. It felt wrong. She watched him walk away with a sigh.

'I'll be back in time to see Julian with you!' he called.

By the time she'd put a second load of washing on, Julian Walkley had arrived, punctual to the minute. He was a very tall, thin man, with sparse, thinning hair cut short all over. He stayed by his car, staring round at the outbuildings, making no attempt to come to the house. As Cameron went out to greet him, he turned with obvious reluctance from his perusal.

Ella watched from the kitchen window. The two men continued to survey the yard and outbuildings, gesticulating, speaking eagerly. She took off her apron and went out to join them.

'What would you like to see first, Mr Walkley?' she asked after the introductions.

'The barn. It appears to be the oldest part of the farm. My goodness you do have a mixture of styles and periods. But they blend harmoniously, I don't know why.'

She'd always thought it was because they'd

been built with love, but you couldn't offer that as an architectural reason.

He walked round the outside of the barn, murmuring a faint commentary, talking to himself more than to them, so they fell back and left him to it, smiling conspiratorially at one another. When they got round to the big doors again, he gestured to her politely to lead the way inside, but she moved to one side, opening both doors to allow him to go first and see the place properly.

He remained in the doorway, not saying a word, staring round the interior. She and Cameron exchanged puzzled glances and she asked, 'Is there — '

But Julian held up one hand for silence. Walking slowly forward, he stared up at the huge beams, nodding slowly, then went across to examine a rough wooden partition, whose slats were battered and patterned by years of use. 'Incredible,' he said softly, fingering the dark old wood.

She relaxed. This was a man who loved old buildings, not one assessing them for their monetary worth.

He continued to walk round slowly, stepping back to study various angles and eventually he ended up next to the huge double doors again. 'Do you realize what a treasure you have here?'

'I think so. I love the whole farm, though.'

'This barn is definitely medieval in structure and I bet if we removed some of the later extensions and additions, we'd even find sections of wattle and daub infill in the inner walls underneath.'

She made up her mind suddenly because she trusted his enthusiasm. 'There's a secret hiding place in here.'

He stared at her incredulously, then stared quickly round again. 'Where?'

She moved forward, pressed the rough wooden panelling on the rear wall in the appropriate places, then stepped aside as it slid back.

'It's in remarkably good condition.' Julian made no attempt to enter.

'My father did a lot of repair work. He loved the place as much as I do.' She took a torch out of her pocket. 'We can all three fit into the hidey hole. Come inside and let me show you how it works.'

It seemed natural that Cameron should put one arm loosely round her waist as they stood in the small chamber, equally natural to link her arm round him in return. Julian had eyes for nothing but the hidey hole. After a minute, she gave in to the temptation to share the old house's secrets for a second time. 'There's more. But I must ask you not to reveal this to anyone else without my permission.'

Both men nodded, so she moved away from Cameron and closed the outer door. Then she slipped her fingers under a particularly rough piece of the wooden plank wall. Using this as a lever, she opened the inner door and revealed a narrow passage. She took the other torch kept ready there and gave it to Julian, then led the way, moving slowly forward to allow them to look around.

'I don't think this passage was here originally, but the later additions to the buildings left this narrow slice, and some enterprising ancestor turned it into a passage. It only leads to the back of the old feed store and you have to wonder why they bothered. See.' She stepped outside at the other end and they followed.

Julian turned to examine the secret door at that end, shaking his head in amazement at the quality of the craftsmanship and watching carefully as she closed it. 'What would an architectural television programme make of this house! I bet there are secrets even you don't know after all these years.'

She looked at him in alarm. 'It's not for sharing with the public.'

'I won't break my word,' he said gently. 'But I'd guess there are other secrets here. There are, aren't there?'

'I know of a few.' But she didn't offer to share any others with them, just continued to show them round the buildings, then brought them back to the kitchen for a cup of coffee.

'Who made enquiries about listing this farm?' Julian asked.

'My ex. He said he was told it wasn't worth it, that the buildings weren't of a good enough quality to warrant preservation.'

'I don't know whom he consulted or how he got that impression. No one I know would have said that without looking at the place — and one visit would have shown them it was genuine and of definite heritage quality.'

She held back her anger as it was confirmed

that, once again, Miles had fooled her. 'My ex wanted me to sell it to a developer,' she said at last. 'My refusal was one of the things that ended our marriage. I think — no, I *know*, that he lied to me many times. I should have checked what he said about the house as well, but I was worrying about Amy's problems just then.'

She bit back any further confidences about that period, when she'd struggled alone to understand her daughter's condition and learn how to deal with it. She'd met other mothers and seen how they hovered anxiously over their children. She didn't want to do that. But even if she'd tried to, Amy wouldn't have allowed it. Amy was a very special young person, and her disability was the least of what made her so special.

She knew how lucky she was to have a child like that and felt sorry for Miles, who couldn't love anyone but himself. She turned her attention back to Julian and saw him shudder.

'It's a good thing you did refuse to sell, Ella. If there's any doubt about whether a building should be listed or not, some of those developers can knock a property down in a single day once they get their hands on it. Then they happily pay the fines and go on to do what they always intended. Willowbrook must definitely be saved and I think you should apply at once for heritage listing.' He became thoughtful as he added quietly, 'I've heard rumours that a big developer is interested in putting something together round here at the moment. Have you been contacted?'

'Yes. I refused to sell again.'

'Again?'

'There was another offer three years ago.'

'Who is it this time?'

'Some company called DevRaCom. Do either of you know them?'

Cameron nodded. 'Yes.'

While he was trying to think what to tell her about DevRaCom, his companion pulled some papers out of his pocket and smoothed them carefully. Ella's attention was on the papers, so there was no need for an answer. He was glad. Now wasn't the time for such revelations.

Julian smiled at Ella. 'I hope you don't mind, but I brought the preliminary listing forms with me, just in case. Why don't you fill them in now, while I have another look at your barn, if I may? Then I'll take them into the local council for you tomorrow and speak to someone I know there. The sooner this is started, the better.'

She didn't hesitate. 'Very well. Good idea.'

★　★　★

When Julian had driven away with the completed and signed forms, Cameron decided the time had come to mention his former connection to DevRaCom. 'I have something to tell you. Can you spare me a moment or two before you go back to work?'

'Yes, of course.'

Just then the phone rang.

'Excuse me.' She picked up the receiver and listened carefully.

'Of course.' Putting the phone down, she said,

'It was Amy's head teacher. Amy's not well. I have to bring her home.'

'Do you want me to come with you?'

'No. It'd look . . . strange. And it doesn't sound serious. But she's not comfortable at school and will be better off here. If you're going to be around, though . . . '

'What can I do?'

'Man the phone in case anyone rings up to book.'

'Do you have a bookings diary?'

'It's on the computer. I'll just bring it up and then if anyone rings, you can check. You don't mind doing that?'

'Of course not.' He grinned. 'Especially if you bribe me with a couple of your biscuits.'

'Done.' She was already seated at the computer. She was out of the house within a further two minutes.

He stood at the window to watch her go. What a wonderful, capable woman she was! How straight her back and how energetic her stride. But she still looked tired underneath it all.

He stayed at the window, lost in thought for quite some time. He wished the phone hadn't interrupted their conversation. He couldn't move forward till he'd set things straight with Ella, and yet he was nervous of her reaction to what he had to tell her.

Surely she'd accept his assurances that he was no longer in any way associated with DevRaCom and had never intended to help take her home away?

★ ★ ★

Rose rang up her cousin to find out Miles's phone number. She intended to ask him what he'd done with the letter Oliver had given him three years ago. Bad enough to break up with the one you loved, but the anguish was magnified when you thought he'd walked away from you without a backward glance, without even a word of farewell.

She was surprised when Cameron answered the phone. He explained about Amy and Rose sighed.

'I'll tell Ella you called. I'm sure she'll get back to you once she's settled Amy down. From the sound of it, I don't think the child's all that bad, just running a temperature and would be better for a day or two off school.'

'Amy doesn't often catch things. I bet she'll make a dreadful patient. Tell Ella not to worry. My little problem can wait.'

It had waited years already, after all.

★   ★   ★

Oliver saw the last patient off the premises with a sigh of relief. For the past hour he'd been finding being shut inside the tiny consulting room increasingly difficult to handle. He'd kept the window open and stood near it in between patients, taking deep breaths, but it was Rose's painting that had been the most help. Several times he'd glanced at the open spaces it showed, wondering how she knew what would help him and feeling grateful to her.

The gift of the painting spoke of more than

just help, it spoke of the connection that was still there between them, her understanding of his needs.

He wondered if he dare go up and see Rose. Before he'd come to a conscious decision, his feet began to lead him out to the back and up her stairs to knock on her door. 'Could you spare a cup of coffee for a tired, thirsty man, kind lady?'

She held the door open without a word.

He hovered outside, unsure whether this was a welcome or a gesture of pity.

She rolled her eyes and yanked him in by the front of his shirt, then let out a groan of exasperation and pulled his face down. 'I swore I'd not do this again,' she growled, then kissed him with tenderness and hunger both.

When the kiss ended, they stayed in each other's arms and it felt right, so very right.

'I've missed you,' he murmured in her ear.

'And I've missed you too, damn you, Oliver Paige.'

He stepped back a little, grinning at this resurgence of the sassy Rose he remembered all too well. 'Coffee?'

'It's only instant. I don't have time to fiddle with real coffee like Ella does.'

'You never did. You were usually too busy painting. I admired that in you.' He wandered round the room, stopped at the big metal box and raised one eyebrow? 'The project?'

She nodded, gave him a long, solemn look and went to unlock it with a key carried on a chain round her neck. She held up one hand in a stop gesture before she raised the lid. 'Don't even think of touching anything.'

Her hands gentle with love, she lifted the top painting from the box, laid it on the table and lifted up the transparent paper stuck to one edge of the card to protect it.

He moved slowly forward, taking in the vivid scene which showed a female wagtail feeding her nestlings. Each feather seemed too real to be merely a painting. It felt as if you could pop a tasty morsel into the cluster of open mouths and see them gulp it down. He let out a long, low whistle. 'This is incredible. Surely you can sell paintings of this calibre and leave the chocolate box art to others?' He flicked one finger disdainfully at the wall, where a painting of someone's pet cat was leaning, ready to be delivered.

'I didn't do these as individual paintings but as a record of the wildlife in the area. They're going into a book. Well, they are if I can sell it.'

'Like the art books of flora and fauna that are issued at enormous expense?'

She nodded as she covered up the painting again. 'You can do only so much by photo. I can use several photos, though, to distil the essence of what I've seen into one painting. That gives me a composition that says more than a photo ever could. I've captured most of the small wildlife of Wiltshire now, and I've finished the main flora.' She locked the box again, slipping the key chain back under her tee shirt.

'Only one glimpse? I'd like to see them all.'

'I have to deliver the chocolate box art in half an hour.'

'And I have afternoon surgery and a couple of visits. May I come back this evening and take you out for a meal?'

'Oh, Oliver, why give ourselves so much pain? Why did you even come back to Chawton? Surely you could have recuperated elsewhere? They need A&E people everywhere.'

'I'm unable to function in emergency medicine and I doubt I ever will be able to again.'

She gaped at him. 'Is it that bad?'

He nodded, throat closing with the pain of his loss, unable to speak.

'But you've built your whole working life in A and E.'

He could only nod again. The damage one drug-crazy man had done went too deep for him to discuss it easily.

'Can you be happy as a GP?'

'Not sure. It's more interesting than I'd thought. I'm not making any rash decisions. We'll see what happens.' He grew suddenly angry with himself for sounding so pitiful. 'In the meantime, I'm coming back tonight, and as many other nights as you'll see me. I'm not going away this time and we *shall* find a solution . . . But Rose, talent such as that — ' he indicated the box ' — comes way before my doctoring. If your other paintings are of the same calibre, then it's *your* career that should matter more than mine.'

She stared at him, open-mouthed.

He held her gaze for a moment longer then said very softly, 'I mean that. And I promise you, I'm not nearly as selfish as I used to be.' Then he glanced at his watch and grimaced. 'I have to go. I'll come by at seven and take you out. If you're working tonight, cancel it.'

'I'm not working. I was going to paint.'

'Don't. We need to talk. You know we do.'

He didn't wait for her to dream up an objection but ran lightly down the stairs, still blown away by that one single painting. He had, quite simply, never seen a bird painting so exquisite.

★　★　★

A man's voice answered the phone, saying simply, 'Willowbrook.'

Delighted that Ella hadn't picked up her call, Stephanie booked a chalet for three days, starting tomorrow, giving her maiden name with a simple Ms. She hadn't called herself Parnell for years. She wasn't sure whether Ella would remember her maiden name, hoped she wouldn't.

When she put the phone down, she heaved a happy sigh. First hurdle passed. Now, she needed to decide what to pack and she wanted to go and buy a present for her granddaughter. Nothing too ostentatious. From what she'd wheedled out of Miles, Ella and her daughter had both spurned his lavish present.

'Books,' she decided. 'You can never have too many books.'

She glanced at the shelves of books in the supermarket as she picked up something for her tea. Nothing suitable there, nothing special enough, just garish books she'd not want to give anyone. So she walked further into town and went into a small bookshop which had opened recently. She'd kept meaning to visit it. Bookshops could provide so much more than supermarkets, not just in expertise, but in variety of stock and willingness to hunt out books for you.

A long, earnest chat with its owner yielded two books she thought Amy might like, books she'd loved herself as a child. Unlike her son, Stephanie had done her research into SMA and knew that her granddaughter was no different mentally to any other child. Why would Miles not listen to her about that? Why had he abandoned his own child — and caused his mother to be kept away from her too?

Packing her suitcase was difficult. Should she dress smartly or casually? Casually, probably. But how casually? Stephanie stared at herself in the mirror with a wry smile. Even though she was retired, she wasn't into jeans, never had been. Well, she wasn't skinny enough for that. She'd fought her weight problem for most of her life and given in five years previously to her body's urge to put on ten extra kilos. Size sixteen wasn't that bad, actually, and it was heaven not to be hungry all the time. She envied women who could eat what they wanted and stay slender. She had to eat 800 calories a day or less to do that.

And actually — she leaned closer to the mirror and studied her skin — the wrinkles didn't show up nearly as much when you were this size. Was it Barbara Cartland who'd said something about being able to keep either a face or a waist as one grew older — and the eccentric author had recommended a face, because that was what people looked at first.

Stephanie grinned at her reflection. 'That'll do me.'

It was amazing how much she'd relaxed since she quit being a high flyer.

In the middle of the night she awoke with a start. She'd been dreaming that Ella had refused to let her stay, refused to let her spend any time with her granddaughter.

She found it hard to get to sleep again.

Surely her daughter-in-law wouldn't be so cruel?

Miles had seemed quite certain his mother wouldn't be welcome at Willowbrook. Was he right? Or was he being manipulative again?

* * *

Ella returned home with Amy, whose cheeks were hectically flushed and who was only too willing to go to bed and be cosseted.

'Do we need to call in the doctor?' Cameron asked.

'I think I might give the surgery a ring. I'm not dragging her in to see them, though.'

'I'll take the drink up. You ring them now.'

She looked at him doubtfully, but when he held out his hand with an imperative little shake, she gave him the glass of hot lemon and honey and went to make the call.

She knew the receptionist from school and

when she'd described Amy's symptoms, Mandy said she'd send Dr Oliver out to see the child. You couldn't be too careful, could you?

Relieved, Ella went back upstairs to find Cameron sitting by the bed reading one of her daughter's favourite books to her. Even as she watched, Amy's eyelids fluttered and closed. Soon she was breathing slowly and deeply.

Cameron stopped reading, waited a moment and closed the book.

Ella beckoned.

'She usually sleeps a lot when she's ill, but she doesn't usually have such a high temperature. If we leave the door open, I'll hear her if she calls.'

'Talking of calls, a woman rang to book a chalet for three days. I've written it down. She's coming tomorrow.'

'Good. The season seems to be starting earlier this year.' And she was glad, because she needed the money this would bring even more than she'd ever needed it before.

Cameron put his arm round her for another of his quick hugs. 'I'm staying around. I may be able to help.'

'Yes. And thank you.' She couldn't remember the last time there had been anyone but herself to rely on. Rose helped when she could, but had her own life to lead — and her own obsession to pursue. Ella knew all about that, had seen one or two of the special paintings and been blown away by them.

What a pair she and her cousin were! She with her obsession about keeping Willowbrook in the family and Rose with her Wiltshire wildlife paintings. She hoped Rose and Oliver would get back together again. They'd been so good for each other, in spite of their differences.

★ ★ ★

Oliver took the call and went out to Willow-brook, happy to renew his acquaintance with the old place. At first glance it didn't seem to have changed, but when he got closer, he couldn't help noticing the small touches that had given it added beauty: flowers, a vista which must have been opened deliberately through the gardens and trees beyond to the lake. Even the sparkling windows seemed to be twinkling a welcome.

When Ella opened the door to him, he was shocked at how drawn her face looked.

'Sorry to bring you out, Oliver, but Amy's doing nothing except sleep and that's so unlike her. This is Cameron O'Neal, a friend of mine.'

The two men shook hands briefly then Ella took Oliver upstairs to see her daughter.

He examined Amy, who was sleepy and unwilling to co-operate, then pulled up the covers. 'I think it's just a very bad cold, but you were right to call me out. If there's any sort of rash, or she starts vomiting, or complains of cold hands and feet, get her to hospital.'

Ella looked at him in horror, well aware of what these symptoms might mean. 'You don't think it's meningitis?'

'No, I don't. But one should always be aware of the possibilities. She looks to be a healthy, well-nourished child.' He patted Ella on the shoulder. 'You've done well, and all on your own. My mother has been singing your praises loudly, and I hear that Willowbrook is doing well. It certainly looks attractive.' He frowned. 'You're looking tired, though. Are you getting enough rest?'

'As much as I can.' Her eyes went back to Amy and he could see she was in no mood to chat. He made a mental note to ask Rose to keep an eye on her. 'You sit with her for a while. I'll find my own way out.'

In the kitchen, Cameron got to his feet. 'How is she?'

'Are you a close friend?'

'I hope so.'

So Oliver repeated his instructions and Cameron nodded, then walked with him to the door.

'I didn't know Ella was seeing someone,' Oliver said.

Cameron gave him a tight smile. 'It's rather recent — but nonetheless important to me. How's Rose? Ella told me you two used to be friends.'

'More than friends. And will be again, if I have my way.'

The two men gave each other a measuring look, then nodded as if to say they'd wait to pass judgement on each other, then went about their business.

Cameron put on the kettle, because he couldn't think of anything else to do, and waited for Ella to come down. If Amy was ill, her mother wasn't going to deal with it on her own

216

as well as run the B&B.

He had no experience whatsoever of sick children but the thought of that bright, happy child being ill upset him, and he was prepared to do anything he could to help look after her.

⋆　⋆　⋆

Oliver arrived promptly at seven, by which time Rose had decided not to go out with him, had reversed that decision, then changed her mind again. Finally she decided she was being cowardly and got ready with grim determination to look her best.

He held out a bunch of flowers and her heart melted. He'd remembered: white roses, her favourites. She went to find the pale green vase that would be just right for them, sitting on the floor by the cupboard; staring at it she realized it was Oliver who'd bought this for her.

'Something wrong?'

She shook her head and held out the vase, then got up slowly, trying to hold herself together.

He stroked the semi-opaque glass. 'I remember buying you this vase at a craft fair. You fell in love with it on sight.'

She nodded. 'I've not used it since you left. I don't know why.'

He reached out and caressed her cheek briefly with his knuckles, then turned to fill the vase at the sink.

As she arranged the flowers, she sought for something casual to say and found nothing.

'I've just been out to your cousin's. Amy's not well.'

She was instantly alert. 'Is it serious? Because if so, Ella will need my help.'

'She has help.'

'Who? Don't tell me Miles is back on the scene, because he'd be no use to her.'

'No. It's a guy called Cameron. He says their relationship is quite recent. Must be, or Mum would have known about it. She picks up all the gossip.'

'I've met him. He seems nice, but she can't have known him long or she'd have told me. I'm reserving judgement.'

'My own sentiments, exactly.'

Silence fell as she finished arranging the roses. He watched her, thinking, as he always had, that she was like a rose herself, a big one full of rich red colour and perfume.

He couldn't resist touching her, so put an arm round her shoulders and pulled her to him for a moment. 'We'd better go now. I shan't be able to keep my hands off you if we stay.'

In near panic, she turned and hurried out of the flat.

He took a deep breath and followed her, held the door of his car open, then drove off without a word.

At least she wasn't indifferent to him. He couldn't have borne that.

They both relaxed slowly and the silence grew almost comfortable. Almost. But there was still just the faintest whisper of tension behind it, the echo of pain and emotions held back for years.

Rose exclaimed in surprise as he drew up at a restaurant she'd heard of, small, very expensive, with wonderful food.

'I hope you like this place.'

'I've never been here before.'

'Dad said it was good.'

Rose rolled her eyes at him. 'You must be rolling in money to come here.'

'I've been careful, but I feel this is a night to celebrate, us going out together again, I mean.'

She wasn't sure about that, felt more as if she was walking too close to a precipice. How together were they anyway?

The menu and food gave them something to talk about — in between long, thoughtful looks at one another.

Once he took her hand and smiled down at it. 'You never do get all the paint off.'

She looked down at his slender fingers. 'And you still have beautiful hands.' The trouble was she remembered what those hands could do to her. Hastily she changed the subject. He let her, but smiled knowingly.

'Do you want a liqueur or cognac?' he asked after the desserts had been cleared away. 'I can't because I'm driving, but you're welcome to have something.'

She shook her head and as they got up to leave, she stopped at the sight of Brett Harding sitting in a corner, scowling at them. She scowled back as she waited for Oliver to pay.

When he rejoined her, he followed her gaze and said in a sharper tone, 'How can that fellow afford to come here? His parents must pay him triple the going rate for a petrol station attendant.'

'The Hardings probably have an account here. Mr Harding is not backward at spending their money on himself.'

Brett was still scowling darkly. His companion, a much younger woman with a very low neckline, glanced from him to them, eyeing Rose up and down with a sneering look, as if she knew herself to be superior in appearance.

'If that fellow gives you any more trouble, let me know,' Oliver said.

'It's Ella he fancies, always has been. Him crashing into my cottage was just an accident, but from what I've heard in the bar, he's telling everyone he blames me for it — though how he figures that out, I can't understand.'

'Well, he's certainly looking at you as if he bears you a grudge.'

She shrugged as they went back to the car. 'It doesn't matter. All Brett ever does is glower and sulk when you upset him. He was the same at school, blaming everyone but himself when things went wrong. I can handle him.'

'He's a grown man now, and I'd guess from what I've heard, and what Dad's said, that he's well into alcoholism. That can change people's behaviour and personalities.'

She didn't pursue the matter. She wasn't afraid of a bully like Brett.

But the encounter had destroyed the quiet, companionable mood and she was both glad and sorry about that. Glad because it wasn't safe to spend time with Oliver, sorry because . . . just because! She wasn't going there yet.

When they got back, she said abruptly, 'I'm tired now. It was a lovely meal, but it's late for me, so I'm not going to invite you up for coffee.'

He smiled and pulled her into his arms, planting a farewell kiss on the end of her nose, something he knew irritated her. He laughed as she scrubbed at her nose.

Rose kept rubbing the damp spot as he drove away and gave it another rub as she got ready for bed because his touch seemed to linger on her skin.

She was a fool to love Oliver still. But if she gave up her life's work, she'd not be herself, so whatever he said, their relationship was leading nowhere — again. Tears welled and overflowed, but there was no one to see them, so she allowed herself the rare luxury of a little weep.

Life didn't always bring you what you wanted. She knew that. And you had to make sacrifices to achieve your dream. She knew that too.

She'd meant to ring Ella and check on Amy. But it was too late now. She'd do it first thing in the morning. Her cousin would have rung if she needed help, and Cameron seemed a nice guy.

13

Amy spent a restless night, one minute feverish, tossing the bedclothes off, then shivering and complaining that she was cold. Ella was up and down several times, checking, fetching a cool drink or simply stroking her daughter's forehead and murmuring soothing nothings.

At five o'clock she gave up yet another attempt to get back to sleep and went downstairs to brew herself a cup of her favourite coffee as a treat and wake-up. Porgy got up from his basket near the door, wagging at her then asking to go out. She followed him, taking the mug out into the brisk air of morning but staying within hearing of the house. She always enjoyed the peace of this time of day, with few man-made noises, unless there were planes flying to and from the nearby RAF base. Today there was only the occasional bird starting its day's work by chattering to its friends.

She looked up, seeing clouds piling up. The air felt damp and she was sure it'd rain later. Maybe that was why she was feeling a bit shivery. It wasn't the warmest of mornings.

After drinking the coffee slowly and with relish, she went back inside to bake some scones. She had this Ms Odham arriving in the early afternoon — it couldn't possibly be her former mother-in-law, surely? How would she deal with it if this was Stephanie? She shrugged. She'd handle that when it happened.

There was also a couple coming around teatime. They'd stayed here before. All three guests had requested an evening meal, so there was that to plan for as well.

By seven o'clock Amy had had a quick shower and was back in bed, toying with breakfast and complaining that her throat was sore and itchy. The slight tremor that sometimes affected the child's hands from the SMA was more in evidence today, though mostly you didn't notice it.

Cameron turned up at the farmhouse soon afterwards, studying Ella with a frown. 'You look as if you slept badly.'

She shrugged. 'Amy was restless.'

'Maybe I can spell you a bit this morning, let you have a nap?'

'Thanks, but I find it hard to sleep during the day. And I've a lot to do. I'll be all right. I can manage without sleep if I have to. Would you like some breakfast?'

'Yes, I'm ravenous. But I'll help you get it and eat here in the kitchen with you, then I'll continue to help you in any way I can. I'm not going away, Ella — nor is our relationship. We can take things as slowly as you like, but we're going to get to know one another very well indeed.'

She gave in to the temptation to plant a quick kiss on his cheek, but she didn't dare stop work or she'd never get started again. Goodness, she was sluggish this morning! She pulled away. 'All right. On all counts.'

'That's great. Now, can I just nip up and say good morning to Amy before we eat or is it better to leave her alone? She's a great kid. I don't like to see her under the weather. You're sure it's nothing more than a cold?'

'It seems like just a cold. And yes, do go up, Cameron. She'd love a visit. I'll call you when breakfast is ready.'

By the time he came down, Ella had fruit and cereal set out, and the bacon ready to fry.

He looked at the single place set at the kitchen table. 'Have you already eaten?'

'I'm not really hungry. I'll just grab a piece of toast.'

He tugged her over to the table and pushed her gently down on one of the chairs. 'Someone who works as hard as you do needs to eat properly.'

She didn't know whether to be flattered or angry. 'Are you bullying me?'

'Yup. Sure am. Someone has to. We don't want you falling ill as well.'

'I'm never ill. I don't have time for that.'

Amy called from upstairs and Ella rushed to answer her. He shook his head as he checked that nothing was likely to burn or spoil in the kitchen. Loving Ella was like treading through a nettle patch. He didn't yet have the right to interfere in her life but — he stopped in shock. *Loving!* Where did that thought come from? Or rather, how could it have happened so quickly when he'd avoided emotional entanglements for years?

He smiled. Well, he wasn't allergic to love. In

fact, it was rather nice to find someone you could care about. He was more than ready to settle down.

Ella joined him again. 'She's hungry now for toast and honey. But she's still feverish and heavy-eyed. It's good that she wants to eat, though, isn't it?'

'Yes.' He watched her as she worked. Was it his imagination, or was Ella looking rather heavy-eyed herself? She'd assured him she never fell ill, but no one could guarantee that.

And before the day was over, he intended to tell her about his background. He didn't want any nasty surprises spoiling the developing feelings between them. But as Miles wasn't likely to be here till the weekend, there was no hurry.

★　★　★

A car drew up at the farm just before two. Ella went out to greet whichever of her guests it was and stopped dead at the sight of her former mother-in-law. She watched warily as Stephanie got out of the car and came towards her.

'Hi, Ella. Are you going to turn me away?'

'No, of course not. But I am surprised to see you.'

'Is it so strange that I'd want to see my only grandchild? Or do you still only permit birthday and Christmas presents?'

'*Permit!*'

The two women stared at one another in puzzlement, then Ella said slowly, thinking aloud, 'Miles told me you were too busy to visit us.'

225

Stephanie gaped at her in such shock, there was no mistaking that her surprise was genuine.

'*Miles said that?*'

'Yes.'

Suddenly tears were rolling down the older woman's cheeks and she fumbled for a handkerchief.

Ella pushed a tissue into her hand and then, as she continued to sob, put her arms round her.

After a while, Stephanie mopped her eyes and blew her nose. 'He's kept me from Amy for three years. *Three whole years!* Why? Why would he do this to me?'

'I don't know. Shh now, shh.'

'You'll let me visit her from now on? You won't blame me for what he's done?'

'I never did blame you. I'd have been happy for her to see you any time. As for Miles, sometimes people are just — ' She sought in vain for a tactful way to phrase it to the man's mother, but Stephanie finished for her.

'Warped. Self-centred. His father was just the same. Handsome face, charming when he wanted to be, and selfish to the core. That's why I left him, and found to my sorrow that his son was cut from the same cloth. I wasn't surprised when you split with Miles. Whatever else, my other son is kind and thoughtful.' She blew her nose again. 'Now, where is my granddaughter?'

'In bed. She's got a heavy cold or maybe a touch of 'flu.'

'You don't look all that well yourself.'

'I'm all right.'

'May I see her?'

'Don't you want to put your things in the chalet first?'

'No. I've missed three years of her life. I don't want to miss another second.'

Arm in arm the two women went into the house. On the way Ella introduced Cameron as 'a friend of mine' and led the way upstairs. She stopped in the doorway of Amy's room. 'I've got a lovely surprise for you, darling.'

Amy looked up and then stared past her at the older woman, a slight frown on her face.

'This is your grandma.'

'I remember you. But your hair was darker.'

Stephanie moved into the room. 'Yes. I've been wanting to see you again for a long time. Can I sit on your bed and talk to you?'

After a long considering look Amy nodded. 'I've got a cold, though. You might catch it.'

'I don't often catch colds.' She sat on the bed and pulled a small parcel out of her capacious handbag. 'I brought you a present.'

The child brightened a little. 'What is it?'

'Open it and see.'

She took it, feeling it through the gift wrapping. 'It feels like books.'

'It is. Old-fashioned ones, I'm afraid. I don't know what girls read today, so I brought two of my own favourites from when I was your age: *Heidi* and *The Secret Garden*.'

Amy had torn off the wrapping paper and was staring in delight at the two books. 'I haven't read these.' She opened the top book, turning at once to the first page and nodding. 'I can read this. I have to ask Mummy sometimes when there are long words, though. I like learning new words.'

Stephanie smiled. 'You can ask me, too. And if your throat's sore, maybe I can read to you for a while.'

Ella was watching her daughter carefully. 'Would you like that, darling?'

Amy went right to the heart of the matter. 'Why haven't you been to see me before?'

Stephanie hesitated.

Ella folded her arms. 'Tell her the truth.'

'Your daddy said you didn't want to see me.'

Amy scowled. 'He was telling fibs. I don't like him. Mummy says I have to see him when he asks but I don't want to.'

'Do you want to see me?'

Another long look, then a slow nod. 'Yes. You look at me. He doesn't.'

Stephanie looked at Ella in shock and she shrugged. Amy was right: Miles did avoid looking at her, especially when she was moving about.

'Well, I'll just go and leave my things in my chalet then come back and read with you, if that's all right, dear?'

When she'd gone, Amy fingered the book cover, smiling in spite of looking tired. 'I like books. And I like my grandma. Won't Nessa be surprised that I've got one as well, now?'

When Ella went downstairs, she found Stephanie weeping again. There was no sign of Cameron and the bacon was still by the cooker waiting to be fried.

Stephanie blew her nose vigorously. 'I'm not

usually so weepy, but I *am* upset. She's a lovely child. Did you ever see such beautiful eyes? And so clear-seeing. You'll not fool that one easily.'

'No.'

'Does Miles really avoid looking at her?'

'Yes.'

'A child of his has to be perfect!' Stephanie said bitterly. 'As if *he* is perfect! I'm sorry he's hurt you, Ella.'

'He's hurt you, too. But he also gave us Amy, and that's worth all the hurt. Come on. I'll show you to your chalet.'

'The man who was here . . . how much of a friend is he?'

'I only met him recently. But things seem . . . promising.'

'He seemed nice. I hope it goes well for you this time but be careful.' She smiled ruefully. 'I don't know why I'm offering you any advice. I wasn't very good at choosing men.'

'I'm taking it slowly, believe me.' Ella sighed. 'If truth be told, I'm too busy to do anything else. Every time we start getting to know one another, something interrupts.'

* * *

While the two women were upstairs, Cameron went outside. Clearly, this was an important encounter, so they needed some privacy. Why had Miles Parnell's mother come to visit? Was she here on his behalf, as a spy, or on her own simply to do what she'd said and see her granddaughter?

His mobile rang and he frowned as he saw who it was. 'Ray. What can I do for you?'

'I've been hoping you'd reconsidered my offer.'

'I told you: I'm not interested.'

'You're still staying at Willowbrook?'

'Yes.'

'I hope you're not trying to pull a fast one on me, lad. We've got the area almost sewn up for a new country hotel and function centre, with contracts for the various blocks of land waiting to be signed. There's only that stupid Turner woman to persuade to sell now.'

'She's not stupid.'

Silence with heavy breathing. 'She's fooled you, then. Parnell tells me she has no idea of the value of money.'

'She has a very good idea of its value. She just doesn't rate it the most important thing on earth. And she's also got a good idea of the value of this place. It's been in her family for centuries and she loves it. Ray, you don't usually go trampling over heritage properties. This place has a medieval barn and — '

'Fake.'

'Did Parnell tell you that?'

'Yes. He used to live there, after all. Her Victorian ancestors put in a lot of fake remains to give them status. That's why it was refused a heritage listing.'

'Check your facts again. It's not fake and it's being listed at this very moment. The inspector came out to see it yesterday and took the paperwork back with him.'

Silence, then, 'Your doing, I suppose?'

'I've been helping.'

'The listing won't be accepted.'

Cameron heard the certainty in Ray's voice and wondered who he'd bought down here. 'I don't like to see historic farmhouses knocked down for — ' He broke off just in time. Ray didn't like anyone to malign his hotels, which were as alike as peas in a pod, whether they were in London or Liverpool.

'For what?'

'For a modern hotel complex that could be built anywhere.'

'Would it make any difference if I asked for your help, for old times' sake? DevRaCom is at a crucial stage in its development and if we're to enter the big league, we can't afford lengthy lawsuits or appeals.'

Read that as DevRaCom was overstretched at the moment, trying to grow too big too fast, Cameron thought. Well, he'd suspected that for a while. 'I'm sorry, Ray. If I could help you, I would, but this is an important piece of English heritage — and anyway, it's her home. Why should she be forced to sell it?'

The phone was slammed down on him.

He immediately dialled Julian's number. 'We have to talk. Where can we meet? Right. I'll be there.'

* * *

When Cameron saw the two women appear in the doorway, he shoved the phone in his pocket

231

and waited till Ella beckoned. He was surprised that this pleasant-looking woman was the mother of Parnell. Her hair was that faded blond colour that a lot of older women seemed to adopt, and she was trim and fashionably clad in designer leisurewear, but she had a warm smile. You couldn't mistake the genuineness of that. He'd read somewhere that it was to do with the eye muscles, and they showed whether a smile was genuine or not.

'Could you show Stephanie to chalet three, please, Cameron, and by the time you get back I'll have some food ready for you. Fine hostess I am!'

'Friend, not hostess,' he corrected.

He walked across to the chalet and waited till Stephanie had brought her car round, then carried her luggage inside.

'It's charming!' she exclaimed, looking round. 'How on earth does Ella manage everything on her own?'

'I don't know. She's certainly a worker.' He gave her an assessing look then added, 'But I'm hoping she'll not be on her own again.'

She cocked one eyebrow at him. 'That serious, is it?'

He nodded, smiling ruefully. 'On my part, yes. I'm not as sure about her. I thought I was immune to love.'

'No one is.' She sighed. 'Well, except for my younger son. Or rather, Miles saves his love for himself. Now, go and get your food and see if you can persuade Ella to rest. I'm coming across shortly to read to Amy.'

Cameron walked into the kitchen and sniffed appreciatively. 'Smells wonderful. Aren't you going to join me?'

'I'm not hungry.'

'Then sit down for a minute and tell me about Stephanie.'

She set a plate of home-made scones, with butter and jam, and a cup of fragrant coffee in front of him and went to fetch a cup for herself.

He ate two scones as she sipped the coffee. She was definitely pale behind those hectically flushed cheeks. Even as he watched, she tried to stifle a cough, which wouldn't be stopped.

'I think you've got Amy's cold,' he ventured, waiting for her to snap his head off.

Instead she sat staring down at the food left on her plate. 'Maybe I have.'

'What is there to do today?'

'The usual. And I'd better get started.' She pushed herself to her feet, but instead of moving off she stood swaying, one hand rubbing her forehead.

He got up quickly. 'You're feeling rotten, aren't you?'

She nodded, then turned round as Stephanie knocked at the door and came in again.

'I think Ella's got the same thing as Amy,' he said. 'She's not feeling well. I was hoping you and I could take over here.'

'My pleasure.'

'I can't just — ' Ella broke off to cough, and when she'd stopped, sat down abruptly. 'I can't believe this! I was feeling fine yesterday, not too bad this morning, but now I — can't manage. I've never . . . But I can't.'

'Let's get you to bed.'

But she wouldn't go until she'd given them a list of things to do and got the food out of the freezer, and even then she was protesting. He lost patience and pushed her up the stairs.

'I'd carry you up like one of those romance heroes, but I'm not Mr Universe, I'm afraid.'

'And I'm not a featherweight.' She stopped in the doorway of her daughter's room to explain that she wasn't well either and would be spending 'an hour or two' in bed. 'Your grandma will be looking after you. Is that all right?'

Amy nodded. 'I like her.'

'And I'll be helping,' Cameron added. 'I'll be the waiter, fetching and carrying food and drinks.'

With a smile the child wriggled down in bed. 'I'm sleepy now.'

'So's your mother.'

It was impossible to persuade Ella to get undressed and have a proper rest, so he compromised by pulling the duvet over her.

When he went back to the kitchen, Stephanie was wearing a big pinafore and clearing up, pausing sometimes to find the right cupboard for an item.

'Did you get her to bed?'

'Only for a quick lie down. She won't get undressed. See if you can persuade her to later.'

'I was shocked when I saw her today. I always remember her being in blooming health. She

234

looks drawn and pale.'

'Do you think I should call in the doctor?'

She considered this then nodded. 'Yes. I reckon she's seriously run down.'

He picked up the handpiece, opened the phone directory that stood under it and found the number of the Chawton Medical Centre. When the receptionist answered, he persuaded her to put him through to young Dr Paige and explained the situation.

Putting the phone down, he smiled at Stephanie. 'Oliver knows Ella, so he's coming straight out. He doesn't have a full case load yet, is still easing into the practice, and he said Rose is worried about her cousin too.'

Stephanie sighed in relief. After a moment's hesitation, she added, 'I know for a fact that she's not asked for any maintenance from Miles, so it must have been difficult to manage, not to mention paying him back. He laughs about that, says he conned her into accepting the loan instead.'

'Well, she won't be coping on her own from now on, if I can help it.' He smiled at her nod of approval. 'The thing is, though, I'm not much of a cook. I can manage simple things, I'm not exactly helpless, but her guests will expect a bit more than that.'

Stephanie smiled. 'I'll take over that department. I am, if I say so myself, rather a good cook. And I suggest we don't tell Ella we've sent for Oliver Paige, just present her with a fait accompli when he arrives.'

'My thoughts exactly.'

Oliver arrived at Willowbrook just after Cameron returned. He rapped on the kitchen door then opened it and poked his head round. 'Anyone there?'

An older woman who seemed vaguely familiar was cooking, looking flushed and singing along with the music on the radio.

He raised his voice. 'Hello.'

She swung round. 'Sorry. Didn't hear you knock.'

'I'm Oliver Paige.'

She beamed at him and switched off the radio. 'The doctor. Don't I remember you being a friend of Rose's from a few years ago? I'm so glad you could come. Just let me take this pan off the heat. There. I'll show you up.' She hesitated, then said in a quiet voice, as if afraid of being overheard, 'I think Ella's run herself ragged managing this place on her own, and this cold or virus or whatever is the final straw. I'm not trying to tell you your business, you understand, but fill you in on the background.'

She showed him to the bedroom, saying, 'You have a visitor.' Then she left them alone.

Ella glared at him. 'Why on earth did they send for you? I'm perfectly all right, Oliver. It's a cold, that's all. I'll be fine by tomorrow.'

He went across and sat on the bed. 'Not like you to snap at people before they've even opened their mouth, Ella. And anyway, I can check up on Amy at the same time, so this won't be a wasted visit. Here, let me take your temperature.'

He picked up her wrist and felt her pulse. 'You look pale, and you've lost a lot of weight since I last lived round here. Is that recent? Intentional? Your clothes look loose.'

'Unintentional. But haven't you heard? Thin is in.'

'When have *you* ever bothered about fashion, Ella Turner?'

She opened her mouth as if to argue, then sighed and closed it again. 'I do feel lousy, Oliver. So weak, and that's not like me. And . . . I'm a bit frightened of giving something to Amy.'

'I'll keep an eye on you both, then. You seem to have some willing helpers, so why don't you seize the chance to have a rest? There's a nasty little virus going round. It doesn't usually last more than a few days, but you can't fight it by willpower alone. You need to rest and let your body do the work.'

'I've too much to do.'

'And that sod is still giving you grief. Rose said he'd been to visit.'

'My cousin is telling you far too much.'

'Never complain that people care about you.'

She went quiet and he followed suit, watching her, waiting to see what she'd say, whether she'd be sensible.

'I can't remember the last time I lay in bed like this,' she said at last with a weary sigh.

'Everyone needs a rest. Carpe diem, Ella. You might not get another chance like this. You could actually do with at least a week off.' He pretended to duck. 'I know. You're not going to take that long. But at least take a day or two.'

'I'll see how I go. You'll check on Amy before you leave?'

'Of course. And I'll keep visiting. Rose would kill me if I didn't keep an eye on her god-daughter.'

'Are you two together again?'

'Sort of. We've still got issues.'

'I hope you're not going to hurt her again.'

'I'll try very hard not to.'

'You didn't give me a letter for Rose last time, you know.'

'I gave it to your husband. You were just across the road at the bank. I could actually see you, but I was running late. Miles couldn't possibly have lost or forgotten the letter in the time it would have taken for you to return to the car.'

'Which means he must have lost it on purpose, though I can't understand why.'

'Sheer malice, I suppose. The two of them never got on.' Oliver stood up. 'Well, what's done is done. I'll make sure I speak to Rose myself from now on when something is that important. No intermediaries.' At the door he paused and grinned. 'I like your new fellow better than the old one, by the way. Much better.'

She threw a book at him, which clattered against the hastily shut door and fell to the ground. People were taking too much for granted. Was it so obvious that she and Cameron were attracted?

He was a lovely man, though.

She gave in to the urge to sleep, just for a few hours.

14

Miles leafed through his mail when he got home after work and frowned at an envelope with *Hannow & Hannow* on the back. Ella's damned lawyers. He remembered those envelopes from the divorce. What did they want now? Whatever it was, he wasn't interested. He tossed it aside, then changed his mind and ripped it open.

'What the hell — '

He sat down and re-read the letter with the utmost care then screwed it up and hurled it across the room. Ella could whistle for child maintenance. She'd not need it if she sold that tumble-down monstrosity. He reached for the phone to tell her just that, then thought better of it and switched on his computer to search for information.

Surely you couldn't be forced to make back payments of child maintenance when your damned ex had never asked for it in the first place?

He used a search engine and read everything he could find on the topic, which left him bewildered. He still wasn't sure whether she could claim back payments, but she could certainly claim ongoing payments, he was pretty sure of that from what he'd read. He found a child maintenance calculator and entered his details, cursing when he found out he might be liable for quite a lot of money per week. Ridiculous! A small child couldn't possibly cost that much. Only ... what if the child was disabled? There would most likely be wheelchairs and such as Amy grew into her teens, not to mention modifications to buildings to accommodate her needs and a special car when she was old enough to drive.

Glancing at his watch, he pulled out his mobile and called a cousin who was a lawyer.

'Steve, I've got a little problem. No, I know you can't promise me anything legally correct in a casual chat. Just give me a little guidance, will you? Thanks. The thing is, my ex is trying to claim maintenance from me for the child and — get this — is asking for three years of back payments. Can she do that? No, I know you're not a divorce lawyer, but you must be able to give me *some* general information. I'm completely in the dark here.'

He listened in growing horror to some of the possibilities — though with each case being judged on its own merits as well as on what the law stipulated, nothing was certain.

It seemed to be important to find out whether Ella was going to the courts for maintenance or to the Child Support Agency. His cousin thought the courts would be more chancy for Miles, because you could never tell which way a judge would jump with regard to the details. Miles was sure he'd read that the Child Support Agency only sorted out maintenance from the day of application, something his cousin wasn't sure of. Trust a lawyer never to commit himself if he could and to stick in an 'if' and 'but' with every sentence.

Whichever avenue Ella pursued, it'd mean Miles's financial details being revealed. And he didn't like the idea of that, not at all.

After thanking his cousin, he set the phone down and poured himself a shot of whisky, downing it in one. He wasn't cashed up at the moment and really needed his investment money back from Ella if he was to keep up appearances till he settled in with DevRaCom. It was shocking what it cost for even a small luxury car.

Something else occurred to him and he cursed. If she did get maintenance awarded, how the hell was he going to pay his own mortgage? He was juggling payments as it was. This place might be small, but it'd been damned expensive and he'd not had much of a deposit to put down, so he was paying a big chunk of his income each month. And his bloody father was no help.

Well, the bitch wasn't getting away with this. He'd been very patient about his investment, but she'd managed perfectly well without maintenance for the past three years and could continue to do so. What he earned was for himself, not for wasting on a child.

Another shot of whisky then he settled down to think hard. He had to put a stop to this once and for all. He wasn't working his butt off to pour money into Ella's purse. No way.

And he wasn't going to let her sabotage this project as she had the other one.

He'd do whatever it took to push that sale through. Short of murder and other indictable offences, of course.

★   ★   ★

Oliver was waiting for Rose when she finished her evening shift at the hotel.

She looked at him warily. 'I'm tired.'

'Don't you want to hear about your cousin?'

'Ella? What about her?'

He explained.

'I have to go out there and help. She — '

'She has two perfectly good helpers.' He explained. 'How about a coffee?'

Rose hesitated. 'I'm not sure it's wise.'

'I'm sure it is. I'm not going away this time.'

'Do you have a better solution to our dilemma? Because I don't.'

'I'm working on that.' He pulled her into his arms. 'Besides, I've found out what happened to that letter I wrote.'

'Tell me.'

'Over a coffee.'

'That's blackmail.'

He grinned. 'Yeah. Neat one, isn't it? You're dying to know.'

She pretended to hit him, then allowed him to take her hand and walk back to the flat with her.

There was a parcel outside the door, badly wrapped, the paper coming off. Rose moved to pick it up, but Oliver kept hold of her arm. 'Don't. The post office doesn't deliver at night.'

She gaped at him. 'You don't mean — you think it might be dangerous? In Chawton?'

'Probably not. But wherever you are, it pays to be vigilant, especially when there are anomalies. Who brought this, do you think?'

242

She shook her head.

'Let me find something to turn it over with. There's an old hoe in the storeroom that they use to weed the garden here. Do not go near that parcel.' He got out his keys and was back with the hoe, which he used to turn the parcel over gingerly.

There was a soft whoofing sound and the parcel exploded. Oliver threw Rose to the ground and covered her body with his, lying there till he realized it was pieces of coloured paper which had fluttered out of the parcel not bomb fragments. He helped her up, a grim expression on his face, and got out his mobile phone.

'Who are you calling?'

'The police.'

'But — it was only a practical joke.'

'Not funny. Whoever did this wanted to worry you. And they've certainly worried me. Ah, Bill. Glad it's you on night duty. Can you come over to the rear of the surgery? Yes, straight away. There was a suspicious package and it exploded. No, not a bomb, a practical joke. But I don't happen to think it's funny. If it had been one of our elderly patients who found it, it could have given them a heart attack. Yes, we'll be here. Me and Rose, who's renting the flat. The parcel was addressed to her.'

As he put the phone away, Rose flung her arms round him. Not averse, he held her close. 'What's brought this on?'

'You covered me with your body, Oliver. You were willing to get hurt to protect me.' She put her hands round his neck and drew his head closer for a quick kiss on each cheek. 'I can't believe this is happening, but I'm glad you're with me tonight.'

He smiled at her. 'Me, too. We'd better not go inside. I don't want to disturb anything.'

'I bet it's that stupid Brett Harding. His idea of a joke.'

'If it is, he'll be in serious trouble. People don't play that sort of trick these days. Terrorism is all too close to everyone's mind.'

They were still standing there when the police arrived.

Bill stared round at the confetti-like paper, and the torn wrapping from the box that had exploded. He questioned them, though there wasn't much more to add, then said quietly, 'I'm calling the detectives out on this. You're right. It could have given someone a heart attack. Better not go up to your flat till the detectives have been, Rose.'

'We can go into the surgery,' Oliver said. 'I could make us all a cup of coffee.'

'Good idea. Night duty always makes me thirsty,' Bill said briskly.

The detectives took it just as seriously.

'Designed to frighten someone,' one of them said grimly. 'As you say, not funny. And I don't think it was intended to be funny. Have you upset anyone lately, Ms Marwood?'

She frowned.

'Brett Harding,' Oliver said. 'We saw him in the restaurant and if looks could kill, she'd have expired on the spot.'

'Don't mention him to anyone. We'll take the parcel away and get a few photos, then you can go into your flat again.'

After they'd gone, Rose swallowed hard. 'I don't want to be on my own tonight, Oliver. I don't want to make love, I just need you here.'

'I'll stay.'

★ ★ ★

Ella stayed in bed for the rest of the day. She hadn't intended to do that, but she fell asleep, surfacing once to hear Stephanie and her daughter chatting happily together nearby. She trusted her ex-mother-in-law, so snuggled down in bed, just for a little longer.

She woke in the dark, feeling disoriented. What time was it?

She gasped when she saw the clock. Ten thirty. How could she possibly have slept so long?

As she was getting out of bed, she stumbled and fell against the dressing table.

There were sounds from downstairs and the landing light went on. Footsteps ran lightly up and Cameron appeared in the doorway.

She pushed past him. 'I have to go to the bathroom.'

When she got back, he was waiting.

'Back to bed, my love.' He pulled the covers back.

'I'm ravenous.' *My love?* Had he said that or had she just imagined it?

'Being hungry is a good sign. Stephanie has left you a few bits and pieces, including a vegetable soup that's delicious. But I can get you something else if you don't fancy that.'

She climbed into bed and slid down with relief. 'Vegetable soup sounds wonderful. I'm feeling a lot better now.'

'Yeah, tell that to the fairies. You're as white as a sheet and don't think I didn't hear you coughing in the bathroom just now. I'm not deaf.'

He was gone before she could answer. When he came up with the tray, she'd managed to brush her hair and was sitting up against the pillows, secretly glad not to have to get up.

As she ate, he sat quietly in the old armchair by the window, not interrupting but obviously keeping an eye on her.

As soon as she'd finished, he came across to take the tray. 'Can I get you anything else?'

She yawned. 'No, thanks. I can't believe it, but I'm feeling sleepy again.'

'That's good. Sign of healing. Look, before you fade on me again, is it all right if I sleep in one of the spare bedrooms here? It'll be easier for Stephanie if I can keep an eye on you and leave her to look after Amy and run the B and B side of things.'

'I'm getting up tomorrow.'

'You can try, but I think I'm stronger than you are.'

'We'll see. And of course you can sleep here. Take the room next to this.'

He tucked her in, smiling down at her and somehow her hand was in his for a moment or two.

'How many bedrooms do you have in the farmhouse?' he asked to prolong the moment.

'Six on this floor, four or five attic bedrooms as well.'

'It's an amazing place. No wonder you love it.'

He watched her yawn and snuggle down. When her eyes had stayed closed for a while, he left the room, stopping abruptly on the landing because he thought he'd seen a woman at the far end. But when he blinked, the figure vanished. It must be the moonlight playing tricks.

He ran downstairs and fetched up his bits and pieces. For some reason he didn't understand, it felt good to be sleeping in the house. As if he belonged here. Or perhaps it was because he was closer to Ella here.

Had she noticed that he'd called her 'my love'? It'd slipped out. She'd shown no reaction. She probably hadn't noticed.

He grinned in the darkness. He was a sad case! Trying to chat up a woman who was too sick to respond.

But her hand had felt right in his. Warm and trusting.

★　★　★

When Rose woke up, Oliver was lying beside her on top of the covers. 'So much for keeping my distance from you,' she said with a wry smile, making no attempt to disentangle herself.

'I didn't want to keep my distance. I'm glad we're together again.'

'We are?'

247

'Looks like it.' He cuddled even closer, his warm breath fanning her cheek. 'And this time we'll find a way to resolve our differences.'

'I'd like that.'

'Can I move back in?'

She hesitated. 'Isn't that rushing things a little?'

'No. Apart from anything else, I'm not having you here on your own while that fool is trying to upset you. Who knows what he'll do next?'

'Why me? He's the one who knocked down my house. I did nothing to him.'

'He's an alcoholic. His brain's muddled. It'll be a while before he pulls clear of that — if he ever does.'

She sighed. 'My money is on Mr Harding Senior. He's got everything else he wanted in life, one way or the other. When he realizes how serious Brett's drinking is, he'll sort his son out.'

'I hope you're right. But I'm still taking no chances with your safety. Brett Harding's mixed up with some bad 'uns. I've seen them drinking together.'

'That's not the reason I want you to move in.'

He traced a line down her cheek with his forefinger. 'I know. I love you, too. That's the main reason.'

★ ★ ★

Since Ella was asleep, Stephanie decided that Amy should have the rest of the week off school. It was only two days, after all.

She said she needed a junior assistant to help

her run the guest house and after being allowed to peep in and see the unusual sight of her mother sleeping during the daytime, the little girl followed her grandmother downstairs.

'You'll have to tell me where everything is and what your mother gives guests for breakfast. I don't know what time that couple in number three wants to eat.'

'Mum writes it down on their card.' Amy went across to the pigeon holes. 'Half past eight.'

'Good. We've got time to sort it all out, then.'

With many giggles at her grandma's ignorance of how things were done, Amy helped get ready, turning to beam at Cameron when he joined them.

'I peeped in and your mother's still asleep.'

'I'll take up some fruit juice and leave it by the bed,' Stephanie said.

They ate together, as near a real family as Cameron had known for a while, although they were almost strangers. He found Amy's grandmother easy to chat to and both of them enjoyed the comments of the child, while Amy was clearly relishing their attention.

That child's as hungry for family life as I am, Cameron thought.

When the guests arrived for breakfast, Stephanie went to explain to them what had happened and crave their indulgence over any mistakes she might make as their stand-in hostess.

After they'd finished eating, they said they'd be out for the day, but would enjoy an evening meal here again, if that was all right, given the circumstances.

'No problem. I do know how to cook.' Stephanie waved them goodbye and returned to the kitchen. 'I'll have to check what's in the freezer. We gave them that casseroled steak last night. It ought to be something different tonight, maybe chicken.'

In the end, she decided to do a little shopping and leave Cameron and Amy to keep an eye on Ella, who was still sleeping.

As she was on her way out, the phone rang. 'I'll get it.'

'I'd like to book a chalet for a couple of nights, starting tonight,' a man's voice said.

'Certainly. May I take your name?'

'Peter Smith.'

'And will you require an evening meal?'

'Do you do those as well as the B and B?'

'Oh, yes.'

'Why not? Save me going out again. I'll be arriving in the early afternoon.'

She put the phone down and smiled at Cameron. 'A booking for a couple of nights.'

'Do you think we should keep on taking bookings?' He looked meaningfully upwards towards where Ella was lying then back at her.

'Yes, I do. I think Ella needs rest more than anything, and if we start turning people away, she'll start worrying about money. Now, this time I really am off.'

Cameron turned to Amy. 'Let's check that the kitchen is tidy and then we'll get a chalet ready for Mr Smith.'

'I know what to do. I can show you.'

'All right. As long as you promise to have a lie

down after we've done it. Your mother isn't the only one who needs to rest.'

She pulled a face, but muttered, 'All right.'

When they went outside she slipped her hand into his and he looked down at it in bemusement before giving it a quick squeeze in return. These Turner women had a way of wriggling their way into your heart.

★ ★ ★

Ella woke feeling well rested but still disinclined to do much. A small handbell was sitting beside the bed with a paper propped up against it, saying, 'Ring for waiter service when you wake.'

She didn't recognize the handwriting. Cameron's, she supposed. She listened and could hear voices downstairs — Amy and Cameron. They sounded happy. There was no mistaking her daughter's gurgle of laughter.

She rang the bell, which tinkled cheerfully, and a moment later she heard footsteps on the stairs.

Cameron came in, carrying another glass of orange juice like the one she'd drunk earlier. 'What would madam like for brunch?'

'Brunch?'

'It's gone eleven o'clock.'

'Goodness. I didn't even think to look at the clock. I think you'll have to call me Rip Van Winkle.'

His gaze was warm. 'I think Sleeping Beauty is more accurate.'

Their eyes met, held, then he reached out for her hand, holding it in both his for a moment.

251

'How are you feeling, Ella? Really.'

'As if I could sleep for a million years. Which is silly, when I've been doing nothing but sleep. I hope this hasn't been too much trouble for you. I can easily get up for lunch.'

'You'll have to fight your way past Stephanie and me, not to mention Amy. No, shh. Listen to me. Oliver says you're run down and need a good rest, a week or two if possible.'

He put one finger on her lips to prevent her speaking, and warmth zipped through her body at even this light touch.

'I've nothing to do with myself at the moment, so I'm happy to help out. Stephanie is loving spending time with her granddaughter and she's a brilliant cook. We just took another booking, so business isn't suffering. Give yourself time to recover properly, Ella. If you don't, you could make yourself really ill and what would become of Amy then?'

Tears filled her eyes. 'That's always been my big worry.'

'I can imagine.'

'But I can't ask you to do this.'

'You didn't ask. Stephanie and I volunteered.'

Tears overflowed then, she couldn't keep them back. And when he drew her close, she nestled against him willingly.

'So you'll let us help you?'

'Yes. But only on condition you don't pay for your accommodation while you're helping out.'

He chuckled and stroked her hair back from her forehead. 'All right. I won't pay for the days I'm helping out. Then, when you're up, I'll start

252

using my week paid in advance. Is that all right?'

'Yes.'

From downstairs they heard Amy singing. It was the voice of a contented child.

'What's she doing?'

'Listening to the radio. She loves music, doesn't she? And she's getting on really well with her grandmother.' He looked at her. 'Something wrong with that?'

'It really hurts to think that Amy's missed three years of her grandmother's company. I'll never forgive Miles for that.'

'Pretty mean thing to do, I agree. Now, let's get you some food.'

She lay back again, feeling limp and so unlike herself she'd have worried if she'd had any spare energy to worry with. As it was, she just let herself go with the flow.

Cameron was wonderful.

And both Amy and Willowbrook were being well looked after.

Life was . . . promising. In spite of Miles and his demand for repayment. She smiled, wondering if he'd got the letter about maintenance yet. He'd be hopping mad. Serve him right. He couldn't have it every which way.

She stayed awake to eat most of the food Cameron had brought up, then felt tired again. She thought she'd thanked him for his help, hoped she had.

Just a short nap . . .

★　★　★

253

Stephanie came back from Chawton with several bags of groceries and another book for Amy, who had just got up after a rest.

'This fell into my shopping bag,' she said with a smile.

Amy flung her arms round her grandmother. 'Thank you. I do like having you here.'

Stephanie turned to Cameron. 'How's Ella?'

'She ate brunch, then fell asleep again. She's looking a little pinker, at least. Anything else to fetch in from the car?'

'Yes, there are a couple more bags. Thanks.'

The day passed quietly, the only interruption being a phone call about the heritage listing. The local officer was excited after Julian's assurance that the place was genuinely medieval in parts and had started processing the listing.

'Thank goodness for that,' Cameron told Stephanie. 'But I think we should keep it to ourselves. Would you mind not telling your son?'

She grimaced. 'When do I ever see Miles unless he wants something?'

★   ★   ★

Mid-afternoon a car drew up and a man got out. Cameron frowned. The newcomer looked vaguely familiar. He turned to Stephanie, 'I think I know that guy and I'd rather avoid meeting him till later. All right if I hide in the family sitting room?'

'Fine by me.'

Amy looked up at him sharply so he put one finger to his lips, winked and slipped out of the room, staying behind the door to listen.

'I have a booking,' the man said. 'Name's Smith.'

'Yes. Let me show you to your chalet. And you wanted an evening meal. We usually serve meals about seven o'clock. Is that all right?'

'Fine by me. Lovely place.' He stared round. 'It looks older than I'd expected. I mean, really old.'

'It is.'

'I'd love a tour.'

'Sorry. The owner is ill. I'm only filling in for the moment.'

'All right if I wander round the outsides of the buildings?'

'If you wish. Please don't go inside them, though.'

When she came back, she went to find Cameron. 'I don't like him. The way he looks round is . . . predatory. I wonder if Smith is his real name?'

'I doubt it. But I don't know what he's called, only that I've seen him somewhere.' He didn't explain about the DevRaCom link. Not yet. He wanted to tell Ella first. But he was determined to keep an eye on that fellow, so went upstairs and found a bedroom whose window looked in the direction of the chalets, standing hidden by the curtain to watch.

Within ten minutes Smith had left his chalet, carrying what looked like a camera. He walked up to the outbuildings, appearing and disappearing between them, then vanishing from sight — but not before Cameron had seen him taking photos.

255

Ella's bell rang and he went along to her room to find her dressed.

'I'm not staying in bed *all* the time,' she said, in the tone of one prepared to argue till she won her point.

'Come down to the sitting room, then. But we'll quarrel if you try to do anything more than sit quietly there.'

She swung her feet over the edge of the bed and stood up, clutching the top of a chest of drawers with a look of surprise on her face. 'I don't think I could do much. I feel as if my bones have turned to rubber.'

'You've got to give your body time to rest. Everyone needs that.'

She shook her head as if annoyed at herself, but didn't move. 'Did I hear a car arrive a short time ago?'

He hesitated, then nodded. 'Yes, the man who booked in earlier. Only I didn't like the looks of him, so I watched out of the bedroom window. He's not wasted any time going exploring and has started taking photos. I'll help you down the stairs, then I want to go out and keep an eye on him.'

She was instantly more alert. '*I* should be doing that. And I don't need help to walk down a few stairs.'

But he still chose to keep his arm round her waist. 'Don't worry, Ella. I'll check up on him as carefully as you would. And if you're feeling well enough later, maybe we can have that talk we keep postponing? I've got something important to tell you.'

She nodded and let her head fall back against the sofa.

Amy came to join them, looking at her mother in a worried way. Cameron spared the time to say gently, 'Your mother will be fine. She just needs to rest for a few days.'

'I can tell her that myself,' Ella said. But the words were without her usual fire.

The girl nodded and sat on a stool near the sofa, her hand creeping up to hold her mother's in a way that showed this had been done many times before.

His heart was touched by the sight of them, both of them under the weather, both bravely facing a world where the odds were against them.

'I'll report back when I can,' he said gently and left them alone.

★   ★   ★

Cameron strolled round the back of the outbuildings to find their new guest trying to get a shutter undone. 'Problem?' he asked.

Smith swung round, looking first surprised then relaxing when he saw who it was. 'O'Neal. Don't know why you're still here.'

'You have the advantage of me. I know your face, but not your name.'

'Smith.' He grinned. 'It really is.'

'The owner doesn't want people going into this barn.'

'I'm not intending to hurt anything, just take a few photos. Why don't you help me? If the place is genuinely old, it's better for Mr Deare to know it.'

'It *is* genuinely old. But I'm not the owner. It's up to Ms Turner whether people are allowed into her property or not.'

The man's expression turned ugly. 'Mr Deare isn't going to like it if you stop me doing my job.'

'As I no longer work for him, that's irrelevant.'

'You won't think so if you cross him. He can make life very difficult for people and he has a long reach. Anyway, from what I heard, he's been very helpful to you in the past. I'd say you owed him a little in return now.'

'Why is he so fixated on buying this place? I can't quite work that out.'

'It's ideal for his purpose, not too expensive, and minimum landscaping needed to provide a decent lake.' He jerked his head towards the farm. 'Of course the house would be below the new water line, but that adds to the romance of the place, don't you think?'

Cameron stood very still as this sank in, then he turned to look at the small lake and the configuration of the landscape. Yes, it'd be relatively easy to move the earth and extend the lake. 'Trouble is, she's not going to sell.'

'Oh, she will. There's always a way. And I hear she owes money, more than she can pay back. She may not get a choice.'

Cameron bit back angry words. 'Whether she does or not, you still have no right to break into her property.'

'You're a fool.'

Smith strode off.

Cameron turned to stare at the small lake and try to imagine it covering this whole area. It'd look great as a lake. But it'd destroy Willowbrook.

He wasn't going to allow them to do that to Ella.

15

They had six guests for dinner that night, because another lone traveller turned up, a taciturn man called Brown who gave them no information beyond his name and who replied to attempts to chat with monosyllables.

By that time Ella had abandoned the battle to stay up and retired to bed, but her two helpers agreed that she looked a bit pinker and not as exhausted.

When they'd cleared up, Stephanie said thoughtfully, 'I don't like those two men. Birds of a feather, I should say. And I'm sure they know one another.'

Cameron frowned. 'You think so? They made no attempt to sit together, didn't exchange a word that I saw.'

'No, but they exchanged glances a couple of times. If Porgy weren't so old, I'd leave him outside to keep watch.'

'I was thinking of camping out in the barn.'

'That's a bit risky, isn't it?'

'I doubt they'd attack me. I was thinking more of acting as a deterrent, making a noise.' But not till after he'd seen what they wanted.

'I'll get you a bed.'

'I think not. We don't want anyone noticing that I'm sleeping there. Just get me a sleeping bag or quilt, preferably an old, dark one.'

She winced. 'You'll be uncomfortable.'

He grinned. 'The object is not to sleep, is it?'

'You'll be tired tomorrow.'

'I can cope with that.'

★ ★ ★

Oliver wandered into town, waiting for Rose to finish work. A big silver car purred to a halt beside him and the window was wound down.

'Dr Paige.'

'Mr Harding.'

'A word in private, if you please.'

Harding reached across, opening the other front door of the vehicle with some difficulty. He was carrying a lot of extra weight since Oliver had seen him, and his colour wasn't healthy.

'We'll just drive round to the park, if you don't mind.'

Oliver looked at his watch. 'I have to be back in quarter of an hour.'

'To see that hippy female,' Harding said sourly. 'I don't know why you bother with her.'

'She's called Rose and she's not a hippy, she's an artist. And a damned good one, too.'

Harding squinted sideways at him. 'You're making a big claim there.'

'I've seen her work. I've also visited art galleries all over the world. I'm sure of what I said. If you'd seen her special project, you'd be blown away.'

'Might pay to buy one or two of her paintings, then, for an investment?'

'Definitely. Now, what did you want to see me about?'

'My boy. He isn't getting any better. Been sneaking out at night. Thinks I don't know. I don't want to upset his mother any more than she is now, but I have to do something.'

'Could be he's an alcoholic, out of control. If he was my patient I could advise him.'

'Advise me instead.'

'These are only general suggestions about alcoholics. I can't be more definite about your son without seeing him. You could take him to another doctor if he won't see me.' Oliver rapidly outlined several avenues of action that might help anyone slipping into alcoholism.

'Brett won't agree to let himself be locked away in rehab.'

'I'm sure you can persuade him, Mr Harding, if you feel it's in his best interest. He should definitely consult a doctor before you do anything, however.'

'If I have to, I'll persuade him, and I'll take him to see a specialist myself. Get some names to me, will you? Just one other thing. About the mix-up at the surgery with that parcel. It was a joke. My Brett's no terrorist. You don't need to press charges, surely?'

'Not if you're certain he'll not go near Rose again.' Oliver had a thought. 'Once he goes in for rehab, we'll see about getting the charges withdrawn.'

Harding nodded. 'Fair enough. It'll give me a bit more push. I'll make certain he doesn't go near her while we're fixing up some rehab. I'll drive you back now.' When they drew up outside the pub, he said grudgingly, 'You seem to have a steady head on your shoulders.'

And that left Oliver wondering exactly what Mr Harding was going to do to persuade his son to let himself be locked away.

He'd stay on his guard till that happened. He wanted Rose to be safe and he didn't want to be looking over his shoulder as he courted her. This time he was going to persuade her to marry him, would not take no for an answer. Would do whatever it took.

* * *

Bright moonlight guided Cameron across the yard with the ragged sleeping bag Stephanie had found. As he pushed the door shut, darkness surrounded him like a heavy cloak, so he stood still and let his eyes grow accustomed to the dimness.

It wasn't totally dark. There were a couple of skylights. But the interior seemed eerie in this light and he didn't move for a while, feeling safer with his back pressed against the heavy wooden door. Which reminded him. He used the spare door key Ella had given him to lock up again. If those men found it locked and opened it, then they were definitely trespassing, if not breaking and entering.

He still felt jittery, which surprised him. He wasn't usually afraid of much, certainly not of shadows.

Even as he watched, light seemed to gather in one corner, shimmering slightly. His heart began to pound and his hair prickled with apprehension. He made no attempt to go and investigate

263

the patch of light. Well, how did you investigate what might be Ella's ghost? It didn't look like a lady, well, only vaguely, just a patch of light that couldn't be explained by anything else.

He cleared his throat, shivering as the sound echoed round the barn, and gave in to a sudden urge to explain his presence. 'I'm here to protect the farm.'

The light went brighter for a moment, then faded and dimmed.

When nothing happened for a few minutes, he let out his breath, realizing he'd been breathing very shallowly. Not like him to be spooked by something. But then, he'd never encountered a ghost before. He'd never believed in such things, but how did you explain Amy's firm belief in 'the lady' and Ella's smiling certainty that there were ghosts here? Not to mention this patch of light that came from nowhere.

He forced himself to walk round the big space, ending up at the place where the secret panel was. He studied it, head on one side. Could he remember how to open it? Not that he was going to need it, but still, he'd found it fascinating.

What had Ella done? He raised his hand and pressed the spot she'd touched, feeling something, a bounciness at the edge of the wood. But nothing happened. Oh yes, she'd pressed in two places, somewhere lower down as well. He ran his hand across the rough dark wood and pressed lower down. Nothing happened. Had he got the right spot? It was hard to tell. He tried again, with the same lack of result.

A shimmer of light played briefly where two

walls met at right angles, lower than his hand and slightly to the right. He froze. Was he being guided? No, it was just a stray moonbeam — wasn't it?

But as he pressed where the light had glowed, the panel swung open with only the faintest grating sound. He let out another long, low breath of air. This was . . . hard to accept. And though he was no coward, his heart was pounding.

The hidey hole was much darker than the main barn, so he stayed in the doorway, looking in, then took a step back and pushed the door closed. It moved quietly, as if well oiled. He didn't know why he'd wanted to open it.

He continued to prowl round the barn, but found nothing else of interest because most of it was empty.

He went to sit on the sleeping bag in one of the low-walled storage areas, leaning against the wall, arms clasped around his knees. It was going to be a long night.

★   ★   ★

The two men met just after midnight, by which time lights in every building at Willowbrook had long been extinguished.

'Y'know, I think this place really is old,' Smith muttered.

'*He* won't like that.'

'He'll want to know the truth, though what he'll do with it is anyone's guess. He's a fast worker when he's got his sights on a new development.'

'Well, let's get started.'

They walked along the grass by the edge of the path, stopping with muffled curses when they found only the soft earth of a flowerbed to walk in.

'We'll need to get rid of our footprints from that afterwards,' Smith whispered.

'Ah, they won't know we've been here. It'll be a jobbing gardener in a place like this and he won't look at them footprints twice.'

'I'm not taking any risks.'

Brown grinned, teeth showing white in the moonlight. 'There are no risks. Trust me, I can get us into the house and barn without anyone being the wiser.'

'Careful here. There's more of that damned gravel. Better go round it where we can. It makes a crunching noise.'

They made their way slowly across to the barn doors.

'Spooky old place, isn't it?' Smith said.

'Yes. Now, the old man wants a quick survey and plenty of photos.' Brown bent to fiddle with the lock, snickering at how easy it was to pick these old locks.

The door made a noise as they started to open it and Brown pulled out a small oil bottle, dripping some on the hinges. But the door still squeaked. 'Funny sort of noise, that. Should be all right now.' But the door squeaked even more loudly and they both glanced nervously at the house.

Brown opened it the minimum amount to slip inside. 'Leave it like that! No one will be awake at this hour, let alone looking out at it.'

'They might if they've heard that noise,' Smith objected.

'Trust me. I've done dozens of these jobs and not been caught. It's more likely to wake them up if we make more noise by closing it. Leave it. We won't be long.'

Muttering, Smith followed his much larger companion inside, nervousness showing in every twitch of his body.

The big man pulled out a torch and flashed it quickly round the inside of the barn, letting the light linger on the old beams. 'They don't build things that solidly these days. Shame this place has to go.'

The door hinges squeaked again.

'It didn't move,' Smith said. 'I was watching and the door didn't move. Why should the damned hinges squeak?'

'Wood settling. Old places always creak. You're making more noise than it is with your complaints.'

Crouched behind one of the partitions, Cameron listened to their muttered conversation, praying they'd not find him. He didn't think they'd linger long.

Smith brought out an infra-red camera and began to take pictures while the other played his torch here and there.

Cameron moved back further, crouching and ready to run as the men came to stand nearby and the torch flashed in his direction. They were taking a very comprehensive series of photos. The wood he was pressing against creaked slightly.

'What's that?' Smith asked.

'What's what?'

'That sound. Something creaked, and it wasn't from the direction of the door, either.'

'It's nothing. How many times do I have to tell you: all old places creak.'

'Well, I don't like it in here. It gives me the shivers.'

'Shut up and finish taking those photos.'

'There. Done.' He shoved the camera in his pocket and turned round, so eager to get out he bumped into the partition and knocked Amy's fairy wand off it.

The wand landed close to Cameron's foot.

'I'd better put it back,' the big guy said. 'It's sloppy work to leave things different.' He bent to pick it up and as he did, his torch played over Cameron's foot. 'There's someone here!' he yelled in shock.

For lack of anything better, Cameron hurled the sleeping bag at him and luckily, it tangled around his head for a moment. But the smaller man was between him and the door, so he could see no alternative but to slip along the wall and activate the secret panel.

He heard the big one call, 'Did he run out?'

'Didn't get past me. Turn that bloody torch on again and stay in front of those doors.'

'The torch won't work.' He clicked it several times in frustration but it didn't light up.

By that time Cameron was inside the hole and had started the door closing. It moved painfully slowly and he felt vulnerable as he crouched at the back of the small space.

Suddenly the torch came on again, just as the door was shutting. Cameron watched the thin line of light vanish then sat down on the bench and leaned back against the wall. That had been a close shave.

In the barn the big man swung the torch to and fro but found no one. 'He must have got out.'

'He did not! I was standing by the door all the time. It's barely half open, so I'd have felt him if he'd tried to push past me.'

'Then where the hell has he gone.' Once again he played the torch methodically to and fro. Once again, it failed suddenly, and this time didn't come on again.

Cursing, they moved cautiously towards the door and went outside again.

The door squeaked even more loudly as they closed it, and with backward glances over their shoulders, they made their way back towards the chalets. Smith stopped to smear their footprints in the soft earth of the flower beds.

'I'll check on these in the morning,' he muttered, and this time Brown didn't object.

At the chalets they stopped to listen but there were no sounds of pursuit.

'Damned if I know what happened back there,' Brown whispered. 'But as long as you got the photos *he* wants, what the hell.'

Inside the hidey hole, Cameron listened carefully. The two men must have left the barn, because their voices had faded to silence. He waited a while, then decided to go out via the inner secret passage, just to be sure of not bumping into them. He'd almost swear he'd heard soft laughter as he made his way down it. Strange the tricks imagination could play. He grinned. If there was a ghost, it had certainly been on his side.

The two men had definitely been sent by Ray, and given the power of money, Cameron was glad he'd warned Julian that someone might have been bribed to bury or refuse the application for listing.

In the meantime, he doubted the men would be coming out again, so he might as well get some sleep.

* * *

Ella woke up as she heard footsteps crunching faintly on the gravel of the yard. She slipped out of bed and went across to the window in time to see two men creeping round the corner of the barn on their way to the chalets.

Just as she was about to get back into bed, she saw another figure appear from the direction of the storehouses. When the clouds slid away from the moon, she saw that it was Cameron. What had he been doing? Had he seen anything?

She switched on her bedside lamp, hoping he'd pop in to see her.

Footsteps came up the stairs and a silhouette appeared in the doorway.

'You awake?'

'Yes. I heard someone outside. What happened?'

Cameron came across to the bed, sitting on

the edge of it, taking hold of her hand. 'Two of our guests have been exploring. I was keeping watch inside the barn because they seemed so interested in it, and they came inside to take photos there.'

'That was far too risky. They might have attacked you.'

'That occurred to me very forcibly once I was actually shut in the barn with them. But when they found me, I used the hidey hole and secret passage you showed us to escape. I hope you don't mind.'

'Of course I don't. I'd have hated anything to have happened to you.'

He raised the hand to his lips, smiling. 'So would I.'

'Tell me exactly what happened, every single detail. Here, you can lie next to me while you talk.'

He moved beside her, wishing he wasn't tired, and she wasn't so run-down, and began to give details of the night's events. When he debated whether he'd seen her female ghost, she gasped in surprise.

'What did I say?'

'No outsider has ever seen Jane Turner until after they've married into the family. You've been honoured.'

'I'm still not sure whether I believe it was a ghost.'

'She doesn't exactly flaunt herself, does she? Just occasionally you can see her clearly, but mostly it's what you saw, shimmering light. I like having her around, though. I always feel she's

271

watching over us. Tell me again exactly what you saw?'

But there was no answer. His breathing was deep and even, and his eyes were closed.

With a smile, she pulled the covers over him and snuggled down beside him. She was tired herself.

She felt safe and happy with him beside her, even though they were acting like a brother and sister. Something would happen between them one day, she was sure. The attraction between them was too strong for it not to. She stared at him in the moonlight. His hair was tousled, lashes veiled his eyes, his chest was rising and falling.

Attraction? Why was she skirting round her feelings. It was far more than an attraction already. She'd fallen in love with him. And if she'd heard him correctly, he'd called her 'my love'.

16

In the morning Cameron woke up to find himself lying next to Ella, who was sleeping soundly. He smiled at the sight of her, but slid out of the bed and crept back to his own room, not wanting to disturb her rest. He had a lot to do today. He glanced at his watch. Seven. Too soon to ring Julian. He'd go out to the barn and check everything there.

The interior of the old building looked perfectly normal in the soft morning light streaming in through the big double doors. Hard to believe what had happened there last night. Had it happened? Or had his imagination been playing tricks?

The door creaked and he spun round, smiling at his own nervousness. There was something rather awe-inspiring about very ancient buildings, he'd always found. He removed the sleeping bag then locked up again and walked down to the lake, standing by the water and sharing the early morning with the birds. Swallows darted and twittered, carrion crows pecked at the ground at the end of the lake where there was a grassy slope fringed by small trees. It'd been mown a couple of days previously and the crows had been grubbing around there ever since.

He'd have to find out more about birds. He was ashamed of how little he knew. He'd buy some binoculars and watch them. That reminded him of the poem *What is this world if full of care, We have no time to stand and stare*. He smiled. It seemed appropriate just now.

He took the time to study the wild flowers scattered here and there. He could recognize daisies, of course he could, but there were others he didn't know the names of. What was that tall rusty-coloured plant, for instance?

A rabbit hopped out into the sun and sat very still. He could see its ears twitch occasionally, but other than that it seemed simply to be enjoying the morning.

With a smile he walked back to the house and began to set the tables for breakfast. It'd be interesting serving the two men he'd last seen in the shadowy barn. Would they guess it'd been him they'd been chasing? It wouldn't matter if they did. They could do nothing about it now.

There were voices upstairs and Stephanie came down, smelling of soap, with her skin rosy.

'Good morning, Cameron. I see you're still in one piece. Did anything happen last night?'

He explained and her smile faded. 'So those men were here to photograph the insides of the farm buildings.'

'Seems like it.'

'Who for?'

He hesitated.

'You know more than you've told me, don't you?'

He nodded. 'Yes. But I think I owe it to Ella to tell her first.'

'Fair enough. But do that as soon as you can

— I'm fairly itching with curiosity. Now, let's get breakfast ready.'

★   ★   ★

Smith appeared first, taking a single table by the window and consuming his meal quickly and neatly, saying he had to leave early. Could he pay now, then he'd be off?

Just as he was finishing, Brown ambled in, nodding to the other man as if to a stranger. He paused to give Cameron a narrow-eyed frown then moved on without a word.

He ate a huge breakfast, complimented Stephanie on the food and asked for his bill.

He left nearly an hour later than Smith.

'And good riddance to the pair of them!' Stephanie said. 'Oh, there's the phone. I'll get it.'

★   ★   ★

Oliver woke up and went into the living room to find Rose already painting. 'How long have you been up?'

She gave him a quick smile, then her attention went back to her work. 'A couple of hours.'

He wandered across and smiled at the painting of a group of fledglings. 'That's not one of your specials.'

'No. But I thought it might sell. I'm a bit over working in a pub. Too old, my feet hurt and I'm having trouble staying polite to idiots.'

'Don't work there then. If we move in together, I can pay the rent and — '

A paintbrush covered in beige paint jabbed towards him and he ducked back.

'I'm *not* going to be a kept woman. Not now, not ever.'

He sighed. 'Half the rent and utilities payments, then. That'd be fair.'

She stopped to look at him very solemnly. 'We've not agreed to live together yet.'

'I thought we had. Have you changed your mind?'

To his dismay tears welled in her eyes. 'Damn!' She brushed them away, smearing paint on her hair.

He caught hold of the brush, put it down and hugged her fiercely. 'Don't cry. I can't bear to see you cry. What's wrong?'

Her voice was muffled against him. 'You.'

'What have I done?'

'Got into my heart again.' Her voice went up a register. 'And there's still no solution to our differences.'

He hugged her close as he said, 'Trust me. I'll find a solution. And if I can't, I'll stay here rather than give you up again. I missed you every single day, Rose, every single hour.'

Now she was weeping in earnest, but also covering his face with kisses. 'I can't bear to give you up, either. But — '

'No buts. Trust me. I'll find a way.'

With a sound halfway between a sob and a chuckle she subsided against him and the paintbrush didn't get picked up again for some time.

★ ★ ★

Miles decided to ring Ella to remind her he was coming to see his daughter the following day and was astonished to hear his mother's voice on the other end of the phone. 'What are *you* doing at Willowbrook?'

'Visiting my granddaughter. And how dare you tell me Ella didn't want me here? I'll not forgive you for that, Miles! I've lost three years of Amy's childhood because of your lies! *Three whole years.*'

'Don't put the phone down.'

'Why not? I don't want to hear more lies from you.'

'I thought it'd be easier on you to stay away,' he said.

'Lame excuse, Miles. You didn't think any such thing. When did *you* ever care for anyone else's feelings?'

He ignored her taunt. Feelings were vastly overrated, if you asked him. 'How long are you staying there?'

'As long as Ella needs me.'

'What do you mean by that?'

'She's very run down, has been overdoing it for years, partly thanks to you not paying maintenance, if I read things correctly. Cunning of you to blackmail her into going without by using the loan. That earned you more money than interest on savings would have done.'

'Mum! Don't — '

'Anyway, Cameron and I are looking after things and making her rest. Amy has a bit of a cold, too. Are you sure you want to come down? You might catch something.'

'Book me in for tomorrow night. We may as well make a family party of it.'

'I'll see if Ella wants to rent you a chalet and — '

'Damned well book me in. With the money Ella owes me, I should have unlimited access to those chalets and not need to pay a penny.'

This time she did put the phone down.

He stood staring at the handpiece, trying to sort out in his mind what was going on at Willowbrook. Then the name Cameron jumped into his mind. She'd definitely said 'Cameron'. It wasn't a common name. Could this possibly be the Cameron he'd seen at DevRaCom, the man who'd been greeted by Ray Deare as if he was an old friend? What was the connection there?

Thoughtful now, he rang DevRaCom and asked to be put through to Deare. He got Miss Bradley instead, and although she was perfectly polite, she refused point-blank to put him through to her employer unless he explained exactly what he wanted to discuss.

He wasn't such a fool as to pass on this information to a subordinate, explaining only, 'It's about Willowbrook.'

'All your dealings have been about Willowbrook. Exactly what do you wish to discuss? Mr Deare is extremely busy this week and he's expecting a call from America at the moment.'

'I'll ring back later, then.' He put down the phone, wondering what to do. Then he realized he need do nothing yet. He was going to see Amy the following day. If Cameron — what was the fellow's surname? — was still there, Miles would know something was going on behind Deare's back.

The brat was proving difficult, though, refusing even to speak to him politely. She needed a good spanking, that one, even if it was unlawful nowadays to hit a child. He wasn't going to buy her a big present this time only to have her throw it straight back at him.

Still, you had to give her credit: disabled or not, Amy had spirit. She got that from his side of the family, he was sure. Ella was a naïve fool, credulous and trusting, always had been. She was born to have people wipe their feet on her.

He spent the next two hours worrying about this Cameron fellow, then tried to ring Ray Deare again, without any success.

'Mr Deare has left for the weekend,' the starchy secretary said.

That was when Miles decided to surprise his ex — and his interfering mother — by going a day early.

★ ★ ★

Cameron rang Julian just after nine and had trouble persuading him to take seriously the possibility of someone at DevRaCom bribing local officials not to heritage list Willowbrook.

'For heaven's sake,' he exploded in the end, 'do you think Deare got rich by playing nicely? He didn't. He got rich by any means he could, believe me.'

'Hmm. I'll have to think about it.'

'What does that mean, Julian?'

'Well, there would have to be someone vulnerable to bribery for it to happen.'

'Then you do believe me?'

'Not sure. Let me have a chat to one of the HR managers who's very supportive about preserving our heritage. I'd hate anything to happen to that farmhouse, especially that glorious barn. Leave it with me.'

'If I can help in any way . . . '

'Doubt it. You don't know the locals like I do.'

Which wasn't the most satisfying result to Cameron, who preferred to handle important matters himself.

He went upstairs, to find Ella showered and dressed, but still looking wan.

She smiled at him. 'I can't believe I found it tiring merely to get dressed.'

'Once you let go, your body takes over and demands the rest it craves.'

'It's certainly demanding it.' She yawned. 'I could lie down and have another nap, but I'm not going to. I wonder how those two men are getting on with their employer — I assume it's DevRaCom?'

'Yes, it is. I've been thinking about them. It was photos they wanted. They made no attempt to damage the place. I don't know whether that's good or bad. But it's out of our hands for the moment. Come and sit in the sun. I have something to tell you.' His watch beeped at him and he sighed. 'First, however, I have a phone call to make.'

'You make a lot of calls.'

'Tying up loose ends for the big changes in my

life. Trouble is, some of the people I need to speak to are in different time zones and work long hours, so I have a narrow window of opportunity if I want to catch them, hence the alarm.' He indicated his watch.

'Yet you don't know what you're changing to, do you?'

'I'm beginning to get a few ideas.' And she was part of them, the central part.

She went downstairs, hugged Amy, who was helping her grandma to cook, and decided to sit outside in the small private patio to the side of the house.

Cameron peeped out a few minutes later after his first phone call ended to see Ella frowning at the water, her book neglected on her lap.

What the hell was she worrying about now?

Then he looked at his watch and muttered in annoyance. Time zone differences waited for no man.

★　★　★

Miles arrived at Willowbrook that afternoon, taking them all by surprise. He breezed into the kitchen without knocking and as Ella had reluctantly gone back upstairs to lie down, found himself confronting only his mother and Cameron.

The two men nodded stiffly when introduced.

Amy hunched down in the armchair, scowling at her father.

'You should have let us know you were coming, Miles,' Stephanie said. 'Surprises aren't always welcome.'

281

He went across to kiss the air above her cheek and when he would have done the same to his daughter, Amy ducked away from him, clutching the teddy so that it came between them.

From his basket in the corner, Porgy growled and hauled himself to his feet.

Amy darted over to him. 'Sit down, Porgy-Worgy. It's only my daddy. He's not going to hurt me.'

But the old dog continued to growl in his throat, on and on.

'Can't you shut that damned animal up?' Miles asked as he'd twice tried to speak only to have the growls rise in volume.

'He seems to dislike you even more than he did when you lived here,' Stephanie said, smiling at the dog. 'Would you like a cup of coffee?'

'Yes. And a chalet for the night. I was in the neighbourhood and thought I'd save myself an extra trip down here tomorrow to see my daughter.'

'I've seen you now, so you don't have to come any more.' Amy said, prudently staying near the dog.

'You're my daughter,' he said pointedly.

'Well, I don't want to be.'

'Get up and sit at the table properly with us and leave that dirty animal alone!' he snapped. 'And I'm sure you have plenty to keep you occupied, O'Neal. Don't let us keep you.'

Cameron didn't feel he had a right to intervene, but he wasn't going to be driven away. 'I'm helping out here while Ella's recovering, so I'll need to come and go. I'll just get those things you wanted from upstairs, shall I, Stephanie?'

To his relief she took the hint and nodded. 'Thanks.'

He didn't knock on Ella's bedroom door, but pushed it slightly open and peeped in. When he saw she was awake, he put one finger to his lips and went inside, closing the door carefully behind him.

She sat up in bed and stared at him in surprise.

'Your ex has just turned up,' he said in a low voice. 'I thought I'd better warn you. Stephanie's holding him at bay in the kitchen and Amy is doing an excellent job of keeping his attention on her.' He grinned. 'She doesn't mince words when she doesn't like someone, does she?'

'No. That child doesn't know the meaning of the word tact.' Ella sighed tiredly. 'I could do without this.'

'Do you want me to send him away?'

'How can you? I can't deny him access to Amy.'

'He's demanding a chalet for tonight.'

'Now that is going too far.'

There were footsteps on the stairs and Stephanie joined them. 'I've left Amy holding him at bay and Porgy still growling, but I can't exactly throw him out. Have you decided what you want to do, Ella?'

'No.' She rubbed her forehead. 'I seem to be swimming in fog at the moment. Not the best way to deal with Miles.'

'Then why don't you give someone else the right to deal with him?'

'What do you mean?'

Stephanie looked from one to the other. 'It's obvious you two are attracted to one another, shines out a mile. Why don't you pretend you're an item — tell him you're engaged to be married? I'm sure Cameron would love to have the right to deal with my dear son and you must admit you're not yourself, Ella. The stress of dealing with my slippery son won't help your recovery.'

They were both staring at her as if she'd thrown a bomb at them.

'Let me tell him.' Stephanie grinned. 'It'll be such fun to see his reaction.'

They both stole a glance at one another.

'I'd like that.' Cameron smiled at Ella as if they were alone. He saw her take a deep breath, swallow hard and then nod.

'Why not? If you don't mind, that is?'

He took her hand and raised it to his lips. 'I'm very happy to be engaged to you.'

Ella blushed but didn't pull her hand away. He wished they were alone, wished he could really kiss her, was terrified of frightening her away. And to his surprise, he wished this engagement weren't a pretence.

Stephanie broke the silence by saying cheerfully, 'What fun! When I think of all the times Miles has pulled the wool over my eyes, I shall enjoy giving him some of his own medicine.'

Cameron gave her a quick, speculative glance and she winked at him behind Ella's back. What did she mean by that? Was she aware of how deep his feelings already ran for Ella?

'Shall I go and tell him?'

'No.' Ella swung her feet off the bed. 'Certainly not. I want to enjoy the fun, too.'

Cameron enjoyed the quick display of lean, nicely curved leg, judging it best to make no further comment.

'Turn your back,' Ella ordered. 'I'm not facing him in my tatty old nightdress.'

He did as he was told. Very reluctantly. As the short nightdress had shown, she had beautiful legs, curved in exactly the right places. He'd seen models on TV with what he called 'chicken legs', so scrawny they had no curves at all. Women like that didn't turn him on at all. But Ella did.

She slid her arm round his waist. 'I'm ready — Cameron *darling*. Shall we make our entrance hand in hand?'

'Definitely.'

★   ★   ★

Miles looked up to see that fellow come in with his arm round Ella's waist. She was smiling at him as if . . . What the hell was going on here? Had O'Neal wormed his way into her bed? The thought made Miles angry. The fellow was using dirty tactics to get the information for Deare. Very dirty indeed. And worse than that, he was poaching on Miles's territory.

He turned to his mother, only to find she was looking at the two of them fondly. When he turned back, he was in time to see them exchanging loving smiles.

He'd put a stop to this before he left, he decided. He'd put in the hard work, dreamed up the concept of a development here and sold the idea to DevRaCom as soon as the property on one side of the farm went up for sale.

'Why don't you take Porgy out for a walk?' Ella suggested.

Amy nodded and left without even looking at her father.

Stephanie beamed at Miles. 'Cameron and Ella are engaged.'

He was lost for words for a few seconds then forced a smile to his face. 'Congratulations!'

'You're the first to know,' Ella said. 'We hadn't even told Amy yet.'

'Sorry if I let the cat out of the bag,' said Stephanie. 'I didn't realize.'

Amy came back into the room, smiling at her mother. 'I forgot my book. I heard what you said, but I'd guessed already. When my friend Nessa got a new daddy, her mother went all soppy, like you've been doing, and *he* looked at her like Mr O'Neal looks at you.'

'Oh. Right. I . . . hope you don't mind.'

'I like Mr O'Neal.'

'You should call me Cameron now.'

'Cameron.' She brightened. 'Does that mean I don't have to see my old daddy any more?'

Miles glared at her. 'It doesn't make any difference to you and me, young lady. I'm still your father. He'll only be a stepfather.'

Stephanie couldn't help chuckling, tried to turn it into a cough and failed.

'Well, I like him an' I don't like you, so I'd rather have him for a daddy.' Amy went across to hug her mother round the waist.

'Come and sit down, darling,' Cameron said. 'You're still a bit wobbly.'

'Perhaps I'd better.' Ella was enjoying Miles's shock, but worried about how this deception would affect her daughter when the truth was revealed. As if she'd have announced a real engagement without telling Amy first!

'I'm here to spend time with my daughter,' Miles said sourly. 'Your affairs are irrelevant to me. Let's hope this one lasts longer than the others. What's the other fellow called who's been chasing you? Brett Something.' He snapped his fingers. 'Harding. That's the one.'

Ella gaped at him. 'You know those are lies. I can't stand Brett Harding and I've *never* been out with him.' She shuddered. 'I never would.'

'So you say now.'

'You always were a poor loser,' Stephanie said. 'Stop telling lies.'

'Believe what you want. I know what she's like. Now, Amy and I are going for a walk.' Miles captured his daughter's hand before she could escape.

'She's been ill. She's not fit to go for a walk,' Ella said. 'Why don't you go and sit outside with her for a while?'

'I don't want to,' Amy wailed.

'Just for twenty minutes, darling,' Ella said.

'I'll get the timer,' Amy said at once, tugging her hand away from her father's and hurrying over to the kitchen bench.

In her haste, she misjudged the distance and fell over.

Cameron got to her first, offering a hand but

not forcing it on her. 'You all right, kid?'

'Yes. I fall over sometimes. But I can get up on my own.'

'I can see that. But friends can help one another and there's no chair in reach for you to hold on to.'

She took his hand but let go as soon as she was standing.

'Maybe she should start using a wheelchair,' Miles suggested.

Frosty silence met this remark, not only from Amy but from the others.

He looked round, puzzled. 'What? What did I say?'

'Kids with SMA usually make their own decisions about using wheelchairs, and it's not always necessary,' Cameron said curtly. 'I'd have thought you'd know that, you being her father.'

Miles glared at him and turned to his daughter. 'If you're all right now, shall we go outside?'

Porgy began to growl again and heaved himself to his feet.

'That stupid creature isn't coming with us,' Miles snapped.

Stephanie said quietly, 'My son doesn't understand about pets, never has.'

Ignoring them all, Miles ushered his daughter outside.

Ella went to the window. 'I'm keeping an eye on them. If it looks like he's upsetting her, I'm going to intervene.' She laughed suddenly. 'Oh my! She's set the timer already and he doesn't like that.'

'I'd back her against him any day,' Stephanie said. 'I reckon she's inherited something of his ruthlessness, so he's not going to find her easy to deal with.'

'He found me all too easy,' Ella said bitterly.

★ ★ ★

In London, one of Ray Deare's PAs took the camera from Smith and left him reporting what had happened to the CEO.

He downloaded the images on to his computer in the adjacent office and frowned, fiddling with them.

He went back and held out the camera. 'It didn't work.'

Smith frowned at him. 'What do you mean, it didn't work? It would have been carefully checked out before I took it out of Stores. How could it not work?'

'See for yourself. There are a few shots of exteriors — rather a nice old barn, but the rest is all fuzzy. You must have had it on the wrong setting for indoor shots.'

'I was using cameras before you were out of nappies,' Smith snapped, furious at being treated like this in front of the big boss. 'Let me see. I'll use my own computer to download.'

Ray watched them go, turned and saw Miss Bradley waiting patiently. 'This project isn't going well.'

She gave him one of her disapproving looks.

'Don't start, Sonia. The situation is urgent and we can't afford to lose this one.'

'You've never acted like this before,' she said, pinch-lipped. 'I don't like underhand behaviour and cheating.'

'I have to do it any way I can. I'll be in the good old *merde* if I don't pull it off.'

Her expression softened slightly. 'Try to find another way, Ray.'

'There isn't one.'

'There must be.'

She waited and when he stubbornly shook his head, she turned and went out, once more in her normal stern persona.

The two of them went way back, he thought, in fact he'd known her longer than anyone else in the company. They'd been close once and he'd even considered marrying her. Then Alicia had turned up, heiress to a fortune, making eyes at him. It had been too good an opportunity to miss.

But he was glad he'd persuaded Sonia to continue working for him.

She didn't often step outside her role as senior executive secretary, though. What had got into her today?

★ ★ ★

After twenty minutes had passed, the timer pinged. Amy stood up at once to go inside the house.

Miles pulled her down again, looking angry.

Ella, who'd been keeping an eye on them, moved purposefully towards the door and went outside to join them. 'Your twenty minutes are

290

up, Amy. And your grandma has a drink and a piece of cake waiting for you.'

'I don't call this reasonable access,' Miles said. 'I'll have to consult my lawyer. I want to take Amy out, have her to myself.'

'You hardly spoke to her just now.'

'I suppose you were watching through the window.'

'Of course.'

He looked at her scornfully. 'You'd do more good by keeping an eye on that boyfriend of yours.'

'None of your business.'

'Oh, I think it is. Did you know he's working for DevRaCom?'

The world seemed to blur around her for a minute as his accusation sank in. 'I don't believe you!'

He shrugged. 'I saw him myself at DevRaCom head office. He's mighty close to the CEO, Ray Deare. Acts more like his favourite nephew than an employee.'

'Cameron isn't working for anyone at the moment.'

Miles shrugged. 'Have it your own way. Only what was he doing at head office a few days ago?'

Suddenly she could stand the sight of her ex no longer. 'It's about time you left. I'm not renting you a chalet and I think Amy's been forced to spend enough time with you for one day.' She gestured to the object on the ground. 'And you'd better take your bar of chocolate with you. Your daughter clearly didn't want it.'

He stood there for a moment, then shoved his

hands in his pockets. 'I'll go, but I'm coming back again tomorrow afternoon. You and Amy had better get used to my visits. And if you've got any thoughts about denying me access, we'll put it to the test in court.'

He strolled across to his car and slid into the driving seat, moving off with an unnecessary swirl of gravel.

She stood watching his car disappear, but didn't go into the house, didn't trust herself yet to confront Cameron.

What Miles had said couldn't be true.

Could it?

Only . . . Cameron had come here at first to inspect the property. She'd assumed he was doing this for the bank. But what if he'd come for DevRaCom? What if he was deceiving her?

Surely she couldn't have been so badly mistaken in a man again?

17

Brett stared at his father in shock. 'You don't mean it.'

'Oh, but I do.'

'Who's been putting stupid ideas like that in your mind? Come on, Dad. I'm not an alcoholic. I just like a drink or two.'

'More than a drink or two. I've not forgotten you crashing my car, even if you have. And when you come up for trial, it'll look better if you've gone into rehab, my lawyer says.'

'But I've cut down on what I drink already.'

'Oh? Then why did I find those empty whisky bottles in the rubbish bin?'

Brett shrugged. 'I'm going mad shut up here. It was just the odd drink.'

'But you've not been shut up. You've been creeping out late at night, taking advantage of the fact that your mother and I go to bed early. I'd have come after you last night except I didn't want to wake her. And then, to crown it all, you had to set a booby trap for Rose Marwood! Didn't it even occur to you that it would scare anybody out of their wits these days, what with terrorists and all? Stupid, that was, involving the police again. That'll not look good at your trial, either. You'll probably get a custodial sentence. How do you think having a son in jail will reflect on me?'

'It was meant to be a joke.'

'Well, it wasn't funny and if you weren't my son, I'd say you *deserved* locking away to teach you a lesson.'

'You won't let them put me in jail, will you?'

'I may not be able to stop them. But my lawyer says it'll help if you go into rehab voluntarily, so go you will. I've found a place where they treat people decently. It'll cost me a fortune, but it'll be worth it to stop you getting in any deeper. I'm not having your mother worrying herself into an early grave because her son's an alcoholic.'

'I'm not going into one of those places. Dad . . . Don't do that to me.' Brett's heart sank. When his father got that look on his face, he knew nothing would change his mind.

'If you're not going into rehab, you'd better move out of here tomorrow and find yourself a new job while you're at it. I'll be cancelling your credit card, too.'

'You don't mean that.'

'I bloody well do. I've had medical advice about this as well as legal, and we need to nip your addiction in the bud before it's too late.'

'What medical advice?' Brett stared at his father. 'The Paiges. It's one of them, isn't it? You always go to them, even though I keep telling you how old-fashioned their practice is.'

'They know their stuff, especially that young one.'

Brett opened his mouth to say what he thought of Oliver Paige, then looked at his father's furious face and pressed his lips together.

'You leave for rehab on Monday morning, early. I'll drive you there myself and hand you over. You'll not come out till you're well and truly dried out, not if you want your job and home back.'

'I'm not going!'

His father stared thoughtfully at his signet ring. 'There's also the small matter of your future inheritance — I'm not leaving my money to a drunken wastrel.'

Brett knew when he was beaten. 'I can't believe you're doing this to me.'

His father's voice softened just a little. 'It's for your own good, so give it a chance, lad. In the meantime, for this last day or two, you'd better knuckle down and work hard.' He looked at his watch. 'Your shift at the petrol station starts in quarter of an hour. Just gives you nice time to walk into town, doesn't it? Leave your car here. You need to start getting fitter. You've put on a lot of weight round your middle lately.'

Without a word, Brett changed into his work uniform and trudged into town, so furious he didn't notice anything or anyone till he passed the surgery and saw Rose going round the back. Bitch! he thought. She'd get her comeuppance one day, if he had to wait years to pay her back. So would her cousin.

As the long day passed, he thought about Rose several times. Pretending to be an artist. Bloody poser! Gradually a plan came to him. He wasn't leaving town without giving her something to remember him by.

And why not deal with her cousin while he

was at it? Though that'd be harder. He couldn't walk out to Willowbrook.

Well, he still had a few good friends and quite a lot of money stashed away. He'd pay them well to help him. He smiled. Some fools liked to pay for their petrol with cash and if you knew where the security cameras were, you could always slip a note or two into your own pocket. As long as you didn't get greedy, no one was any the wiser.

And if his Dad thought they'd turn him off booze at this rehab place, he could think again. There was nothing wrong with a drink or two. Absolutely nothing.

How would he manage without a drink to wind down at the end of the day? What would he do with himself if he couldn't go out for a pint with the lads? He shuddered at the mere thought.

★　★　★

Ella took refuge in her bedroom for the rest of the day. She didn't intend to confront Cameron about whether he was working for DevRaCom until they were alone together and not likely to be interrupted.

It took all her self-control, however, to remain calm when he came up to chat to her or bring her a drink.

'What's wrong, Ella?' he asked on his third visit. 'You've been very quiet since Miles left.'

'I'll tell you later, once Amy is in bed. We'll go out for a walk. I'm tired of staying indoors.'

He opened his mouth to say something, shut it

again, then gave a little shrug. 'Very well. In the meantime, try to rest. You're looking stressed again.'

'Thanks to Miles.' She saw with relief that this had stopped Cameron's questions for the moment.

Later, Stephanie came upstairs to put Amy to bed, then paused outside Ella's bedroom, before coming to stand at the foot of the bed. 'What did my son say to you?'

'Nothing important.'

'I saw how quiet you were after he'd left, and you've been avoiding Cameron ever since, so it must be important, to you at least.' She waited and when Ella said nothing, said earnestly, 'Don't listen to anything Miles says. He has a way of taking the truth and twisting it out of shape.'

'Mmm.'

'All right, you're not going to confide in me, so I'll butt out. But don't do anything hasty on Miles's say-so.'

Ella could only manage a half-smile in response to that and when Stephanie came round the bed to give her a hug, the smile slipped completely and she clung to the older woman, her chest heaving as she fought against tears.

The thought that Cameron had been deceiving her was like a knife in the guts. He couldn't — surely he couldn't be associated with DevRaCom?

If he was . . . maybe she'd as good as lost her farm already.

An hour later Ella went downstairs, taut with determination to remain calm and logical during their discussion.

Cameron was sitting reading the newspaper, but set it aside and stood up the minute she came into the room.

'Ready for our walk?' she asked, not managing a smile.

'Of course.'

'We're only going down to the lake, Stephanie. We won't be long.'

'Amy will be all right with me. Don't come back without the smile you lost today.' Absent-mindedly she patted Porgy, who was sprawled across her feet, but she was watching the pair of them very intently.

Ella pressed her lips together and closed her eyes for a moment, but couldn't say anything without bursting into tears, so led the way out.

They walked in silence to a bench by the lake, a favourite spot of hers. 'We can sit here,' she said.

'And you can tell me what's upset you so.'

She took a deep breath. 'Miles said you were working for DevRaCom, that you're here to help persuade me to sell Willowbrook.'

'He likes to distort the truth, doesn't he?'

'Yes. But . . . you didn't come here by chance. I thought you'd been sent by the bank, but I've still heard nothing from them. You could easily be here on behalf of DevRaCom.'

'I was sent here by DevRaCom,' he began carefully, 'but — '

With a cry of anguish, she stood up and fled. She'd thought she was prepared for him to admit it, but she wasn't. She couldn't bear — *just could not bear!* — to hear another word he spoke. Nothing could excuse such a deception, nothing! Pretending to love her, to care about her. Pretending to care about Amy, which was even worse.

And all the time he'd been working with DevRaCom, the company which was trying to take their home away from them.

She heard his footsteps pounding after her, so took a short cut through the bushes, following paths only she knew, hearing him stumble and curse as she left him behind among the bushes.

⋆　⋆　⋆

Miles didn't go back to London, but booked into a cheap motel for the Friday night. He had a small job to do for DevRaCom, an envelope to pass on. He suspected it was bribery, but they hadn't told him what the envelope contained and he hadn't asked.

His meeting wasn't scheduled until late so he watched television as he waited for the hours to crawl past.

He smiled a few times about his last conversation with his ex. He'd certainly upset the apple cart where she and O'Neal were concerned. She was still so naïve, she'd believe anything you told her. Some people never learned.

Why wouldn't she realize it was best to

299

capitalize on her asset and sell the old house while it was still worth something? He was actually giving her some sound financial advice there.

And why was his mother interfering? She shouldn't have taken early retirement, clearly had too much time on her hands these days. He didn't get people's obsession with grandchildren, or children, come to that.

He frowned at the thought of Amy, annoyed that his daughter had taken against him and refused to be charmed. She would hardly speak a word to him, and she'd rejected both expensive and inexpensive presents.

Ella must have been poisoning the child's mind against him, that was the only explanation. Everyone knew how kids loved presents.

His mobile phone rang half an hour before he was due to leave for the meeting.

A man's voice said baldly, 'I can't keep that appointment.'

'Oh? Any special reason?'

'I can't do what you want. The listing is already being processed.'

'*What?* You said you could help us stop it.'

'Yeah, well, I didn't know how much local interest this house would raise. Even if I tried to stop it, I'd get nowhere — all I'd do would be lose my job. The guy who's pushing it through quickly came to see me. He'd heard someone was trying to stop the house being listed and — '

'He knew what you were going to do? You must have been careless.'

'No, I wasn't. I swear I wasn't. He's clever.

Too clever. And well connected locally. I wouldn't want to cross him. Sorry.'

Before Miles could think what to say, the call was ended and although he dialled the number he'd been given for use in emergencies, no one answered. He cursed the man and went to stare out of the window of his motel room.

If Willowbrook was listed and this project fell through, his hopes of a comfortable rise in his standard of living would come to nothing.

Who had found out that someone was prepared to help DevRaCom stop that listing? Not Ella, that was sure.

O'Neal? Could it be him? But he had no local connections, surely? And why would he work against DevRaCom?

How that old ruin was still standing after all these years, Miles couldn't figure. It should have fallen down centuries ago. Or been burned down. A vision of it in flames danced before him.

No, he wasn't going there. He wasn't risking prison, not for anyone.

But surely there was something he could do to make sure Ray Deare got what he wanted, and therefore gave Miles what he wanted most, a high-level job?

There had to be some way to retrieve the situation.

He tapped his fingers on the windowsill, drumming them again and again.

Not through Ella. She'd not sell whatever he did, he was sure of that now. He'd tried everything he could to persuade her, had observed her when he was visiting Amy. No use trying to sweet talk her again. And anyway, he didn't want to. He preferred his women pliable and feminine, not scrawny and dressed like a tramp.

Then he had an idea. It was a long shot, but hell, what had he to lose? Only a day or two more in the area.

He'd got another access visit to Amy lined up, so that not only gave him an excuse for staying in the district, but would allow him to continue watching what was going on at Willowbrook.

Never take your eye off the ball!

He picked up the phone and dialled the number on the advert he'd seen when leafing through the community newspaper.

★   ★   ★

Cameron chased after Ella, but she turned suddenly and seemed to vanish. He paused then tried to follow her through the bushes, but they seemed dense and branches kept slapping him in the face or tangling in his sweater. He waited, listening, but there were no sounds of anyone moving, just a light breeze whispering around him.

Damn Parnell! And damn the interruptions that had stopped him telling Ella the truth earlier today!

How the hell was he going to get her to listen to him now?

He turned and walked slowly back to the house.

Stephanie was sitting in the kitchen and from

the expression on her face, Ella had got back.

'She wants you to sleep in the chalet again,' Stephanie said, 'and if I were you, I'd do that, for tonight at least. Best let her cool down before you try to talk to her.'

'I can't just leave things like this.'

'Do you work for DevRaCom?'

'I did. But I severed any connection with them soon after coming here. And I only came to give Ray Deare my opinion on whether the place was really old, or a fake, not to persuade Ella to do anything she didn't want to. Your son is the one who set up the sale, who saw the potential for a hotel development.'

She gave him a long, level look.

'I'm telling the truth.'

'I believe you. But Ella's been deceived and hurt before, and she's very run down, so she's not thinking logically or reasonably'.

'I'll go up and get my things.'

'She's packing them now. I'll bring them down to the chalet shortly.' She went to get a key from the board. 'Please. Go now. She's distraught. This is definitely not the time to confront her.'

'Very well. I'll take your advice on that. But I'm not leaving Willowbrook till she's listened to me.'

'Quite right.'

That comment consoled him a little as he paced up and down in front of his chalet. Unless he was very much mistaken, Stephanie not only believed him but wanted the two of them to get together. It was always good to have an ally.

When she brought his suitcase and laptop, she

said, 'I can't stay. We'll talk tomorrow. I want to keep an eye on her.'

He nodded and took his things inside.

But although he got out his computer and tried to work, he couldn't settle. When he realized he'd been playing solitaire for over half an hour, mindlessly twitching the cards around, losing more games than he won, he shut the computer down and flung himself on the bed.

Sleep eluded him, however, and in the end he went outside and sat staring at the water until long after midnight.

⋆　⋆　⋆

Ella spent a similarly restless night. At two o'clock in the morning, she crept downstairs and wrote a letter to 'Mr O'Neal' asking him to leave her property forthwith and enclosing a cheque for the money he'd paid her in advance. She took it up to bed with her. She'd deliver it in the morning.

Amy peeped into the bedroom at eight o'clock the next morning, smiled to see her mother awake and came in for her usual morning chat.

Ella couldn't turn her daughter away, so tried to listen and respond appropriately, but found it hard to concentrate after so little sleep and with so much on her mind.

'I'm glad I'm going back to school on Monday, Mummy, but I'm sorry I missed Friday. It's our News Day. I could have told everyone about you and Mr O'Neal getting married and — '

'We aren't getting married. It was just pretend.'

Amy looked at her as if she'd suddenly grown two heads. 'But you said you were! You said it to everyone. Were you telling *lies?* You always tell me not to do that.'

'It was to stop your father being a pest. I didn't have time to explain it to you yesterday.'

'But you and Mr O'Neal were cuddling.'

'We were just — acting. Amy, I — '

But her daughter shoved her away and flung out of the room.

Ella lay on the bed, trying desperately to work out what to say to make things better between them.

She must have dozed off because next thing she knew it was nearly nine o'clock.

She crept downstairs with the letter, ready to dart back if Cameron was there. To her relief, there was no sign of him, just Stephanie working in the kitchen. 'I'm sorry. I went back to sleep. Where's Amy?'

'Playing house with Porgy in the barn. I keep nipping across to check on her.'

'Has Cameron had breakfast?'

'Yes. I told him I didn't need his help this morning.'

Ella passed the letter from one hand to the other, then told herself not to be a coward and put it on the kitchen surface. 'I've — um — written to ask him to leave. Would you please deliver this to him for me? I don't want to see him.'

The older woman's gaze was sympathetic but

she made no move to pick up the letter. 'Have you let him explain himself?'

Ella hesitated then shook her head.

'Then I think you're jumping the gun, so I won't deliver the letter. It's not like you to be unfair, my dear girl.'

'But he *deceived* me! He was working for DevRaCom and you know they're the ones pressuring me to sell.'

'I'm not sure you know exactly what he was doing here or what he was doing for DevRaCom. He says he isn't working for them now, and I believe him.'

'Please. I don't want to see him again. I daren't take the risk of — of getting involved. There isn't just me to consider this time, there's Amy.'

'If you two break up like this, Miles will have got what he wanted. He might not want you himself, but he doesn't like to think of anyone else having you. He was like that with his toys, even as a small child.'

'And with his clothes. He'd never give them to the charity shop, kept things I knew he'd never wear again.'

'Miles is rather clever at finding someone's weak spot and using it for his purposes, as you should know by now.' Stephanie crossed the room to put her arms round Ella for a hug. 'Go and see Cameron. At least do him the courtesy of letting him explain. It's only fair.'

Ella bent her head. Fair. Was she being unfair? Was there still hope? 'I'm not thinking clearly, am I?'

'No. But you've not only been ill, you're still under a lot of stress, worried about your home. Cameron will understand, as I do.'

'Will he?'

'Of course he will. He loves you.'

Ella gazed at her. 'How can he? And how can I think of love when everything's in such a tangle that I don't know where I stand? I'm probably going to lose the farm, whether it's heritage listed or not, because I owe Miles so much money that he can take me to court to get it. I can't seem to get past that.'

'If love waited till everything was smooth sailing to strike, I doubt anyone would fall in love. More to the point, how did you feel about Cameron before this cropped up?'

'I was — getting fond of him.'

'I thought so. Go and see him, Ella. Be sure you know the truth before you start making decisions.' She smiled. 'But not like that. I'd suggest a shower and doing something with your hair first.'

'I should listen to his side, shouldn't I?'

Ella went back up the stairs, caught a glimpse of herself in the mirror and exclaimed in horror. Definitely not like this. Her hair was lank, her eyes shadowed and she was wearing a tatty old dressing gown that had seen far better days.

She didn't want Cameron to see her like this. Had she looked as bad the previous day?

Galvanized into action, she hurried into the bathroom.

★ ★ ★

In the kitchen, Stephanie listened till the water started running, then hurried along to the end chalet, where she found Cameron packing his suitcase. 'For goodness' sake, she'll be here in a few minutes. Do you really want her to find you getting ready to run away from your quarrel?'

'You can't quarrel with someone who won't talk to you. I've been waiting for her and she's not come. She's always up early, so what else could I think but that she's not changed her mind, won't trust me.'

'She fell asleep again after Amy popped in to see her, hasn't been up long.'

'Oh.'

'Give things a chance, Cameron.'

'I want to, but she's terrified of getting into a new relationship, thanks to your damned son. And maybe I've been rushing her, maybe I'm fooling myself and she's not fallen for me as I have for her.'

Stephanie rolled her eyes. 'You're both acting like teenagers in love. In my opinion, she does care about you.'

He stared at her. 'You really think she does?'

'Yes. Look, she's coming to see you in a few minutes. Talk to her, tell her exactly what you're doing here and most important of all, how you feel about her.' She glanced at her watch. 'I must get back. I don't want her to know I've been talking to you.' She patted his arm. 'Cheer up. This is love, not war. I'm going back via the barn. I'll make sure Amy doesn't interrupt you.'

When Stephanie had dashed off, he stared down at the suitcase for a few moments, then started pulling things out, shoving them into the drawers anyhow. He zipped up the suitcase again and put it away. Better check that he looked decent. He'd flung on his clothes anyhow this morning.

'She was right. You were running away! I'm ashamed of you,' he told his reflection then brushed his teeth again and combed his hair.

He had known Ella just under two weeks. Could you really fall in love so quickly? How did you know it was the real thing? Love with a capital L. This wasn't a business deal, to be approached with tactics, knowledge and logic, it was, quite simply, the most important thing that had ever happened to him — and the most bewildering.

He began to pace up and down, willing Ella to hurry up, dreading her arrival, more unsure of himself than he'd ever been since he was a teenager. He could tackle a hostile consortium and prove them wrong financially, but tackling one woman, one dear brave woman, had him shivering in his shoes.

What if Stephanie was wrong and Ella didn't love him?

What if Ella didn't believe his explanations?

18

Oliver suddenly realized that since he'd got back with Rose, he'd not had any more nightmares, and that his episodes of feeling trapped and breathless had been fewer and less severe.

'What are you looking so happy about?' his father asked during a break in the Saturday morning surgery.

'Me and Rose.'

'You're together again? When you didn't come home at night, your mother said you'd have made it up with her. We both hope it's for good this time. We're fond of Rose.'

Oliver grinned. 'So am I. I never stopped loving her all the time I was away, Dad. Never. The big problem now is to find a way to keep us both here in Wiltshire because she can't leave. She's still working on that project.'

'You can always work in the practice with me.' He held up one hand to stop Oliver replying. 'Don't say anything now, just keep it in mind. But I'll understand if you want to find something else to do. I can always get another partner or two, you know. I'm not the only doctor on this planet who still believes in personalized medicine.'

'I know. And I'm grateful. I'll let you know about that as soon as I figure out where I'm going.'

'How is the other thing?'

'Much better since I've been back with Rose.' He laughed softly. 'She hasn't changed, not in any way that matters.'

'Good.' His father frowned. 'Still obsessed with that project, is she? I mean, it's been years now. How long is she going to put her life on hold for it?'

'If you'd seen the quality of her work, you'd understand why it's taken so long, and why it's worth it. Anyway, I'm moving in with her permanently. I suppose it's all right if we stay in the flat?'

'Fine by me. I can rent out that old cottage easily enough once it's repaired.'

'Good.'

'Are you going to get married this time?'

'I hope so. I intend to take her away for a romantic weekend in a luxury hotel and discuss that matter rather seriously.'

'Good idea.'

When Oliver had gone back to work, his father picked up the phone and called his wife. 'Mary? You were right. He's moving in permanently with Rose and he's going to ask her to marry him.' He listened to her excited comments and laughed. 'I don't think we'd better mention grandchildren to him yet, my love.'

Then he turned with a sigh to his next patient. He'd known Graham Harding for years, was on various local committees with him. The man's blood pressure was dangerously elevated and nothing would persuade him to change his lifestyle. Still, John always went through the motions each time, repeating his instructions about losing weight and getting some exercise.

When he'd finished saying it all over again and passed over the new prescription, Graham didn't move but sat fiddling with the piece of paper.

'Something else you need to discuss?'

'I'm taking Brett to a rehab place your son recommended. We're going on Monday. I'll see him into it myself.'

'Good. I'm sure it's the right thing to do.'

'It doesn't feel right to lock your only son away. You're lucky with yours. He's always been a high achiever.'

'Yes. I am. And Oliver's back with Rose, permanently, we hope.' John smiled fondly. 'They're going away for a romantic weekend. I'd not be surprised if we don't hear wedding bells soon.'

'Good for them. I'm really glad for you.'

John patted the other man's arm after they'd both stood up. 'If anyone can help your Brett, these people at the rehab place can. You might find he's a changed person when he's off the booze. It does happen.'

'But what if they don't help him?'

John shrugged helplessly. There was no answer to that. Some people couldn't be saved, whatever their loved ones did, and that left emotional scars.

★   ★   ★

Brett listened to his parents chatting over lunch, not paying much attention to what they were saying till he heard the name 'Paige'. He was suddenly on the alert.

'John Paige was telling me Oliver and Rose are going away for a romantic weekend. He thinks they'll be getting married this time round.' Graham looked sourly at his own son. 'Pity *you* didn't find a nice girl and settle down. It might have been the making of you.'

'So you've said — about a million times. I do not want to lumber myself with a wife, children and mortgage, thank you very much.'

'What do you want to do with your life? You know . . . afterwards?' his mother asked cautiously.

Brett tried to think of some soothing reply, but nothing came to him. What did he want? he wondered. Not to work at a damned petrol station. To get away from this dump of a village, maybe. Yes, he wanted that. But what to do with himself in order to achieve that was more than he'd ever been able to figure. He didn't have any particular talents or interests, never had had. What he enjoyed most was hanging out with the lads at the pub, swapping jokes and yarns. The group kept changing, depending on who was getting married or divorced. They all had unskilled jobs. In fact . . . they were all losers like him.

He hated that thought. Anger boiled up inside him. It was all right his father nagging, but the only women Brett could have married were tarts he'd not look twice at if he didn't need sex.

And now, to cap it all, his own father was locking him away, blackmailing him into going.

Well, they'd not find him an easy patient in that place.

He was suddenly unable to stand it for a

moment longer. 'I think I'll go out for a walk.'

'Where?' his father barked at once.

'Just — out. Walking. Unless you intend to lock me in my room all weekend?' He saw his mother lay her hand on his father's arm and shake her head. Even these two oldies had one another, he thought, with another surge of bile.

He left the house straight away, not daring to hunt for a coat in case his father changed his mind. It was warm enough, had been quite a good start to May, and if it came on to rain, who cared?

It was while he was standing near the War Memorial on the small mound in the centre of the park that what his father had said suddenly sank in. Oliver Paige was taking Rose away for the weekend.

The flat would be unoccupied.

It was a perfect time to get back at the bitch. See how she liked having her things taken away from her, as his life was about to be taken away from him.

Only he'd have to do it very carefully, wait longer this time and not go out tonight till his parents were both deeply asleep. And he'd have to call in a few favours as well to borrow a car and set up a good alibi. No, he'd not set up an alibi. That'd look suspicious. He'd just say he'd been asleep in his own bed if anyone asked.

He'd visit Willowbrook tonight as well. He smiled. Easy to know what would upset the Turner bitch.

* * *

314

Ella walked slowly down to Cameron's chalet, her stomach churning with apprehension. He was waiting for her outside, his expression solemn. He looked like a polite stranger, not his normal self. She nearly turned and ran back to the house, then stiffened her spine. What? Had she turned into a jelly or something? She had always prided herself on facing up to life and dealing with it.

'We need to talk.' She was pleased her voice didn't wobble, though she felt very short of air.

He moved forward. 'We do indeed.'

As he took her hand, she felt sure all the oxygen had been sucked from the room and she couldn't stop her fingers quivering in his. She tried to pull away from him, but he wouldn't let go.

'Please let me finish what I was trying to tell you last night, Ella. I came to Willowbrook to do a quick check on whether the place was really old, or a fake. That's all. I was asked to come by Ray Deare, CEO of DevRaCom, who had been told it was a nineteenth-century fake. I emailed him that in my opinion parts of the farm were genuinely several centuries old. I then said that as far as I was concerned, that ended our business connection, just as I've ended things with all my old clients over the past few months.'

'You let me think you were from the bank.'

'I know. And I apologize for that.' He hesitated and his voice faltered. 'You see, I'm not used to falling in love, and — well, I fell rather heavily for you, and it happened so quickly it threw me off balance.'

As she waited for him to go on, a tiny seed of hope began to blossom inside her. If he'd spoken glibly, she'd have been far less inclined to believe him, but he kept fumbling for words, gesticulating, running his free right hand through his hair — while all the time he held on tight to her hand.

'I knew Ray was keen to buy Willowbrook and I didn't want you to think I was supporting him on that. I've made a mess of it, I know, but can't we get past that somehow? I'm not trying to help anyone cheat you out of your family home. I'd never, ever take on an assignment to do that, whether I knew the person or not. Someone else has been feeding him false information.'

He paused, watching her reaction so anxiously she didn't know what to say.

Miles, she thought. It must have been him, not Cameron.

She was as uncertain about what to do next as he'd said he was. Did she dare trust him? Could they move forward?

Then suddenly it came to her that her daughter and her dog had both trusted him instinctively. Porgy went to lean against him and be stroked. Amy chatted away to him, her face alight — and he listened to her, didn't treat her any differently from other children. Surely that meant something?

But there was one other thing to clear up, something else that her untrustworthy ex had told her. 'What were you doing in London when Miles saw you at DevRaCom a few days ago?'

'Tying up some loose ends in town, saying a

few goodbyes, and answering an urgent message from Ray to go and see him. He helped me a lot when I was starting up, is a friend of my father's, and I owe him, so I went. He didn't believe I really was changing track, you see, wanted me to undertake a rather prestigious project for him in the Middle East. I went to see him face to face because I thought he deserved that much from me. I turned his offer down, though.'

'Why?'

'I'm not burnt out, but I will be if I go on as I have been doing. Or else I'll grow insensitive, like others I've seen.' He looked down at their linked hands. 'I think you and I have both been working far too hard, trying to fit too much into our lives.'

She nodded. That was the simple truth. 'I didn't have much choice. I was sure determination would carry me through, that I'd manage to save my home. But life doesn't offer many miracles, does it?'

'I think me coming here, us meeting, is as near a miracle as you can expect. But . . . there's something else I need to tell you.'

She looked at him anxiously.

'I found out that if Ray gets hold of this place, he intends to make a bigger lake, and that'll mean drowning the house. Which is why he particularly doesn't want it to be heritage listed.'

She stared at him in horror. 'How did you find that out?'

'From one of those two men who came to get photos of the place. I'd met Smith before at DevRaCom so he thought I was on their side and talked to me.'

She couldn't move for a moment and when she spoke, her voice came out as little more than a whisper. 'Would Deare really do that?'

'If he thought he could get away with it, yes. He uses heritage properties when it suits him, but only when it's good for business to flaunt his restoration work. I'd guess he's overstretched himself lately and needs this project to go ahead for all sorts of reasons, the main one being business confidence. But he's also a very stubborn man, and if he's set his heart on something, he prides himself on getting it. Don't underestimate him. And don't trust him. Your ex is involved in setting up the Willowbrook project, as you know. Parnell will have a big stake in the sale going through, probably a permanent job with DevRaCom. Ray always rewards people who deliver.'

She drew a long, shaky breath. 'I feel like an ant facing a giant.' Then she gave him a long, slow look, and without any other reason being offered, she knew he'd told her the truth. He wasn't working for her enemy. He did love her . . . and she loved him. 'I'm sorry I flew off the handle last night.'

'Your emotions are bound to be up and down. You've been near to a breakdown, Ella, and . . . '

For answer she raised their linked hands to her lips and kissed his fingers. Her voice stronger and more certain, she added, 'I do believe you and I intend not only to get better but to save my home.'

With a groan of relief he pulled her into his arms and they stood holding one another, smiling slightly, not saying anything at first. Then they moved into an embrace, not rushing, taking their time, enjoying the kiss, the closeness, the sense that something was very right between them.

It was he who pulled back after a while, because this was not the time to make love to her. When that happened, he wanted to be sure there would be no interruptions, and that their surroundings were rather more romantic. 'If you'll let me, I'll work with you to save Willowbrook.'

'It's a lot to ask.'

'You didn't ask. I volunteered.'

Her smile was glorious. 'I never thought I'd meet someone who could say that. Thank you. I'd be grateful for your help.'

'And can I move back into the house?'

She smiled again. 'Don't you like my chalets?'

'They're very comfortable, you thought of so many details other places leave out, but . . . it didn't feel right leaving the house. I've not only fallen in love with a woman, but with her daughter, her house — ' he paused and grinned ' — and even her dog. I didn't realize I was searching for a home when I decided to change my life, but I was.'

'It's the most wonderful home anyone could have and I'm happy to share it with you. Now, let's go back now and tell Stephanie and Amy that we've sorted things out between us.'

'She's a wise woman, Stephanie. She told me to hang in there last night or I might have fled. Strange that she's working against her own son.'

319

'You'd have to know Miles to understand, and know his father too. They're very alike. It must be so sad for her to be working against her own child.'

'She's got you and Amy, though. She's a great grandmother.'

'Talking of Amy, I told her we'd only been pretending to be in love. She was so upset.'

'We'd better go back and tell her it was a misunderstanding and that we're never going to quarrel again. She'll understand, I'm sure.'

'Do you really think we'll never quarrel?'

'Sadly, no. You're no doormat and I'm used to having my own way. We're bound to disagree sometimes, but let's promise never to let the sun go down on a quarrel.'

'My parents used to have that rule. It's old-fashioned but — '

'It's a good one.'

*   *   *

They heard a sound in the barn, so turned towards it. Smiling, they stood in the doorway and watched Amy talking earnestly to someone or something, waving her magic wand, then closing her eyes as if making a wish.

'She's at a fanciful age,' Ella murmured.

'She's delightful.'

At the sound of their voices, Amy turned round. She said nothing, but she missed no detail of how they were standing, her eyes going to their enlaced hands then back to their smiling faces.

'We've made up our quarrel,' Ella said. 'So we came to tell you first of all.'

'Does that mean Mr O'Neal is going to be my new daddy?'

Ella gulped. This was diving right into the deep end.

Cameron didn't flinch, just said gravely, 'I hope so. But these things take time. Your mother and I have to get used to one another, see how we go on living together, see how you like having me around before we can get married.'

'I already like you being here,' Amy said. 'And so does the lady. She comes here to see me sometimes. She watched me making a wish today and she smiled, so I knew it'd come true.'

'What was your wish? Or should I not ask?'

'It's all right to tell once the wish has come true. I wanted you to live here with me and Mummy . . . and for my old daddy to go away.'

Ella gave his hand a quick squeeze. 'We'd better go and tell Stephanie now.'

'I'll come with you.' Amy picked up her teddy and wand, going confidently to take hold of Cameron's other hand.

He looked down and felt a lump in his throat. He knew she wasn't an angel, that she'd be naughty and troublesome at times like all children, but dammit, he liked her and enjoyed her company. Miles was a fool.

As they began walking towards the house, Stephanie came to the door, her face grave, and beckoned to them to hurry. 'Ray Deare's secretary is on the phone. He wants to speak to you, Ella.'

The rosy glow faded abruptly from the day as she hurried into the house and picked up the phone. 'Ella Turner here.'

A woman's voice answered, cool and impersonal. 'One moment, please. Mr Deare is waiting to speak to you.'

'Hello, Ms Turner. Ray Deare here, CEO of DevRaCom.'

'I know who you are. What can I do for you?'

'I wondered if we could meet face to face and discuss your property.'

'I don't think there's anything to discuss, Mr Deare. Willowbrook is my home and I have no intention whatsoever of selling it, to you or to anyone else.'

'You don't waste time on small talk, do you?'

'No.'

'Could we still meet?'

Cameron was signalling to her, so she said, 'One moment please.' She covered the phone. 'He wants to meet me.'

'Get him to come here,' he whispered. 'Let's show him the house he's trying to destroy.'

She nodded then uncovered the phone and held it between herself and Cameron as she spoke, so that he could hear everything. 'I don't see any point in us meeting, because I'm not going to change my mind. But if you wish, you can come to Willowbrook.'

'I was thinking of sending a limo to fetch you up to London. I'm a busy man.'

'Not possible. I'm a busy woman, with a daughter and business to care for, and no subordinates to take over.'

'Just a minute.' The phone went dead apart from a faint beeping sound, then there was a click and Ray said, 'Very well. It's about time I looked at this place of yours for myself. How about I come down tomorrow?'

'Weekends are my busy time. We have guests in the chalets.' She winked at Cameron and waited.

'Monday, then.'

'Very well. But you won't change my mind about selling.'

'Perhaps you can give my secretary directions.'

'Mr O'Neal will do that better than I could.' She handed him the phone.

'Hello, Miss Bradley. This is how you get here . . . '

When he put the handpiece down, Ella let out her breath in a whoosh of relief.

'You did well,' Cameron said. 'It's not everyone who can make Ray come to them.'

'I don't want to see him at all.'

'I think it'll be good for him to see what he's trying to destroy. This place is very impressive, you know.'

'Will that do me any good?'

'I don't know. He does seem unusually keen to get this project up and running. Strange, really. He used to be quite interested in antiques and history. Or his first wife was. I don't know about this wife. It's worth a try, anyway.' He studied her face. 'Time for you to rest now, I think. You're looking tired again.'

She smiled at him. 'Yes. But I'm feeling much better today — and much happier.'

'So am I.' It was a moment before either of them moved, then they went to find Stephanie, who was looking after Amy, to thank her for her part in bringing them together.

Afterwards Ella went upstairs and Cameron was despatched to the shops for more supplies of fresh fruit and vegetables, since another family had booked in.

★　★　★

When Ray put the phone down, Miss Bradley came into his office and closed the door. 'I think I should go with you on Monday.'

He looked at her in amazement. 'You don't usually get involved in DevRaCom's projects.'

'I've heard so much about Willowbrook that I'd like to see it for myself.'

He looked at her suspiciously. 'What are you up to, Sonia?'

'Keeping my eye on you.'

'Well, keep your eye on the main game as well. You know how badly we need that project to go ahead so that we can demonstrate that the company is still in expansion mode. And we don't want the project to cost us a small fortune, either.'

She gave him one of her bland smiles. 'I'll arrange for a limo to pick us up on Monday and then I'll cancel your appointments for the day. Eight o'clock suit you?'

He shrugged. 'It's a waste of time your coming, but I'll be ready.'

'Will Mrs Deare be joining us?'

'Why not invite the whole management team and make a party of it? No, Petra damned well won't be coming. Why should she? She's never even tried to get involved in the business side of my life because she knows I'd not stand for it.'

'You seem to have been going out without her quite a lot lately. You're not exactly the world's most faithful spouse.'

He gaped at her. 'My private life is none of your business.'

'Just curious. I do field some personal calls. I've been with you a long time.'

His expression softened. 'Best executive secretary a man could have.'

'I won't go on working for you if you do anything dishonest to get hold of Willowbrook, though.' She turned and left the office before he could reply.

It was a full minute before he realized he was still gaping open-mouthed at a closed door, a further minute before he went back to sit at his desk.

He didn't take her words lightly. She never made threats she wasn't prepared to carry out.

But hell, a man couldn't run his business to suit his secretary. You could always get another secretary . . . though perhaps not one of Sonia's calibre. He thumped his clenched fist down on his desk. She knew his ways, dammit, could think on her feet, didn't need telling what to do half the time. He *needed* her.

He couldn't dismiss what she'd said, either. She had a way of making an observation every now and then that cut to the quick. And when he'd disregarded her rarely offered advice, he'd invariably regretted it.

He thumped his desk again to vent his annoyance but it did no good, so he flipped open his appointments diary. Meetings for the rest of the morning, even though it was Saturday, and there was no one on the list he really wanted to see. Suddenly he couldn't bear the thought of it. What was the point of being CEO if you couldn't do something for yourself occasionally? He pressed the intercom. 'Cancel my meetings for the rest of the day, Sonia. I'm going to the golf club.'

'Certainly, Mr Deare. I'll see you on Monday.'

He didn't look at her as he walked out, but could feel her eyes following him. Her words followed him, too.

I won't go on working for you if you do anything dishonest.

What he was doing wasn't against the law. Not exactly. Hell, a man had to fight to stay on top, didn't he?

19

Miles spent the whole of Saturday, well into the long May evening, searching for other options to save his credibility and the future he desperately wanted with DevRaCom. By the time he got back to the hotel, he was exhausted and had found nothing. Since he needed to be careful with his money and had seen the prices they charged for meals at the hotel, he went next door to the pub and bought a substantial meal at a quarter of the price.

Then he went to sit in the bar, where he got chatting to a group of guys who were throwing back the booze like it was water. You could pick up a lot of information from locals so he lingered, eking out his drink but still imbibing more than usual. It didn't matter. He'd not see these guys again.

One of them knew the best jokes Miles had heard for years. Even as he laughed loudly, he mentally noted down the joke for future use. He'd definitely not heard that one before or the next few the guy told. This encounter would pay off at business meals.

As closing time drew near, the others started planning how to pick up a friend who was being given a hard time by his father.

Miles didn't pay much attention till a name he knew cropped up, then he set down his glass and fiddled with some spilled booze, listening carefully.

They didn't think he knew the district, so were only partly guarded about what they were saying.

After he left them, he walked back to his room smiling. He wasn't going to do a thing to stop them. Why should he?

★ ★ ★

The following morning Miles woke up with a start when his alarm rang, grimacing as his head began thumping with a hangover. He swallowed two painkillers and waited for the pounding to subside a little before picking up his mobile. He was definitely not interested in breakfast.

'Ah good, it's you, Ella. Look, I'm still in the area, had another job to do, so I could come and see Amy this morning before I go back to town.'

Her voice was chill. 'It's too soon to come at all, Miles. You need to give her more time between visits.'

'It's not too soon for me.'

'Come this afternoon, then. Morning really isn't convenient.'

'All right.' He had an inspiration. 'Look, I know you don't like me taking her away from Willowbrook, but how about I take her and Mum out for a drive? That way, you won't have to worry about her and we'll have something more interesting to do than sit and stare at one another.'

The silence went on for too long, but he waited her out.

'Just a minute,' she said at last. 'I'll ask Stephanie.'

He could hear the murmur of voices, Amy's shrill yelp of protest and his mother's deeper tones.

In the end his mother came on. 'Miles, how about we do it next weekend?'

'I have a right to see my daughter and I want to see her today, before I go back to town. Are you going to help me or not?'

She sighed. 'Could you leave it till Sunday then? We're frantically busy here today because all the chalets are booked, so I'm needed. I definitely can't come out with you this afternoon.'

He scowled at the faded hotel wallpaper. Stay in Wiltshire for another day? Then he shrugged and decided to go with the flow. Maybe fate was giving him a nudge. The extra day would give him time to pursue the final lead from yesterday, the one the guy he was dealing with had reckoned wasn't likely to come to much. 'All right. Sunday it is.'

'Very well. Amy and I will come out with you for an hour or so. But no longer than that. Ella will still need my help.'

'I'll pick you both up at about eleven thirty on Sunday morning. We'll have lunch somewhere then return.' He disconnected before she could argue, then phoned the real estate guy.

★ ★ ★

Rose set off with Oliver on the Saturday afternoon for an unspecified destination. All he'd told her about their trip was to pack an overnight bag and something smart to wear for dinner.

'I don't like letting the pub down,' she

grumbled as she got into the car.

'I have something very important to tell you.'

'You could have told me here.'

'No. This is special. We need to get away from here to do it properly.'

'Oh, very well.' But it wasn't well. She'd lain awake next to him worrying last night about what she was getting into. She'd been alone for three years, had lost the habit of being a couple. And now she was getting used to Oliver again, the man whose body and thoughts had once been almost as familiar to her as her own. He had something important to tell her. What?

That he was going away again?

What else could it be? Would he try to persuade her to go with him? Was that what this weekend was for? 'Where are we going?'

'It's a surprise. Wait till we get there.'

'I don't like surprises.'

He gave her one of his warm smiles and she nearly went into melt-down inside. How was she to cope when he went away this time?

'You'll like this surprise, Rose.'

She gave up protesting, leaned her head back and let him drive, allowing her thoughts to wander. He didn't interrupt. They'd always been able to enjoy silences as well as conversations.

When he pulled through an impressive gateway which had a name that was a household word for luxury discreetly carved into the stonework, she leaned forward in shock. 'Oliver! I've read about this place. It costs a fortune to stay here!'

'You're worth a fortune — or rather, our relationship is.'

She said nothing as they signed in at reception then went up in a lift filled with mirrors, soft music and even real flowers in a small vase on the wall. The mirrors showed her a woman in clothes that weren't nearly elegant enough for this hotel — and a man who was watching her with a faintly anxious smile. Why? What did he have to tell her?

When they were shown into a suite, not just a room, she couldn't hide her dismay. 'This is costing far too much!'

'Humour me. Just this once. Come and look at the view and stop counting the pennies.'

'It's the pounds I'm counting,' she muttered but went with him to the big picture window to stare out across a stunning landscape that had her itching for her camera. It was undulating countryside, not grand but infinitely beautiful in a soft, English way, with delicate spring foliage and darker evergreens delineating the patchwork pattern of fields and copses. Closer to hand were flower beds, set with a blaze of colour that looked magnificent against the creamy Cotswold stone of the hotel and outbuildings.

'They say the gardens here are rather special. We can go out and explore them later.'

'I'd like that.'

He left her side and she swung round in time to see him locking the door of the suite.

'Alone at last, my proud beauty!' he mocked.

She clasped one hand to her bosom. 'No, no, my lord! You shall not have your wicked way with me!'

'Shall I not?'

And heaven help her, she ran across the room and fell into his arms. It was love they shared, not lust, every touch, every kiss an offering. Passion rose slowly but surely in them both but they didn't hurry. If she was to have only this, then she'd seize the moment with both hands, because he was Oliver, her Oliver, the only man she'd ever loved.

As she lay in his arms afterwards, she realized her face was wet with the joy of their lovemaking.

He kissed her tears and she saw that his eyes were overbright, too. 'I could stay in bed with you all day and all night, Rosie mine, but I have a few things planned, so I'm afraid we'll have to get up now or it'll all be wasted! We'll start with a spa, then we'll wine and dine in a restaurant that is world famous.'

'I've not got the clothes for a restaurant like that.'

'I know. But I picked something out for you.' He laid one hand across her lips to prevent a protest. 'Let me spoil you, Rose, spoil and love and cherish you all weekend long.'

After the spa he led her into the bedroom and opened the wardrobe on his side. 'I sent this on in advance, so that they could press it.'

The dress was deceptively simple, a deep, subtle shade that was neither maroon, nor purple, with a soft, layered skirt that had threads which shimmered. The skirt whispered around her as she moved and a close-fitting top showed off her figure to perfection.

She couldn't protest when she saw the elegant

woman in the mirror. Just this once, she wanted to be truly beautiful for him, to give him memories he would never lose. 'I couldn't have chosen better myself.'

He fastened something round her neck and she stared down at a locket.

'It was my grandmother's. Mum sent it. She thinks you should have it now.'

'I — don't know what to say.' Was this a farewell present? But why give her his grandmother's locket? It didn't make sense.

'Don't say anything. Just go with the flow.'

He'd brought an evening suit for himself, the severe elegance of it making him look like a celebrity at a film premiere. She'd forgotten how well he scrubbed up, but he never could get his ties straight, so she went to adjust this one. 'I've never seen you look quite like that! So formal.'

'I had to attend a lot of official functions at my last job.' He kissed her cheek. 'You're even more beautiful than I'd expected, Rose. Now, let's go down. We don't want to be late.'

Their table was in a secluded corner. The menu had her mouth watering. But when the food came, she had trouble swallowing it.

'Oliver, this is like a stage production,' she whispered. 'I can't stand the suspense any longer. Please tell me why we're here. If you're going to your next job soon, just tell me. You brought me here to try to persuade me to leave Wiltshire with you, didn't you?'

He looked at her in surprise. 'I've already promised that I won't tear you away from your project.'

'Yes, but what about *your* needs, *your* job? How can you possibly stay?'

'I have a solution of sorts. It depends on you.' He took her hand. 'Darling Rose, will you marry me?'

She gasped, had been preparing herself mentally for a farewell. Emotion blocked her throat and she couldn't force words out, could only blink at him in mute shock.

'May I not have an answer?'

There was only one answer possible. She knew it now. She couldn't give him up, just . . . couldn't. 'Yes. Yes, I will marry you, Oliver.'

His lips curved slowly until the smile lit up his whole face. 'I've not bought you a ring, because I thought you'd want to choose one with me. An antique, perhaps? I can't see you wearing a stark modern diamond. But your answer makes me happier than I can ever remember. Rose darling, I will love you and cherish you all the days of my life.'

'And I you. Oh, Oliver, is this really happening?'

'Yes. And this time we'll not let anything stop us.' Or anyone, he thought grimly. He still had a bone to pick with Miles Parnell about that letter.

'But your job?'

He put one finger on her lips. 'We'll work that out together, but I won't take you away from your Wiltshire project, I promise. Trust me.'

And she did.

* * *

In the middle of the night Cameron was woken by the smell of burning. He came instantly alert, sniffing, jerking upright in bed, then getting up and running across to the window.

Faint orange light was flickering in the barn, he could see it through the high dusty windows. Shouting at the top of his voice, 'The barn's on fire!' he thrust his feet into his shoes and ran down the stairs in his pyjamas, dragging on his dressing gown as he went.

Voices called out behind him and he yelled again, 'The barn's on fire! Come quickly!'

He grabbed the fire extinguisher and barn key from near the kitchen door and rushed out into the darkness, feet crunching on the uneven surface of the yard. The big double barn doors wouldn't open. He tugged frantically, but couldn't get them to move. What had happened to them? How could a fire have possibly started in an empty barn?

Ella shoved him aside and tried the doors, but though the key turned easily, no tugging and heaving would budge the doors.

And all the time, light was flickering inside the barn, showing through the windows above their heads.

Cameron tried again, but it was impossible to move the doors. Then he had an idea. 'Can we get into the barn through the secret passage?'

'Yes. This way.' She tugged his arm and he followed her, only then realizing she too was carrying a fire extinguisher.

'Keep Amy away from the barn, Stephanie!' she yelled over her shoulder.

It seemed to take a long time to get the secret passage open from the outside. Every second he was expecting the barn to explode into a major conflagration. He had to let Ella lead the way along the tunnel, but he worried all the way about how rashly she would act at the other end.

As she disappeared into the darkness of the tunnel, he followed her blindly, trusting to her knowledge of these ancient ways to keep them safe.

'Stop a minute!' she called, but he bumped into her before he could do that. He stood close to her in the darkness, hearing her fumbling for something.

Suddenly a light came on and she shone the torch that was kept in the tunnel on the panel, pressing and pushing the old wood and waiting for the door into the hidey hole to move slowly aside.

The smell of smoke was stronger here, but not overpowering, which he didn't understand. If the barn was alight, they should be having trouble breathing by now, surely?

As the next door that led into the barn began to open slowly, he tensed, ready to drag Ella back down the passage if she appeared to be in any danger. On that thought, he grabbed her arm, just in case she behaved rashly. 'Don't move out until we're sure it's safe!'

'I'm not stupid. Hold your extinguisher at the ready.'

There was a fire in one corner of the barn near the doors, a fire which smelled acrid and made them both cough. But it wasn't burning out of control, rather it seemed contained. How could that be?

The fire gave enough light for them to assess the situation, which was like a scene from a nightmare, all flickering light against shifting darkness, with dark smoke gathering and heaving about above them.

'The fire is only burning in that corner,' he muttered. 'Let me go first.'

He didn't wait for her agreement, but led the way across the barn. Suddenly something shimmered in front of him. Thinking it was another fire starting, he stopped, extinguisher at the ready. But it wasn't a fire; it looked more like an electronic barrier.

'It's the lady,' Ella breathed next to him. 'She's blocking the way. Can't you see her arms spread out? Don't move forward.'

He couldn't believe this was happening, could only see a shimmering mass, not a figure. But that was enough to stop him in his tracks.

'She's gesturing to move to the left.'

'I don't believe this,' he muttered, but did as Ella said nonetheless.

The patch of faint silvery light, totally different from the smouldering oranges and yellows of the fire, stayed where it was as they moved round it.

He pulled himself together and concentrated on the matter at hand. 'Aim your extinguisher to the right. I'll do the left.'

She was pointing her nozzle even as he finished speaking and the two of them soon had the blaze under control.

He sniffed. 'Can you smell that?'

'Yes. A strong smell of paraffin. Oh, Cameron, surely this hasn't been done on purpose!'

He hated even putting it into words, it was such a horrifying thought. 'I think it may be arson. Best not to touch anything. Let's see if we can open the doors from inside.'

To their amazement, there was no difficulty whatsoever in opening them now. 'Why the hell couldn't I get them to budge before?' he wondered aloud. 'Mind you, it's lucky they stuck. We'd probably have fanned the flames if we'd opened them, the fire was so close to this end of the barn. As it was, we had time to put it out before opening up.'

They stood breathing deeply in the fresher air just outside the door, wiping their watering eyes and keeping an eye on the spot which had been burning in case flames flared up again.

Stephanie's voice cut through the darkness of the yard. 'Is the fire out?'

'Yes. But you'd better call the fire brigade anyway,' Ella said. 'And no one should go back inside the barn till they come. Cameron and I could both smell paraffin.'

'Arson?'

'Looks like it.'

A figure appeared out of the darkness on the other side of the yard, one of the guests. 'What's happened?'

'There's been a fire in the barn,' Cameron said. 'Not a major one and it's out now. We have fire extinguishers in place everywhere, as you may have noticed in your chalet, so we put it out quite quickly. However, we've called the fire brigade just to make sure there aren't likely to be any more problems.'

'Oh.' He stood for a minute or two in the light streaming from the kitchen windows and door staring at the barn. 'Smells awful, doesn't it?'

'Yes. I hope it's not too bad in the chalets.'

He grinned, teeth showing lighter against the barely distinguishable features of his face. 'My wife wouldn't notice. She sleeps like the proverbial log.' He yawned. 'I'll get back to bed now, then, if there's nothing I can do to help.'

They heard him talking to someone back along the path, presumably another guest coming to investigate.

'Your fire precautions certainly paid off,' Cameron said.

'I care too much about the place to take risks. I don't economize on things like safety.'

Amy came to stand beside her mother. 'It's not going to start burning again, is it?'

'No, but just in case, if I tell you to run back to the house, you're to do so at once,' Ella said.

She sounded like her old self, Cameron thought, crisp and decisive.

'I promise, Mummy. What's arson?'

'When somebody sets a fire deliberately.'

'That's terrible. Oh! My dressing up clothes will all be burned. And my wand.'

'We can get you some more clothes, darling. And another wand. Was Teddy in the barn?'

'No. He was safe in bed with me.'

'Then things aren't too bad.' She hugged the child close, standing shivering as the sky slowly turned grey, knowing Amy needed reassurance, gaining reassurance herself from the child's warm body. This was what mattered. The barn and farm counted for so little against the life of her daughter.

After a while she sent Amy inside to Stephanie, but couldn't bear to move too far away from the barn herself, felt she had to keep an eye on it. She watched Cameron pacing up and down the yard, frowning sometimes as he stopped to peer into the barn to check that the fire hadn't started up again.

Why would someone set light to the barn deliberately, Ella wondered? Why the barn and not the house? Who could have done it?

Miles? No, she couldn't imagine *him* risking prison.

DevRaCom? Now that was something she could imagine much more easily. The company had a lot of money at stake. But even so, they had enough money to get an arson job done properly, not botched up. This seemed more like the work of amateurs when even she could smell the paraffin.

Who else was there who stood to gain by her barn being destroyed? She couldn't think of anyone.

⋆ ⋆ ⋆

It seemed a long time till the fire engine arrived. When it stopped, they explained to the man in charge that they suspected arson, after which none of the firefighters went inside.

The chief firefighter checked everything then

came to speak to her. 'It's obvious the fire is out, Ella. Good thing we set you up with the right extinguishers, eh?'

'Yes. Thanks for coming out so quickly, Jim.'

'We'll stay here to make sure everything's safe, but it'll be light soon, so as long as there isn't a flare up, we'll wait before we go inside. We don't want to destroy any evidence. You're quite sure you smelled paraffin?'

'Absolutely certain. We both did.'

'Then I'll call in our arson investigators. You know, you might as well go back into the house as stand out here and shiver.'

'All right.' But before they opened the farm door, Ella grabbed hold of Cameron to stop him and asked in a low voice, 'Would DevRaCom do something like this?'

'I doubt it. They're not perfect, and they don't mind trampling on a few toes, but they don't go in for criminal activity, as far as I know. What about your ex? He's still in the neighbourhood, isn't he? Could he have done it?'

'I don't think so. It doesn't seem at all the sort of thing he'd do. Miles uses words and tricks to get what he wants, and I doubt he'd ever risk prison. I may be wrong. He may be desperate enough, but . . . ' Her voice trailed away and she shook her head. 'No, I just can't believe it of him.'

At the door she turned to stare at the figures of the firefighters, dark outlines under a sky that was getting lighter by the minute. 'I hope they catch whoever did it and lock him away for a good long time. First someone broke in and trashed my house, now this. Why me? Why Willowbrook?'

'I don't know, but I intend to find out.'

'We shall find out.'

He smiled. She was definitely getting better.

20

Rose woke early but Oliver was already awake, lying smiling at her.

'How soon can we get married?' he asked.

'As soon as your future is settled.'

'O ye of little faith!' He pulled her closer, scattering kisses on her hair and forehead indiscriminately. 'I have an interview for a part-time lecturing job at Bristol University. If I get it, things will be perfect. The rest of the time, I'll work in the practice with Dad.'

'But that's taking you right out of A and E work.' She felt him go tense.

'I don't think I want to go back.'

She knew then there was more to it than the brief outline he'd given her of the incident. 'Tell me the full story, Oliver, every last detail of what happened to you.'

She listened in growing horror as she heard how he'd been taken prisoner by a man high on a cocktail of drugs, and locked in a chiller cabinet too small for a man his height. Of how he'd been trapped there for many hours before the negotiator had managed to talk his captor down. He'd recovered from the hypothermia but the psychological damage had been much more serious.

'I think I'll go mad if I'm ever shut into such a cramped space again. Even small rooms like the consulting room at the surgery can be troublesome. I don't like cities, either, have to steel myself to enter them. They tell me it'll improve, but at the moment, Chawton and the Wiltshire countryside suit me down to the ground. I feel I can breathe here.'

'Oh, Oliver.'

'The nightmares don't come when I'm with you,' he finished. 'I'm getting good sleep for the first time in months.'

She lay quietly, body against body, one hand laced in his.

'I've never told anyone the full details without breaking down before,' he confessed.

'I feel honoured. But Oliver, you worked so hard. That man's destroyed your future.'

'Only partly. I'll still be lecturing in A and E organization and methodology. And I'll still be in medicine. And actually, general practice is more interesting than I'd thought, so I'll get myself properly qualified in that.'

'Will that be enough?'

'I don't know. If it isn't, we'll work something else out. I've been forced to move on, so I'll make a new life with you, here. In that sense, that man did me a favour because he sent me back to you.'

'*Worry about things you can change and accept those you can't with good heart*,' she said softly.

He chuckled. 'My psychiatrist says the same thing — but in much fancier words and he charges me a fortune to say it.'

As they drove back to Chawton after a leisurely buffet breakfast, they were both quiet again, but it was the silence of happiness, of two people in tune with one another.

Oliver braked abruptly as the surgery came in sight. They couldn't drive behind it to park, because there were crime scene tapes outside it and across the side entrance. A police car was parked there and an officer was on guard duty.

'What the hell's happened?'

As they got out of the car and hurried towards the surgery, the officer came towards them. 'Do you have business here, sir?'

'I live here, above the surgery,' Rose said. 'What's happened?'

'I'm afraid there's been a break-in.'

She felt the world spin around her and terror choke her throat. 'My trunk!'

          ★   ★   ★

By mid-morning, it was clear that the fire in the barn had been deliberately lit. Expert investigators came in and moved carefully through the building, sifting the ash, sniffing. They too could smell paraffin.

'We don't need the sniffer dogs this time,' the officer in charge told Ella. 'It's rather an amateur crime.'

'Are there any clues as to who may have done it?'

He pointed to the ground. 'There are footprints in the dust. Good thing you didn't tread on them. They're fragile things, easily wiped out. But we've got photographs of them now. Good thing you couldn't open the outside

345

doors, too, or you'd have fanned the blaze.'

Ella looked at Cameron. 'That's where the Lady stopped us walking.'

He was shaking his head, muttering, 'I don't believe this. I don't.'

'I do.' She looked round the barn. 'How much damage is there, do you think?'

It was the arson officer who answered. 'Surprisingly little. You've been lucky, caught it in time.' He pointed up. 'There's smoke blackening round that area, of course, but not much actual damage, as far as I can see. The blaze was contained in this area, probably for lack of fuel. Fires are chancy things. Seem to have a will of their own sometimes.'

'That's the more modern part of the barn, the part which matters least. It's being heritage listed at the moment, because those parts — ' she pointed to them ' — are medieval.'

He whistled. 'You don't say! Got any idea of who might have done it?'

'No.'

'We'll bring the police in, then.'

'Would you like a cup of coffee?'

'Perhaps later? I've got things to do.'

He got into his vehicle and they saw him make a phone call then sit writing busily on some papers on a clipboard.

As Cameron and Ella walked back to the house, she said quietly, 'Is it possible the Lady was watching over us, preserving those foot-prints?'

'Until I came here, I'd have laughed at the mere idea. I didn't even believe in ghosts. Now

'. . . I don't know what I believe. Only, I did see something in the barn last night, we both did. And I can't explain what it was. It didn't look like a woman to me, just a shimmer of light.'

Ella gave a rueful smile. 'I didn't think it worth mentioning our ghost to the arson investigator. He'd have thought I was crazy.' She reached out to open the house door, then stopped, giving Cameron a brilliant smile, looking fully alive again. He felt himself relaxing. Whatever had made her ill seemed to be passing.

'I think you're meant to be here, to stay, to be part of our family, Cameron.'

'I hope so.' He kissed her quickly on the cheek and followed her inside. If that meant living with ghosts, then that's what he'd do.

But who had set the barn on fire? He didn't want to live with the fear of a recurrence.

If it wasn't DevRaCom or Miles, the only person he could think of from his limited acquaintance with Ella was Brett Harding. Why would that fellow suddenly come back here? From what he'd heard, Brett was off to rehab on Monday. And anyway, with court cases pending against him, he'd surely not risk committing another offence? No one could be that stupid.

★　★　★

Miles drove up the track to the farm, braking at the sight of the fire investigator's marked vehicle. So those guys he'd had drinks with last night hadn't just been boasting. Someone really had tried to play a nasty trick on Ella.

A quick glance round showed the house intact, and the activity focused on the barn. Pity. He'd have been in a much better position if the house had burned down.

He got out of the car and walked towards the kitchen, knocking on the door. No one seemed to have noticed his arrival, so he knocked again and entered.

His mother turned round from where she was clearing up. 'Miles! I'd forgotten you were coming.'

'You always were a loving mother. What's been going on here?'

'We had a fire in the barn — deliberately lit, they think.'

'Did it do much damage?'

'No.'

'What a pity!'

She glared at him.

He spread his arms wide. 'I'm not going to lie and say I care about this dump.'

'No. You only lie when it suits you. Well, thanks to the fire, we're a bit behind, so I'm not ready yet to go out with you and neither is Amy.'

'I can wait. How about a coffee? The freebie stuff in my hotel tasted like dishwater.'

'I'll put the percolator on.'

Footsteps on the stairs made him turn to see Cameron come into the room.

Miles scowled. 'You're beginning to seem like a permanent fixture.'

'He is a permanent fixture, don't forget,' Stephanie said with relish. 'He and Ella are engaged.'

'I thought you might have reconsidered it. You'll regret it, you know. She's married to this house and you'll come way second to it.'

'We both love Willowbrook. It's a magnificent old place.'

Stephanie broke the awkward silence that followed. 'The coffee will be ready in a few minutes. I'll find Amy and get her ready.'

Miles sauntered across and took a chair, sitting astride it leaning his arms on the chair back to watch Cameron, who had started to put away the breakfast pans Stephanie had been washing.

'So what's with this fire?' Miles asked after a while.

'It was arson and you'll be one of the suspects.'

'Me? Why me?'

'Because you'll benefit financially if this house can't be listed. But don't worry. You're not the only suspect. DevRaCom's in the frame too.'

'Biting the hand that feeds you with a vengeance now, are you?'

'I was only ever a consultant, and DevRaCom wasn't my biggest client by a long chalk. I don't condone crime, whoever commits it.'

'You seemed pally enough with Ray Deare when I saw you.'

'If it's any business of yours, I've known Ray since I was a lad because he's a friend of my father's.'

Amy's voice floated down the stairs. 'I don't *want* to go out with him!'

Miles saw the other man fail to hide a smile

and felt his irritation ratchet up a notch. 'Where's Ella?'

'Cleaning out the chalets.'

'I'll go and speak to her.'

'You leave her alone. She's upset about the barn. She doesn't need upsetting further.'

Before Miles could speak, his mother came down, followed by a sulky Amy, clutching the scruffy teddy bear.

'I'm not having that filthy old thing in my car,' he said at once.

'You always were petty,' his mother said. 'We'll be quite happy to stay at home.'

'Oh, bring the damned thing, then. Why don't you bring the kitchen rubbish bin while you're at it.' Not his usual standard of wit, he decided, but the headache was still lingering. He led the way out, settled them in the car and drove off.

The restaurant he'd decided on the day before was large, furnished in garish plastics and full of families with small children. He didn't usually go to places like this, but he wasn't wasting more money than he had to on the brat. 'What do you want to eat?'

Amy folded her arms. 'Nothing.'

He looked at his mother. 'What shall I order for her?'

'Nothing. We can't make the child eat if she doesn't want to.'

'She can watch me eat, then. I'm ravenous.' He ordered a large meal and consumed every mouthful of it, while his mother toyed with a salad and Amy sat looking more and more miserable, clutching that scruffy teddy to her

350

narrow chest. Clearly the child had been spoiled rotten because of her disability. It'd do her good to face the consequences of her rudeness and go hungry today.

He tried to chat to his mother, but though he prided himself on keeping up with current affairs, she was almost monosyllabic and showed no interest in any topic he raised.

In the end he took the pair of them back early.

⋆ ⋆ ⋆

Clutching Oliver's hand, Rose went up to her flat, stared for a moment or two at the devastation she found in the living room, then went straight along to the spare bedroom.

Her tin trunk was missing.

She could neither speak nor move for a few moments.

She heard Oliver cursing fluently beside her, and felt his arm go round her waist. Closing her eyes, she let him explain to the police officer what was missing and exactly why it was so precious to her, not opening her eyes again till the man addressed her directly.

'I'm sorry, Ms Marwood. We'll do our very best to get it back for you. What about the rest of your things?'

'They don't matter.' She felt as if her whole life had been ripped apart by this theft. And when the burglars found nothing they could sell inside the trunk, they'd probably destroy it. Her life's work for the past few years! The work for which she'd given up the man she loved.

'Please, Ms Marwood. Try to think.'

She couldn't hold back the tears. 'I don't care about anything else. But I have nothing of value, no jewellery, nothing except that trunk.' She turned to Oliver. 'Take me out to Willowbrook. I can't stay here.'

Looking anxiously at her white face, at all the signs of severe shock, he did as she asked, settling her in the car seat as if she was an octogenarian and driving out of the village at a steady pace, not trying to talk, watching her carefully every time he could take his eyes off the road safely.

★ ★ ★

Ray arrived at the farm just after lunch, as arranged. 'Go slowly up the drive,' he instructed the chauffeur.

'It's pretty countryside, even nicer than in the photos,' he commented to Sonia. 'What could be better for our purpose? Absolutely unspoiled.'

'Somewhere zoned for development would be better for a start.'

'That can be fixed. We have a supporter on the local planning committee who's willing to help us. Someone who seems hostile towards our Ms Turner, for reasons he won't specify. And anyway, the government's encouraging more rural development these days. You know they are.'

'The sort of people who go to your conference hotels don't give a damn for whether the countryside is unspoiled or not. They're either getting married or they're eager beavering on a training course.'

He didn't bother to argue. She'd been prickly all the way down here. He'd not have allowed it in any other employee.

The huge vehicle rolled slowly round the side of the house.

'What a beautiful old place it is!' she said softly, her eyes still on the house. 'Anyone can see that it's genuinely old. Your scout lied to you, Ray.'

He shrugged. 'It not only has to be old to be heritage listed, it has to be special in some way. This house is common or garden Georgian. The National Trust has quite enough of those on their lists. I checked it all out — '

He stopped talking as the car came to a halt in the yard behind the house and he saw the incident tape across the entrance to the barn, the fire service vehicle and the police car parked to one side.

'What the hell's been going on here? Don't tell me it caught fire! How sad.' He gave a wolfish grin. 'With a bit of luck, that barn has been damaged beyond repair. Cameron said it was the oldest part of the farm. The wood's bound to have been well dried out and would burn easily.'

'If you've been involved in this fire, Ray Deare, I won't be at work tomorrow — or any day after that.'

That annoyed the hell out of him. 'Do me a favour! Would *I* do something so crude, not to mention criminal?'

He got out of the car without waiting for the

chauffeur to open the door or for Sonia to answer his question, and walked across to the barn. Two men who had an official look to them were inside, discussing something and pointing.

Sonia followed him, waving to Cameron, who'd seen them arrive from the kitchen doorway and was now walking across to join them.

'What's been happening here?' Ray asked.

Cameron came up to them and explained.

'Much damage?'

'Just a bit of smoke blackening. The arsonist was incompetent. Welcome to Willowbrook anyway. We'll show you round the place later. Sonia, it's lovely to see you. To what do we owe this extra honour?' He went through the usual air-kissing ritual with her then steered them towards the house.

'I came to keep an eye on him,' she said, ignoring Ray's rumble of annoyance at this. 'What pretty gardens! In fact the whole place is delightful.'

Inside the house Ella was waiting for them. The rooms, as Ray noted sourly, shone with cleanliness and with that extra something that said this was a well-loved home. No matter how hard he tried, he couldn't get this effect in any of his hotels.

He moved forward, hand stuck out. 'Ray Deare, CEO of DevRaCom.'

'Ella Turner, latest in a long line of Turners who've owned Willowbrook,' she tossed at him before shaking hands.

He blinked in surprise and studied her with

greater attention. Parnell had said she was stupid. She didn't look stupid to him. 'Pleased to meet you.'

Cameron moved forward to stand beside Ella. 'She's also engaged to me and I'm now an official member of the group eager to save Willowbrook.'

Ray's smile faded. 'You two are *engaged*? You always did move fast. Congratulations. That explains why you wouldn't help me.'

'I'd not have helped you anyway. Once the arson inspector's left, we'll show you a barn built six hundred years ago, complete with secret passages and friendly family ghost.'

'Now that I'd like to see,' Sonia said cheerfully. 'But if that coffee tastes as good as it smells, I'm going to beg a cup first.'

Cameron took them to sit in the conservatory and Ella brought in the tray she'd already prepared.

'Good coffee,' Ray acknowledged.

'The coffee's better than what we serve in the hotels,' Sonia added. 'Perhaps you'd tell me its name and I'll order that sort from now on? Ray would happily drink any brown liquid if you called it coffee.'

Ray studied the biscuit. 'Nice biscuits, too. Have that homemade look. Where do you get them?'

'I make them myself.'

'She'll be happy to sell you some recipes,' Cameron said.

'I'll be in touch,' Sonia said at once. 'We have nothing as good as these.'

Ella blinked from one to the other. Miles had said she could sell her recipes. She hadn't believed him. For once, he'd been telling the truth.

After some more chit-chat, Ray said with the abruptness for which he was famous, 'What will it take to persuade you to sell Willowbrook to me, Ella?'

'I've already told you: there is nothing — *nothing at all* — that will make me sell my home.'

'Everything has its price.'

'No. Some things are beyond price.'

'I hear you owe a lot of money.'

Cameron joined in. 'I'd not let my future wife lose her home over a mere fifty thousand pounds, now would I?'

Ray breathed deeply.

Someone knocked on the door just then and Ella went to answer it, her conversation clearly audible from the conservatory.

'We've got all the information we need,' a man's voice said.

'It's the arson inspector,' Cameron whispered.

'You can clear up now, Ms Turner, but if I were you, I'd take photos beforehand for the insurance people. Just one thing. Do you recognize this? It's the sort of so-called lucky piece that usually hangs on a key ring.' He held out a small metal figurine. Its shape was twisted by the heat, its colours were burned off, but its glass eyes still twinkled malevolently.

She recognized it at once. 'Yes.'

'Ah.' The inspector waited.

'Brett Harding has one like that. I can't say whether this one is his, of course.'

'I saw him with one like it, too,' Cameron said. 'When I had an altercation with him for trying to rape Ella.'

The police officer stiffened. 'Are you sure of that?'

She nodded.

'Why didn't you report the assault?'

'I didn't want to cause trouble in town.'

'You mean with his father.'

'Yes. I'm sure I don't need to tell you that Mr Harding is very protective towards his son.'

'So Brett Harding might have a grudge against both of you?'

'Yes.'

'We'll question him, see where he was when the fire was lit. We'll be in touch.'

Ella and Cameron watched them drive away.

'Why didn't we think of Brett?' she asked.

'I did. But I couldn't see him doing something like that.'

'He's an alcoholic, may not be thinking clearly.'

'Well, let's hope we've found the guilty party. If he did set the fire, he'll be lucky to get away with it. Modern forensic methods can detect minute traces of smoke and accelerants on people's bodies and clothes even after an arsonist has tried to wash himself clean. He'll definitely go to prison if it is him, what with the other offences.'

'Serve him right. Now, let's get this over with.' She went back into the conservatory. 'Perhaps you'd like to see the barn now, Sonia, Mr Deare?'

Inside, it still smelled of smoke, but with light pouring into the building through the big double doors, it was clear the damage really was limited to one of the more modern corners.

Ray looked up to the roof, stared at the huge sawn trees used as supporting beams, turned round slowly on the spot to look at the barn, whistling softly as he stared. 'Your husband lied big-time about this place.'

'Yes. But Miles hasn't been my husband for a while.'

'You could still withdraw your heritage application, if you chose. I'd find a way to preserve this barn, have it moved stone by stone if necessary.'

She smiled. 'I'm still not selling.'

'No. Now that I've met you, I can see that this is rather special. Pity.' He went up to stroke the bottom of one of the huge beams. 'A cruck barn. I never thought I'd actually touch one.'

Ella looked at him in surprise.

Sonia nudged Cameron and went to link her arm in Ray's. 'Leave it be, Ray. It belongs here and so does she.'

'I still need that new development.'

Just then they heard a car draw up and Ella moved to the door to see who it was.

'Miles is back. And my daughter looks upset. Excuse me.'

★　★　★

As he drove into the farm Miles saw a limousine parked to one side with a chauffeur sitting in the driving seat reading a newspaper. 'Who does that belong to?'

'None of your business,' Stephanie snapped. 'It's someone to see Ella.'

'I'll find out what she's up to when we go in.'

'There's no need whatsoever for you to come inside.'

He laughed, ignored this and led the way towards the house without waiting to help Amy out of the car. He hadn't wasted the last two hours only to miss some of the moves Ella was making. It just showed it paid off to visit the brat.

But Amy fell over again and started sobbing. Fed up of her, he turned back and yanked her to her feet. 'Stop that squalling! You're not hurt. You fall over all the time without crying. I've seen you.'

She shoved him back unexpectedly, taking him by surprise so that he caught his heel in the crazy paving and pitched backwards into the soft earth of the flower bed.

Amy's tears changed to laughter, but one look at his expression as he started to get up and she went hurrying into the house.

He brushed himself down, trying in vain to see over his shoulder. 'What's my suit like at the back, Mum?'

Stephanie clicked her tongue in exasperation, but her maternal instinct made her move forward and brush him down. 'There. Your suit will live. But it'll need dry cleaning. I can do nothing about the muddy bits, so keep your face towards people you want to impress, don't turn your back. You should let the mud dry and brush it off before you have the suit cleaned.'

Furious, he followed her inside.

Amy was sitting munching a biscuit. She looked at him warily.

The sound of Ella's voice made him ignore his daughter and move on to the sitting room. By the time he'd got to the door, he'd realized who one of the other voices belonged to: Ray Deare. He had not the slightest hesitation in walking in on them. If something was going on between her and DevRaCom, he wanted to know about it.

'I've brought our daughter back safely, Ella. Oh, hi Ray! And Miss Bradley, too. How are you?' He ignored that sod Cameron.

Sonia gave him a frosty nod, Ray a quick one, before he turned back to his hostess.

'You haven't heard the last of this, Ella. I don't give in at the first obstacle or I'd not have built DevRaCom to what it is. You'll be hearing from me.' On this excellent exit line, Ray got to his feet and walked out.

With a shrug and a wink at Cameron, Sonia followed.

Miles tagged on behind them, ignoring his ex.

*   *   *

When they were alone, Ella turned to Cameron. 'What part of *No* does Ray Deare not understand?'

'Don't underestimate him. He's a juggernaut

360

when he wants something.'

She plumped down on the sofa with a groan. 'How long is this going to go on? I can't get on with my life with threats hanging over me.'

He sat beside her. 'Don't forget there are two of us to face the world now.'

She relaxed a little and took his hand.

'We'll start by paying Miles back what you owe him.'

She opened her mouth to protest.

'I know you were going to sell your family jewels, but I don't see any need for that. I have plenty of money.'

'I'm not marrying you for your money.'

'Hey, pull your claws in. I know that. It'd be more accurate to say I'm benefiting from marrying you by being able to live at Willowbrook. I really did fall in love with the place that first day, you know.'

She relaxed still further. 'Do you really love it?'

'Yes. And the first time I stopped in Chawton, I felt at home in the village too. I've never had that, a real home, a permanent place to live.'

She leaned over to kiss his cheek then said, 'Perhaps Ray will back off with you on my side.'

He nodded, though he wasn't optimistic. He didn't trust Ray and he knew how much was vested in this development, maybe even the whole future of DevRaCom. That thought worried him more than he'd admitted to her.

21

Miles followed Ray to the limo. 'I've another suggestion for you. How about we go somewhere and discuss it?'

'If it's going to give me as much grief as this one has — '

'No. It's something I found out purely by accident and I don't want anyone else overhearing what I have to tell you.' He jerked his head towards the chauffeur and whispered, 'What would you say to a new development near here that would cost a tenth of what this one would?'

'What do you mean by that?'

'It's not something I want to discuss here. Look, there's a hotel in Chawton, the Old White Horse, and they do afternoon teas that are to die for. How about we go there and find a quiet corner where we can chat?'

Before they could move away, Oliver drove up to the house, with a weeping Rose slumped beside him.

Miles stared at them. What the hell next? Then he remembered something he'd overheard. None of his business, but . . . He turned to Ray. 'I'll meet you at the Old White Horse. I know these two. I have an idea about what's upset them and I may be able to help. Give me half an hour.'

Ray was frowning at him. It was Sonia who answered. 'All right. I think we should all help others as much as we can.'

Miles blinked at her. This coming from Ms Iceberg herself?

Then he hurried towards the farm. It was impossible to resist the temptation to become the hero of the piece, right under the eyes of Cameron O'Neal and his ex.

★ ★ ★

As they drew near Willowbrook, Oliver said gently, 'Don't give up hope yet.'

Rose looked at him as if he was blurred, then brought him back into focus again. 'I'm so glad you're with me.' She wiped away more tears but others followed.

At the rear of the house they found a huge limo and more crime scene tape.

'Something's happened here as well,' Oliver said. 'Rose, try to pull yourself together. Ella may be in trouble too.'

She nodded, but he wasn't sure she could cope with anything else, so after he'd helped her out of the car, he kept one arm supportively round her as she stumbled towards the house.

Neither of them noticed Miles, because the limo drove away just then, obscuring him from view. He did nothing to attract attention, waited till the others had gone inside and followed.

★ ★ ★

Inside the house, Miles heard Ella exclaim in shock at the sight of Rose. 'What's wrong?'

Unashamedly eavesdropping, Miles listened as both cousins explained their troubles to one another. He saw how tenderly Oliver hovered over Rose, and indeed, Miles was shocked himself at how distraught she looked. In fact, he actually felt sorry for the poor bitch. He'd never liked her, but this went way beyond what he'd ever have done to anyone. After all, those paintings sounded as though they were really valuable.

If he'd known exactly what was involved he might have tried to stop those guys, or at least, called the police anonymously. It was a stupid crime. No benefit to the perpetrators. Those guys would do better to stick to joke telling.

He drew a deep breath, relishing the thought of being a hero, then walked in and said loudly, 'I might be able to help you, Rose.' He was pleased by the way they all fell silent, staring at him as if he'd come from Mars.

It was his mother who spoke. 'What do you mean, Miles?'

'I may know where they've dumped the trunk.'

Oliver moved towards him, an expression so ugly on his face that Miles involuntarily took a step backwards.

'Are you involved in this?'

'No!' He fended the idiot off with one hand. 'It's just that I overheard something in the pub last night. It didn't make sense till I heard you explain about the burglary, then it suddenly clicked what the guys had been talking about.'

'Where might they have dumped my trunk?' Rose asked, going to the heart of the matter.

'In the lake here.'

She let out a wail of anguish. 'Then the paintings will be ruined.'

'I once heard you boast about storing them in a water and fireproof container,' Miles said. 'You told everyone in the village about your special box.'

'Waterproof is one thing, being dumped in the lake for hours is another. And anyway, how will we know where to look?'

'There may be footsteps or signs of where they've been. The ground's always damp near the edge,' Ella pointed out.

Oliver jabbed one finger at Miles. 'Do not try to leave. In fact, you can come with us to hunt for the box.'

'But I have an appointment in the village.'

'It can wait.'

'I'll keep an eye on Amy,' Stephanie said, watching with interest as two tall men escorted her slender, medium-sized son out of the house. Ella followed with her arm round Rose, who still looked white and shocked.

'Can we go with them, Grandma?'

'Better not, darling. We'll only get in the way. And anyway, someone has to stay near the phone. Would you like something to eat now?'

'Yes, please.'

'Why didn't you have something at lunch-time?'

'I don't want anything from *him*. I won't have him for a daddy.'

That was sad, Stephanie thought. Her son was missing so much. It was obvious now that he'd been using Amy to keep an eye on Willowbrook. What was equally obvious was that the child sensed he didn't care for her.

★ ★ ★

When a policeman knocked on the door, Mr Harding opened it.

'We'd like to speak to Brett Harding.'

'Why?'

'We need to question him in connection with an arson attack.'

Mrs Harding spoke from behind him. 'Come in. I'll fetch my son.'

'Linda, I'm not sure that's wise.'

'I couldn't sleep for worrying. I heard him go out last night. If he's been doing something else wrong, I'm not protecting him, and neither are you.'

Brett was pink and glowing after a very long shower. He sat down smiling and denied having left the house, denied having been involved in arson.

'We'd like to search his room,' the female officer said.

'Not unless you have a search warrant,' Brett said quickly.

'On the contrary, this is my house,' his father said, 'and they can search anywhere they want.'

'I'll go up with you. My husband will stay with our son.' Linda led the way out.

'Why did you let them do that?' Brett asked in a whisper.

'Because as your mother said, we're not

protecting you if you've done something else stupid.'

The officers came down, shaking their heads. 'Nothing there.'

Brett smiled triumphantly at them.

'Just a minute,' Linda said suddenly and left the room.

She came back a moment later with a laundry basket. 'These are my son's things. And they smell of paraffin.'

The officers sniffed. 'These are his clothes?' one asked.

'Yes. I did our washing yesterday. This is all recently used stuff.'

'Mind if we take them away?'

'Not at all.'

'Brett Harding, I'm arresting you on suspicion of . . . '

★   ★   ★

It was ridiculously easy to find the box, because the guys who'd dumped it in the lake had made little attempt to hide the signs of their visit. The rushes were trampled, mud still showed gouges where something heavy had been dragged. And indeed, the box wasn't even in very deep water. The top showed clearly, about a foot below the surface.

'They must be pig stupid,' Cameron said in disgust.

'They weren't the brightest buttons on the planet, from the way they were talking,' Miles admitted. 'How are you going to get it out?'

'We are going into the lake and if all three of us try hard, we should be able to heave it out of the water.'

'Sorry. Can't do that in this suit. It cost me a fortune.'

Oliver smiled, not a friendly smile, looking at Cameron. They nodded at one another and in one swift movement pulled Miles into the water with them.

'You're either with us or with them,' Cameron said.

After one look at his face, a tight-lipped Miles helped them drag out the box. By the time it was on the bank, they were all three soaked and muddy.

Rose rushed forward. 'Let me open it. I have to know if anything can be saved.'

Cameron moved between her and the box. 'Not yet. It's covered in mud. We need to clean the outside before we even try to open it. Let's go and get Ella's trolley to put it on. That metal's heavy.'

Miles trailed back behind them, sickened by the ruin of his good suit and anxious to make his appointment with Deare.

Seizing his moment while Cameron and Oliver were man-handling the trunk and trolley, he slipped into his car, shuddering at what the mud would do to his upholstery, and drove off. He stopped at the end of the drive to change into his tracksuit. Fancy meeting Ray Deare dressed like this.

★ ★ ★

Cameron looked up. 'That sod's escaped.'

'He's had any punishment he was due,' Ella said.

'What do you mean?'

'What my ex loves most in life is his fancy clothes and his own appearance. Unless I'm much mistaken, you've just ruined a very expensive suit. And we've also ruined the plans he'd been making to show DevRaCom how good he is at setting up developments.'

'I should go after him and punch him in the face for stopping my letter getting to Rose three years ago,' Oliver muttered.

'They can't prosecute you for getting him muddy; they can for assault,' Ella said. 'Let's concentrate on the box.'

*　*　*

In Chawton, a bedraggled Miles explained about the rescue of Rose's box, with himself figuring in a central role. He went on to describe another plot of land he'd found, one without encumbrances, one about to be released under some new zoning laws. 'It's not for sale yet, so we should be able to get it quite cheaply.'

'Good lad,' Ray said. 'You've done well.'

Sonia regarded him with less favour but said nothing.

'Serve the Turner woman right,' Ray added. 'She's lost a great opportunity.'

'I think she's kept what's most precious to her,' Sonia said, but the two men ignored her comment.

Cameron and Oliver carried the box into the utility room. It took them over an hour to make sure it was clean and dry in every crevice.

They all stood back as Rose keyed the numbers into the lock, her hand trembling. Holding her breath, praying for a miracle, she opened the trunk and everyone swayed towards it to see what state it was in.

Rose burst into tears, sobbing so hard against Oliver's chest that everyone else had tears in their eyes too.

'They're all right. Check for me. They are, aren't they?' she sobbed. 'I'm not fooling myself. They're safe.'

Cameron stepped forward to lift the transparent cover off the top painting, showing it to be unmarked. 'It's gorgeous.'

'They're safe, darling. The box really was waterproof.' Oliver folded Rose in his arms.

He had to repeat his reassurances twice before she could make sense of what he was saying, then she nodded, still clinging to him and weeping more softly in sheer relief.

'They'll be quite safe here,' Ella said. 'I'll lock the outer door of this room. You and Oliver can have one of the chalets tonight. He can go back into the village and fetch some of your clothes.'

'No need,' he said. 'We've been away for the night. Our cases are still in the car. And . . . we have some good news for you. Rose has agreed to marry me.'

The mood suddenly lightened. Ella hugged

her cousin, then hugged her again for good measure.

The two men shook hands.

'We're getting married too,' Ella said, and the kissing started again.

After they'd calmed down, they went into the kitchen and told Stephanie and Amy the news.

'And I want you to be my bridesmaid,' Rose told the excited child. 'Will you do it?'

'Even if I walk funny?'

'Who cares how you walk? I want my favourite relatives at my wedding, and that means your mother as matron of honour and you as bridesmaid.'

'I'm going to be Mummy's bridesmaid, too,' Amy crowed in delight. 'And I'll have a new daddy, just like Nessa!'

We do hope that you have enjoyed reading this large print book.

Did you know that all of our titles are available for purchase?

We publish a wide range of high quality large print books including:
Romances, Mysteries, Classics
General Fiction
Non Fiction and Westerns

Special interest titles available in large print are:
The Little Oxford Dictionary
Music Book
Song Book
Hymn Book
Service Book

Also available from us courtesy of Oxford University Press:
Young Readers' Dictionary
(large print edition)
Young Readers' Thesaurus
(large print edition)

For further information or a free brochure, please contact us at:
Ulverscroft Large Print Books Ltd.,
The Green, Bradgate Road, Anstey,
Leicester, LE7 7FU, England.
Tel: (00 44) 0116 236 4325
Fax: (00 44) 0116 234 0205

Other titles published by
The House of Ulverscroft:

CHESTNUT LANE

Anna Jacobs

When novelist Sophie Carr rescues a man hiding in her garden from a group of paparazzi, she finds that her neighbour is ageing pop star Jez Winter. She's loved his music for years and knows he's had a tough time lately: an intruder having slashed his face, then a car accident putting his ability to play music at risk. Life's not been easy for Sophie either, losing her husband just as she was taking off as a novelist and having difficulties with her control freak son William and her daughter Andi, who is into recreational drugs and has lost her way in life since her father's death. And Sophie also has a secret to hide. One that makes her very wary of getting involved with Jez.

YESTERDAY'S GIRL

Anna Jacobs

The Great War opened up an exciting new career for Vi in London. But that was yesterday. Now, the war is over, her husband is dead and she needs to pick up the pieces of her life. On her way home she meets a man who needs her help. Recently demobbed, Joss Bentley has no job or home, and with his wife dead, there's a new baby to care for — and it's not his. As he searches grimly for its real father, he runs up against people who will use any means necessary to conceal dark secrets . . . and Vi finds herself faced with conflicting loyalties. Whichever way she moves it seems she'll hurt someone — or they'll hurt her . . .

KIRSTY'S VINEYARD

Anna Jacobs

Four years ago Kirsty was left broken-hearted when her husband, the love of her life, was killed in a car accident. Despite being in her early thirties she has put her life on hold since, focussing on her work at the local library and moving in with her brother, Rod. Then she meets Ed James, a cancer-ridden and lonely old man, whose family only cares about his money. Kirsty is shocked when he leaves her all his money and his estate, an Australian vineyard, when he dies, disinheriting his nephew. But there is a condition attached to his legacy: she must give up her life in England and live at the vineyard — in a remote corner of New South Wales — for at least one year . . .

TOMORROW'S PROMISES

Anna Jacobs

Ellen Dawson is glad when the Great War ends, but sad that Lady Bingram's Aides are to be disbanded. She can't bear to go back into service again after working as a driver and mechanic in London. But she is forced by her mother's illness to accept her old position as housemaid in order to stay in the small Lancashire town . . . and her stepfather will stop at nothing to get her under his control again. Meanwhile, Seth Talbot is facing great difficulties when he takes over as local policeman and tries to bring order to a town where the law has been flouted for years.

MRIA
12/8

CITY LIBRARIES
·y.gov.uk/libraries

Return to ....
or any other Aberdeen City Library
Please return/renew this item by the last day shown. Items may also be renewed
by phone or online

CU 4/15.

28 MAY 2015

1 1 AUG 2015

1 3 NOV 2015

21/12

R 12 /18

WITHDRAWN

X000 000 037 5316

ABERDEEN CITY LIBRARIES